ARRESTED
PLEASURES

By the Author

In Helen's Hands

Arrested Pleasures

ARRESTED PLEASURES

by

Nanisi Barrett D'Arnuk

2020

ARRESTED PLEASURES

ISBN 13: 978-1-63555-684-1

This Trade Paperback Original Is Published By
Bold Strokes Books, Inc.
P.O. Box 249
Valley Falls, NY 12185

First Edition: June 2020

Credits
Editors: Barbara Ann Wright
Production Design: Stacia Seaman
Cover Design by Jeanine Henning

For Ti

CHAPTER ONE

I was jolted awake by the train pulling out of the station. The abrupt start was enough. I sat up in time to catch the name on the platform.

"Damn! I missed my stop." I took out the map in my pocket. *Wow! We're already on the border of Rebinia.* The next stop was Nové Ville, across the border.

I'd have to pay for a train back and make my transfer to Hungary, and it would put me back a day, but I wasn't too worried. I had been going to Budapest to review some smaller hotels. If I could write anything, that would cover the entire trip.

You see, I loved to go places, and the very best part of traveling was that I get paid to do it. I had a job with a major travel magazine so I'd traveled quite a lot, much of the time alone. I visited new hotels or popular sites and reviewed them for the magazine, or I visited little-known places and made them popular. It felt like quite a responsibility. I could make or break a vacation destination or help a small family business.

When I reviewed a place, it was always a big deal. My by-line, "as reviewed by Katherine P. Lowe," brought a lot of prestige to a place. I'd been told that people really believed what I wrote and planned or rearranged entire vacations because of it. Of course, it made me feel pretty special, too, but I had to keep reminding myself to not get a big head about it. I had to be direct and honest. It was a responsibility I couldn't forget. If I wasn't reviewing someplace, surely someone else would…eventually.

I would write off the Verona to Budapest part of this trip this time. I'd been in Verona with my three best friends, Paula, Judy, and Amy. We had met in college, the University of Washington, and had bonded when we realized that we were all lesbians. We made it a habit to travel together at least once each year.

Now my friends were going to Greece, and I was headed to Budapest and Krakow.

"Are you sure you don't want to come with us?" Amy had asked me last night as I was packing. She was the unofficial leader of our group, basically cooler than the rest of us, and had opinions about a lot of things. If none of us had a specific need or want, we let Amy decide.

"I've never been to Austria, Hungary, or Poland," I said. "I have visas for all of them. We know so little about the smaller hotels."

"You don't speak the languages, do you?"

"I know enough German to get by. I have my electronic translator, and I've got dictionaries. Besides, someone's always willing to help. It's a great way to meet people and make new friends." I'd made many friends along the way, some I still corresponded with but most not. It was one of the perks and also a hazard of traveling as much as I did.

"You're more adventurous than I am," Amy said. "I'd never travel alone in a strange country."

"Why? You're cute. A lot of people would help you."

Amy laughed. She was tallish, five-foot-six, and her light brown hair was in a pixie cut. "You like talking to strangers. And you have one of those faces that says safe. You'll probably meet some cute little native."

I was only five-four with short dark brown hair. I chuckled. "Well, that's always a possibility. I'm very…friendly."

"Uh-huh. *Friendly* is not the word I would have chosen," she said with a sardonic smile.

I flirted a lot, but I was too uncertain of myself to make a move on some woman who lived a thousand miles away. Yes, I'd learned that with Hannah.

We both laughed. "Well, I wish you were coming with us." She gave me a quick hug.

"I'll meet you in Amsterdam in three weeks."

She sighed. "All right."

"If I've been delayed, I'll call." I turned back to where I was loading my suitcase.

"Let's have a few drinks before you go."

That was my first mistake.

The train ride through Austria had started beautifully, the scenery spectacular, through the rolling countryside with the Alps in the distance. I'd been wanting to visit Austria ever since I'd seen *The Sound of Music* for the sixth time and reviewed the Trapp Family Lodge in Stowe, Vermont.

Oh yes, Stowe, Vermont. I hadn't thought of her recently. No, I hadn't *allowed* myself to think of her: Hannah, the one flirtation I regretted. Not that I shouldn't have flirted, but that I hadn't been able to stop it once I started. We'd been inseparable for a month, and then, well, neither of us came away unscathed. I sometimes wondered what would have happened, where I would be now, if I had stayed.

I'd been doing my reviews for a little over a year when I was sent to review the Trapp Family Lodge in Stowe, Vermont. The week had started wonderfully. The rooms were unbelievably beautiful, the food superior, and the service exceptional. It wouldn't be hard to give it five stars.

I was stunned when I saw their menu. It was predominantly German, with wiener schnitzel, bratwurst, and spatzle, which I had expected, but they had local flavors, too: maple glazed quail and river trout. The wine list was over the top. They advertised more wines than most places. They even offered a bottle of Chateau Mouton Rothschild for fourteen hundred dollars. They had their own wines and a wide assortment of beers. Yes, it was expensive, but not more than the usual big resorts. I dined on some of the best my first night there, the next lunch and for breakfast on the third day.

Then I ordered room service.

The waitress who delivered my meal was the most beautiful woman I'd seen in ages. She had long, dirty-blond hair, braided and curled up on her head, and the most enthralling accent I'd ever heard. She was slightly taller than me, and her shoulders and hips were wide and feminine in the scrumptious way that curves are, and her bearing was overwhelming. It was then that I decided I needed to brush up on my German.

I'd flirted with staff before, but this one flirted back, and I fell right into her web.

"I'm Hannah, your server." She took the dishes off the serving tray and arranged them perfectly on the table in my room. "Would you like me to open your wine?"

"Yes, that would be great."

She deftly uncorked the bottle and poured a bit into my glass. I did the whole taste-testing thing, and she filled my glass.

"Are you enjoying your stay?" she began, and we were off on a long conversation about the lodge and why I was there while I ate.

"And so, you're out of here on Monday?"

"Yes, I was planning to stay for a few days longer, but I really can't afford it without my expense account. I mean, I could afford the room or the food, but not both. I did want to go hiking. This part of the country is beautiful."

She looked at her watch. "When I'm off duty, can I show you the nightlife?"

Was she was seriously hitting on me? "Real nightlife? In the mountains of Vermont?"

Hannah laughed. "Let me show you."

"Am I dressed okay?" I still had on my tan slacks and a yellow soccer shirt.

"Perfect. Let me go sign out. I'll be right back."

She took the tray with the dishes and left. I went into my bathroom and freshened up, but she was back before I knew it. Her hair was unbraided and falling around her shoulders. She was in slacks and a T-shirt. She pulled me toward the door.

"I have to show you the real Vermont. I saw you check in, and you were alone, so I figured you'd need company after a day or two. Come on."

"I have a rental car."

"Leave it. We'll take mine."

Hannah's car was an older sedan, slightly messy in the back seat, but not unlike the one I had in Seattle. We drove into Stowe and wound through the streets until she stopped at a brightly lit alley. The buildings had no windows, and there wasn't a sign to advertise where we were. When she opened the door to let us inside, music boomed out. There were quite a few people inside, some dancing, others standing around talking. I checked out the crowd. It was a gay bar! I turned to look into Hannah's eyes.

She raised an eyebrow. "Okay?"

I had to smile. "Okay."

"Is beer all right? Or would you rather have wine or something hard?"

"Whatever you're drinking."

She bought us dark lagers and drew me onto the dance floor, each of us clutching our drinks. What an unexpected night. After we'd danced for what seemed like hours, we walked to the side of the room, hand in hand, to stools along the wall. Hannah drew me into her arms and planted her lips on mine. I didn't push her away, so we stood there making out like two high schoolers.

And were the kisses ever good. I hadn't been kissed like that in a long time. I could feel the heat getting higher and higher and my panties getting wetter and wetter. Finally, she whispered, "Let's go home."

I gladly let her take my hand and lead me outside. I didn't even think to ask what she meant by home, but we were soon pulling into a driveway of a large house just outside of Stowe. Two other cars were already parked there.

"This is home?" I asked.

"For the time being. I share with three other girls from the lodge, but we each have our own room." She squeezed my hand, got out of the car, and ran around to help me out. We rushed inside, up a flight of stairs, and into her room. I didn't even look around. I merely let her lead me to her bed.

"Hannah," I started to say, but she pressed her lips to mine and pushed me onto the soft mattress. We were naked within seconds. Her breasts were large, and my face fit comfortably between them. That was all I could concentrate on.

Her hand roamed my body and came to rest on the hair between my legs. She reached inside me with two fingers, and I was even more lost than I had been. I didn't think. I'm not sure I even breathed. I let myself float, wanting to feel her fill me.

We made love through the night.

When I woke, I looked up to see Hannah standing in front of her mirror, freshly showered and in her uniform.

"Good morning," I said.

She sat and leaned in to kiss me.

"I was just going to wake you. You have a choice, stay here and sleep until I come back after lunch, or you can get dressed and come back with me now. Your choice."

"I'll go back now as long as I can see you later."

"Of course." She kissed me again. "Then you have to get up. The bathroom is at the end of the hall." She stood and held out her hand to help me up.

I wanted her badly after that. I wanted her to want me. I went back to the lodge. I wrote my review, and I waited for her. She was in charge, and I loved that. She knew what had to be done.

"Check out of the lodge," she told me when I said I had completed my review. "You don't need to be here. Bring all your things to my place. I have two days off, and I can take them tomorrow. I'll switch with someone."

I changed my plane ticket for three weeks later, when I really had to be home. That night was even more amazing. Her roommate, Liesl, cooked sausage, fried potatoes, and greens for everyone, then Hannah took me back to her room.

"Now that I have you totally to myself, what am I going to do to you?"

"Make love to me," I said. "And I'll make love to you."

"Yes, me first." She pushed me back and crawled on top. She kissed her way onto my neck. I threw my head back and let her have her way with me. I was ready for anything...or so I thought.

I was floating above her mattress as I lost all connection to the real world. When I came, I arched up off the bed. I was finally able to open my eyes as I looked up into those dark blues above me. She grinned at me with a very sly expression.

"Now, I'll show you how pleasurable this can be."

I looked over to find my hands were bound to her bed with long silk scarves. I couldn't move. "Uh, Hannah..." I started to say as I pulled on the restraints. I wasn't sure I liked this stuff. I'd heard of it but had never done it.

"No. Don't. You'll enjoy this. You won't have to worry about giving me what I want because I will take it. All of it. All of you." She knelt between my legs. "I want all of this...all of you." And she plunged into me. I screamed as I started to writhe, not sure if I was really enjoying myself. My emotions were all over the place.

"Please, let me loose," I whispered.

She planted a hard kiss on my mouth, her tongue entering into me as her hand delved in, too. "No, my dear, I want you here just as long as I can keep you." She backed down, licking my body until she reached my clit. I spread my legs wider as she licked and sucked me into the hardest orgasm I had ever had. She was right. The added restraint, being without control, added so much to the act. In a way, it was liberating having no responsibility, simply letting it happen.

Several hours and many orgasms later, she untied the scarves. I curled up into her arms.

"I think I'm falling in love with you," she whispered.

"Me, too."

The next three weeks were unbelievable. While she worked, I read and drove around Vermont to see as much as I could. But when she wasn't working, we were together: hiking, shopping, talking, and making love, most times with me tied to the bed. It felt right; it felt complete; it felt like heaven. The one thing we avoided was talking about me going home. In fact, the few times it came up, we talked around it.

Then came the day I had to think about going home. "Hannah, this has been incredible. I—"

She placed her hand over my mouth. "Don't say another word." She wrapped me tightly in her arms. "I don't want you to go home. I've fallen in love with you. Will you stay here with me?"

I wasn't sure how to say it. "I think I love you, too."

"Then stay here."

"Oh, Hannah, I want to."

"But?" She sighed deeply. "You can't. I never asked. Do you have a girlfriend?"

"No. Not for several years."

"Then stay here."

"It's so tempting." I didn't want to have to leave. The silence between us lengthened and lengthened.

"But it's not compelling." She looked away. "I know I don't make as much as you, and I don't have a degree, but I have plans and investments. I will be very rich someday."

"Honey, it's not about your income or education. I have dreams, too. I love what I do. I love to travel. I'm not ready to stop. Maybe in a few years, when you get your plans going and I've seen the world—"

"No, I'm not doing a relationship three thousand miles away. I want you in my bed every single night, beside me every day. I will not fuck you by mail or over the phone."

I could only stare into her eyes. We stood there for several minutes, neither of us making a move. I wanted to hold her, to kiss her, and tell her how much I loved her.

She shook her head. "No," was all she said as she marched out to her car and drove away.

She didn't come back that night, and she wasn't at work the next morning when I stopped by the lodge to say good-bye. I sent her a long note when I got home, but it was never answered.

I wanted to run back into her house and throw myself on her bed. I wanted her to tie me down with something heavier than silk. I contemplated taking my paycheck and buying a one-way ticket back to Vermont. I ached with regret for weeks, months. It was the hardest thing I had ever done.

After that, I still flirted from time to time, but I backed away if it was seriously returned. It was safer traveling and staying alone. If I had survived Hannah, I just might survive anything.

CHAPTER TWO

I had missed Austria. why, oh why, had I fallen asleep and missed half the country? I felt like an idiot. I had ignored the very first lesson I'd learned in my travels: Do not drink alcohol before you travel. I guess I shouldn't have listened to my friends last night.

My watch said 5:27. Had I slept that long?

I sat back and tried to figure out what to do. I'd have to spend the night in Rebinia and catch a train back in the morning or whenever the next one was. I'd be a day late, but I could still get to Budapest. That would teach me. No staying up all night, and remember: *No drinking before traveling.* Right, no drinking. None. Nada. Not a drop.

As we passed the border, the train slowed to a stop, but a minute or two later, started up again, this time filled with Rebinian military.

I looked up when a soldier stopped next to me and said something in Rebinian.

When I looked up with a question on my face, she repeated herself in German, asking for my passport.

I smiled and nodded, then reached under my seat where I had stashed my backpack, my purse, and everything I had with me.

I didn't feel it. I got down on the floor and looked under the seat. There was nothing there. In a panic, I looked under the seat in front of me and all around the area.

"My passport has been stolen," I cried in German. "My whole backpack! And everything I had with me."

It was a good thing I hadn't put all my money in there. I felt in my back pocket. That money was still there.

The soldier called to one of her friends, and they talked for a minute. The other soldier left. "Sit down," she said in German.

I sank onto the seat. She was a cutie, and I loved women in uniform. She had short hair, a medium brown, and did I see freckles? *Come on*, I scolded myself, *this isn't the time to look at women. If I am going to get cute with someone, I'd better save it for someone who can help me.* My passport was missing. I hoped there was a US consulate in Nové Ville. If there was, it wouldn't be too hard to get it replaced. But if not? How far away was Pergue?

When the train pulled into the station in Nové Ville, the soldier stood beside me until the departing passengers left. Then she ushered me off the train and into the transport office in the station where there was a man in a military uniform.

"I am Major Paol Grvenski. I've been told you have no passport," he said in German.

"My passport and all my belongings were stolen on the train," I said. "I need to talk with the nearest United States embassy. I was planning on going to Budapest." I smiled my most endearing smile. "I was going to transfer earlier, but I slept through my stop." I grinned and tried to show my embarrassment. Maybe he'd give me a little leeway. Even if my German was poor, at least my expressions might work. I always relied on cute and charming to get me through tough situations, and this was one of the toughest.

The major asked me a series of questions: who I was, my home address, where I was coming from, where I was going and why. He also asked the names of the women with whom I'd been traveling. I told him all about my job and my travels.

"Sit down and relax while I talk with the adjutant. I'm sure we can get this cleared up without a lot of trouble." He smiled and nodded as he left. I looked around the office. It looked as if it was used only on an interim basis in circumstances like tonight.

He didn't return for several minutes. I looked for something to help me pass the time. There were no reading materials, not that I could read Rebinian, but there might be maps or pictures. When I didn't find anything, I sat impatiently, waiting. He hadn't answered my question about the embassy. Should I take that as a good thing or bad? Should I be worried? I was always hopeful, believing that the best was right around the corner. Somehow, I wasn't so sure tonight. I got up and paced, then sat back down. He was gone an awfully long time. What was taking him so long? All they had to do was phone the embassy and verify that Katherine P. Lowe was a valid person. Come on. Come on!

"Well, Miss Lowe," he started as he finally came back. "We'll get you settled into a hotel room while we verify your information. There's a train back to Austria at noon every day. I'm sure we'll have everything cleared up, but it may take a couple days to get you another passport."

"I understand. Thank you for your help."

We stood and shook hands, and he handed me off to another soldier.

I was taken to a place about five blocks from the train station where my escort helped me book a room and explained to the owner why I had no identification. It felt funny checking into the hotel without luggage. I'd never done that before, although I knew people who did, but those were usually for clandestine reasons. Mine was not.

And so, I settled into the small room with a single bed, a chest of drawers, a chair, and a small table beside the bed. It was nice and clean and smelled fresh. I'd have to share the bathroom with the other four guests on the floor. It was clean, too, although a male guest had left his shaving things on the counter. I could live there for a couple days, and I'd get to see some of Rebinia. All that remained was the clothes I had on and the paperback book I had fallen asleep reading. That would do me no good now, not with my mind going a thousand miles an hour in all sorts of directions.

Then I realized how hungry I was. I hadn't had breakfast that morning, and I'd slept through lunch. I hoped this town had restaurants open in the evenings. I walked into the hall and saw the soldier who'd helped me book my room sitting in the stairwell. He stood when he saw me. Was he guarding me or keeping me prisoner? I told him I was hungry, and he nodded. He ushered me downstairs. He seemed to know where there was food available at that time of night.

Walking the streets of the little town at night was strange. There weren't a lot of streetlights, but then, there never were in small towns. I did feel safer with my escort beside me, but he didn't say a word when I tried to make conversation. We walked until we came to a little bistro. I wasn't sure what I ordered, but it turned out to be some sort of meat pie with a side of potato fritters. It wasn't expensive, and I still had some money after paying for the room and my food. The meal was quite tasty. I'd have to remember this place. There were a lot of people who looked like regulars. Everyone seemed to know each other, but then, that was the way in a small neighborhood.

I studied the place while I drank my cup of very strong black coffee. It was cute, with only a half dozen booths and four tables. It was clean, and the smells coming from the kitchen would make anyone hungry.

Then I walked back to the hotel with my escort. I waved good night to him as I went back into my room to try to get some sleep, that was, if I could quiet my mind. I was still trying to think through all the things I had to do.

The next day, I got up at mid-morning and back into the set of clothes I had. A different soldier was sitting in the stairwell, and like the one last night, he walked with me out onto the street. He was no more talkative than the last. I told him in my broken German that I wanted to get something to eat, and he followed me to the same bistro. I got a cup of coffee. I had less than a hundred dollars in my pocket, I'd have to be frugal until I could get my credit card replaced. I needed to find a phone so I could report it stolen and get the address of the hotel for them to mail me a new one. So many things I needed to replace, and my worst problem was finding a phone I could call from. I should have just relaxed for a moment until I could talk to Major Grvenski. I told my soldier that I wanted to talk to him, but he only looked at his watch and said, "Too early."

With nothing better to do, I decided to explore the city. My soldier wouldn't let me get lost or wander into places I shouldn't. The neighborhood around the bistro looked charming, and I strolled, looking into store windows and examining the old architecture. There were potted plants everywhere and benches so I could sit and rest. I really missed my phone. If I had it, I could take pictures and do an article on this place.

I could see the beautiful, enormous white castle at the edge of the city. It looked astonishing. The many-hundred-year-old buildings surrounding it were absolutely charming. Anyone would want to see it. Of course, it would be even more charming, more astonishing, more intriguing, and much more calming if I had my phone, my credit card, my passport, and a change of clothes...*any change of clothes.*

Later that afternoon, I was walking down the main street when a military car pulled up next to me. "Major Grvenski wishes to speak with you," one soldier said. It was the same cutie from the train. Oh, good. Maybe this was all cleared up. I looked at my watch; it was almost five o'clock.

The other officer opened the car door, and I got in. It was only two or three blocks to the government office. The city's crest over the door and the intricate carvings around the windows and doors amazed me. No one did work like that anymore.

The soldiers left as the major and I shook hands in his office on the second floor. I sat in the chair across the desk from him.

"There are two things we need to discuss." He took a breath. "First of all, the government of the United States says there is no record of a Katherine Lowe in Seattle, Washington."

I froze. "What? That's not true. Of course there is. I've lived there for fourteen years. I went to school there, and I've had the same address for the past four years. Have them check at Washington University in Seattle. I graduated ten years ago. I was born in Port Angeles, Washington. I have family there, and I graduated from high school there."

Oh my God. Am I rambling? Stop it. Get it together. Take a breath. How could they not find me? I knew who I was. Why didn't the government? I paid taxes every year and had them taken out of my paycheck every month. Certainly, someone must know me.

"They said the only record on any database for a Katherine P. Lowe in Washington State is for a woman who is seventy-six years old."

"Yes. That's my great-aunt, my grandfather's brother's wife."

"There are no Lowes in Seattle. Would you like to tell us who you really are?"

Oh my God. Did someone delete a page out of the files? There were a half dozen Lowes in Seattle…not related to me but with the name Lowe. I frowned. "I'm Katherine Lowe." I was starting to hyperventilate.

He stared at me suspiciously. "Do you have friends who can identify you?"

"Not here. I have a friend in Amsterdam, but my traveling companions are in Greece." I started to sweat. "Their itinerary and addresses were in my backpack."

He nodded as he seemed to consider my information. "What is your friend's name in Amsterdam?"

"Bobby…ah, Robert Bowen. But I don't know his address."

"And what does Mr. Bowen do for a living, so we have a start at finding him?"

"He's a bartender at a gay bar. I don't remember its name."

He wrote it down. "And there's no one else here who can identify you?"

"My friends should be in Odessa tonight." My hands shook. I slid them under my thighs so he wouldn't see, but what if he thought I was reaching for a weapon? I locked my hands behind my head. "I don't remember the name of the hotel they're staying at. That was in my backpack, too. I do know it's a small place where they speak English."

He stiffened. "I'm sure there are a lot of places there where English is spoken." He almost growled. "It is only in the United States that people refuse to speak two languages. I was surprised you speak German."

I sat back and nodded. Yes, most Americans only spoke

English. "I don't know anyone near here, but I'm sure there are a lot of people in Washington who can identify me. My professors at UDub all know me. I used to work in the bookstore on campus."

"UDub?"

"The University of Washington in Seattle. Dub rather than a double-u."

He wrote that down. Then he pressed a button on his phone. "Would you come in here for a minute, please?" he asked.

A gentle female voice responded. The same woman who'd brought me here came into the room. She closed the door and stood in front of it as though blocking anyone from leaving. Why would she need to do that? Did I need to run?

"Now, Miss…Lowe," the major said as if he still didn't believe that was my name. He reached under his desk. "Is this yours?" He placed a blue backpack on his desk.

"It looks like it." I looked more closely. There was that broken stitch on the top zipper and a grass stain on the side where I had dragged it across the lawn. "Yes! That's mine. Where was it?" My chest relaxed, and I could take a deep breath very easily. But why all the questions about my identity if he had it all right below his desk?

"This was found in a restroom on the train. Are you sure this is yours? There was no identification."

I was stunned. "Really? My passport was in it. In the front pocket."

He opened the front pocket and reached inside. There were a couple twenty-dollar bills and a few euros that I'd gotten in Italy. "No passport," he said.

No passport but the money was still there? What the hell? Why would anyone do that? It didn't make sense.

"Now let's take a look inside the main chamber." He opened the big pocket and reached inside. He withdrew a package of facial tissues, a tour book about Budapest, my electronic translator, some flyers about tourist places, and a small notebook. Everything with my name on it had been removed.

"This is your writing," he said, not really a question, but he waited for a confirmation. He handed me the notebook.

"Yes," I confirmed as I thumbed through it. I had written the name of each place I wanted to visit on every other page so I'd have room for notes. "My wallet, my plane ticket, and phone were in there."

"But they left the currency. Do you really think someone would steal your identification and not your money?" He glared. That had been my thought, too. Was someone setting me up for something?

I frowned. This was not only strange, this was damned frightening.

He pulled out my T-shirt and jeans and placed them on his desk. He took a deep breath. "There is no identification, but we found these packages." He reached into the backpack and withdrew a good-sized Ziploc of what looked like marijuana and a smaller plastic bag with black chips of something.

My stomach clenched. My heart had a hard time beating. "Those aren't mine."

"But this is your backpack."

"Yes, but the drugs aren't mine. I don't do drugs."

"You've never done drugs?" His voice was getting harder and harder.

"Well…I did some when I was in college. Most college students in the US try drugs a time or two." *Oh, damn, why did I admit that?* "But, even if I did, I wouldn't bring them into another country. That would be stupid."

"Then why did you try to bring drugs into this country?"

"I didn't. Those aren't mine." Good God, this was a nightmare.

His eyes narrowed as he picked up the notebook. "Are these the places you were going to meet someone to sell these? Or buy more?"

I couldn't believe what was happening. I never did anything illegal when I traveled. I checked laws wherever I was going to make sure I didn't make a mistake. That was my biggest fear, to be in jail in a country where I didn't know the language. Hell, to be in jail anywhere, no matter what language, was the most frightening thing I ever thought of. Was this really happening to me? No! No! No! Oh, merciful God! Why was this happening? I wanted my mom.

"It would help a great deal if you'd tell us your real name," he insisted.

"I'm Katherine Penelope Lowe from Seattle, Washington, in the United States of America. I have a degree from the University of Washington in Seattle."

"What did you study?"

"English literature. I'm a writer. I told you, I write for a travel magazine."

"Well, you're going to have a lot of things to write about…and a long amount of time to write them. Because, Miss Whoever-you-are, you are under arrest for drug trafficking."

"What? No. That can't be. I didn't bring those drugs here. I swear it. I'm not a criminal. Someone else did that. I'm being set up. Please! Believe me. I didn't do it."

He stood there looking at me.

"Can I call my family?"

"Not until you tell us who you are." He looked at the young soldier. "Lieutenant, take her below."

"Wait. *Wait…*" I started to exclaim as she grabbed my shoulder. Before I knew what was happening, she'd snapped a handcuff onto my right wrist and was pulling my left arm back to shackle it, too. "Let me talk to someone at the embassy."

"If we knew which embassy to call, we'd be more than happy to. But until you're honest with us, there's nothing we can do."

She pulled me back as she opened the door and pushed me out of the room.

Oh, God. This is turning into the worst nightmare I could ever imagine. Arrest? Drug Trafficking? Good God. I'd never do something like that. I'd never even think of attempting something like that. Why was whoever had stolen my stuff doing this to me?

My stomach clenched, my heart raced, and my eyes filled with tears. It probably wasn't good that I'd eaten because it was threatening to come back up. I never imagined being this scared. Was I going to vomit or cry? Or both?

There was a second soldier in the outer office who looked up as we came out. The lieutenant said something that I couldn't understand as she closed the door behind us. He chuckled and stood. They both seemed quite amused that I'd been arrested.

In the outer office, the lieutenant spun me around. "Do you have anything sharp in your pockets?" she asked. "You don't want to be charged with attempted murder if I get cut."

I looked up to see the other soldier draw his pistol. Oh, God! Now was not the time to hold anything back. "I have a mechanical pencil in my right-hand pocket."

She patted my pocket to feel for the pencil and carefully reached inside to remove it. Systematically, she removed everything and felt my whole body, under my breasts, between and down my legs. She unstrapped my watch and took my rings off, then lifted the cuffs of my jeans and felt around my ankles to make sure there were nothing hidden in my socks. She found the hundred I always kept there when I was traveling. She removed it and added it to the pile of my other things. She even felt around the waistband of my jeans.

The other soldier went through the things she had taken out of my pockets and started to write a list. When he finished, he turned the page around and pointed to a line at the bottom that had one word and an X. He picked up his gun that he'd set on the desk and stepped back. I felt her remove the cuff from my right hand. He handed me a pen and pointed to the form.

I assumed he meant me to sign it. I took the pen and looked at the form. It was all in Rebinian. I had no idea what was written there, and I didn't want to sign anything if I didn't know what it said.

I told them so. They both looked annoyed, but the man pointed to each word and translated into German. I knew that was no guarantee, but I figured I'd caused enough trouble, and they were getting angry about it. So I scribbled my name on the line. When I had, he put my possessions and the form into a large manila envelope and sealed it. He wrote something on the outside.

The lieutenant relocked my hands, said something to her counterpart, and pushed me into the hallway.

She led me through the corridors and stairwells. *Why do all old buildings smell the same? Is it the stacks of paper? The sweat that*

has accumulated there for centuries? The ink? The lack of fresh air?
I shook my head. Why was I worrying about that now? Did it make
a difference?

The musty smell in the lower level told me it wasn't used very
much. We went through a door that led to a corridor of a half dozen
jail cells. She opened one and motioned for me to step inside. The
sound of the lock sliding into place was much too loud. It felt like
shock waves traveling through my body.

I turned, and she motioned for me to step over to a slit in the
bars and turn around. She reached through the bars and unlocked the
cuffs. I turned back around to see her hooking the handcuffs onto
her belt.

She said something in Rebinian.

When I didn't understand what she'd said, she sighed, then she
repeated her order in German. "Take your shoes off." I bent to untie
them and pulled my sneakers from my feet. Instead of taking them
from me, she said, "You are not allowed shoelaces. Take them out.
They can be used as weapons to harm yourself or one of us." She
waited while I pulled the laces from my shoes and handed them to
her.

"Let me see the shoes, too," she said as she put the laces into
her belt. As I handed each to her, she turned it upside down and
shook it, then inspected the sole. When she was certain they were
not dangerous, she handed them back to me.

The lieutenant stared through the bars. I could feel her eyes
assessing me as she scanned my body. "It will be easier if you
cooperate," she said in German. "The next twenty years do not have
to be totally unpleasant." Then she turned, dimmed the lights, and
walked away.

I gasped. I couldn't get my breath. Tears started out my eyes,
and I felt like I was going to pass out. Had she said twenty years? Or
had I translated it wrong? *Please, God, let me have misunderstood
her.* And wait, was that a warning? Or a threat? Why was this
happening? Why? Why? Why? Would all the horror stories I'd
heard about Eastern European prisons become real?

I stumbled to the toilet in the back corner and fell to my knees. Then I lost what little I had in my stomach.

I finally got to my feet and leaned to the small sink that was part of the toilet tank. I tried both faucets, but only the cold water worked. I swished it around in my mouth to wash the feel and taste of vomit away.

I sank down on the bunk and looked around. There was nothing in this ten-by-six cell except the bed and the toilet-sink. That was divided from the rest of the room by a low wall to give some semblance of privacy. The space was too small to even *try* to hide. The only light came in through the bars.

Twenty years? No. Not twenty years. It couldn't be. I'd be over fifty by then. No, we'd get this cleared up. There had to be someone who could identify me. All I needed to do was to contact them. Anyone who could help me. The US embassy, the Red Cross, my mother, maybe my congressman or senator…anyone. How could there not be a record of me in Washington State? Someone was trying to set me up…someone who saw me on the train and figured they could get out of their crime by foisting it off on me and letting me take the heat. No, I would not be someone's patsy. *But how can I prove it?*

There had to be some record of me somewhere. There had to be. I knew who I was…didn't I? Was I beginning to question my own sanity? No. I would not let anyone make me do that.

Maybe they called the wrong person? The wrong agency? There had to be an explanation.

Then I stopped. But how did he know about Aunt Katie?

Tears ran down my face as my stomach cramped. I couldn't breathe. I threw myself onto the bunk. I was shaking. I'd never been this scared. Why was this happening to me? Did someone hate me *that* much?

After a few moments and several deep breaths, I jumped to my feet. How could I sit still? I wanted to call someone, to get this cleared up. I didn't want to wait until tomorrow. I needed to get it done now. Before I went out of my mind.

I paced the cell. Occasionally, I'd sit, but I couldn't stay for long, so I was back up on my feet a few minutes later. I felt like banging my head into the wall to see if I was truly awake. I paced and worried all night.

A guard came into the hallway and looked in on me three or four times. There were two different guards, but neither said a word nor acknowledged my questions. They merely looked in on me and walked out again.

Finally, exhausted, I fell onto the bed.

CHAPTER THREE

I was awoken the next morning—well, I assumed it was the next morning, it might have been just a few minutes later—by someone tapping on the bars. As I sat up, a guard slipped a tray of food through the shelved slot beside the door. He nodded to me and walked away.

Damn. I am *in jail.* It hadn't been a nightmare.

I wanted to turn over and go back to sleep to see if it would go away, but there was a paper sticking off the tray. I didn't dare hope that they'd found out who I was.

I got up and took the tray back to the bed. I opened the note. Someone had taken the time to translate it to English. *Court appointed lawyer meet: 10:00 a.m. Court arraignment: 11:00 today.*

I looked as far up and down the corridor as I could. I couldn't see a clock, and my watch had been taken. I lifted the napkin that covered the food. It looked like a potato pancake, a pastry, and a cup of black coffee. I bit into the pastry. It had a plum taste. The potato pancake was a little spicier than I thought it would be, but the taste was nice. I took a bite of each and went to wash my face. I wished I had a mirror. I imagined that my eyes were red with all the crying I'd done.

As I was finishing the coffee, the same lieutenant who'd brought me in last night came into the corridor. She handed me a small towel with a toothbrush and a tube of toothpaste, a clean shirt, some underwear, and a pair of jeans. I checked the sizes and decided they'd fit.

"Fifteen minutes," she said. Then she stood back to watch me change.

I sighed. *No time to be modest.* I stripped down and put the new clothes on.

The jeans were a little big, but they only fell around my hips a bit and weren't going to fall off. The shirt was fine.

I took the toothbrush and started to brush my teeth. I didn't know what the flavor was, but it wasn't the cool mint I usually used. At least I had something. I washed my face and my pits. I turned back around to see her still watching me.

"A least I smell better," I said in English. She smiled. "Do you understand English?"

She frowned.

"I know you speak German," I said in German.

"*Ja*," she said.

"That's good. At least we can communicate about something."

"You have a good lawyer," she said.

"I hope so. I really am not a drug dealer."

She looked at me without any emotion, then handed me my shoelaces. I sat down and put them on. "Come." She beckoned as she took the handcuffs off her belt. "Your hands behind you through here."

I turned and backed up to the bars and slid my hands behind me through the opening. I felt her handcuff me, and then she turned to unlock the door. I went out into the hallway as she ushered me back upstairs.

A very regal-looking woman was waiting for me in a room on the main floor. She seemed to be in her late thirties or early forties, and she looked stunning. She was blond and had on a stylish business suit and perfect makeup. In any other situation, I would have been attracted to her, but now was not the time for infatuations.

A pad of paper sat on the table in front of her. The lieutenant removed the handcuffs, and the lawyer motioned for me to sit opposite her as she asked me something in Rebinian.

I was confused. I shook my head.

"What is your native language?" she asked in German.

"Oh. English. I do understand some German."

"Then we're even. I understand some English." Her accent sounded thick.

Wow. Someone was listening to what I said. That was new. "Phew. I'm not always sure I'm saying the right thing."

"Then we'll help each other. I am Attorney Jocelyn Buza. Now, what is your name?"

"Katherine P. Lowe."

She looked at me skeptically.

"Really," I said. "Katherine Penelope Lowe from Seattle, Washington, USA."

"The major said you'd say that, but no one's been able to confirm it."

Could she help? Would she? "I'll give you my parents' telephone number. I don't understand what's happening. I was born and grew up there. I went to school there. I have parents, a grandfather, and a sister. I have a lot of friends." I knew I was rambling, but this was the first person who really listened to me. I'd give her any information she asked for if she could get me out of here.

"Then give me the information, and I'll see what I can do."

I told her my family's names: Frank and Shirley Lowe; gramps Francis Lowe, Senior; and my sister Pamela D. Lowe. I gave her addresses and telephone numbers. When she'd written that down, she put her pen down and turned to me.

"You're facing quite a list of charges. If the judge agrees to hear them, you'll be charged with drug trafficking, entering the country without a passport, illegal entry into the country to commit a felonious act, and refusing to cooperate with federal authorities. All of which are felonies. A half-kilo of marijuana and twenty grams of heroin were found in your possession. With that amount, you're looking at a total of twenty-three years in prison."

Oh my God. I couldn't get my breath. I felt like I was going to pass out.

"Why don't they just execute me and get it over with?" I asked in frustration and disbelief.

She smiled and placed a hand on my arm. "If we convince them to let the sentences run concurrently, we're looking at only eleven years."

"Eleven years? I didn't do anything." *Holy shit.* Eleven years in a foreign prison for something I didn't do? That was something from a movie or a spy thriller, not real life.

"All right." She smiled. "Tell me what you think happened."

We talked for the next forty-five minutes about my train ride, my background, home life, and activities. She was easy to talk to and had a warm smile.

"Do you have a husband?" she asked.

I shook my head. I didn't know what to say because I wasn't sure how this country viewed homosexuality, and all I needed was another charge.

"Are you a lesbian?"

Well, I couldn't lie to her. "Yes," I said softly.

"Are you ashamed of that?"

"No, I didn't know how it was viewed here, and I didn't want it added to my other charges."

She took a deep breath. "Yes, there are many places that frown upon it. We won't mention it to this judge."

I nodded.

"I think the best thing to do is to get a continuance until I can contact your parents and the US embassy in Pergue or in Washington, DC. It might take a few days, but we'll get this taken care of. I don't want you to worry. I'll handle everything."

There was a sudden feeling of hope. At least it sounded like she was working for me. "I hope so. Thank you."

"Come on. We don't want to keep the judge waiting." She straightened the pages and slid them into her beautiful hand-tooled leather briefcase.

The judge was a gruff-looking older man. He had a lot of white hair, but I could tell it had once been light brown. He talked with the prosecutor and Jocelyn for a moment, but it was all in Rebinian, and I didn't understand a word.

Finally, Jocelyn changed to German. "Your Honor," she said,

"my client only speaks English and German. Might we conduct this hearing in German so she can understand?"

He looked at the prosecutor, who nodded. The gavel hit the desk. The clerk repeated the charges for my benefit.

"The drugs were found in a sack that the defendant admits is hers." The prosecutor looked convinced that that was all that was needed.

"Your Honor," Jocelyn said, "that is all circumstantial evidence. The backpack was found in a public restroom. Anyone could have put the drugs in it. What we're asking for is to delay the trial for a few days so we can contact more people to identify my client and gather additional information and evidence."

The judge was silent as he studied her face. He sucked in his cheeks and looked at the prosecutor, who nodded. "All right. I will delay the trial."

I almost hugged Jocelyn. That was the best thing I'd heard in the last twenty-four hours. We exchanged glances, and I wanted to tell her how happy that made me, not that I thought I was out of the woods, but at least the trees weren't so close together.

"But," the judge continued, "this court does not have time for another trial for over two months."

My head whipped to Jocelyn, my eyes wide. Two months? Two months? Sixty days? I had to wait that long?

Jocelyn patted my hand and whispered, "Trust me." She sat.

"The prisoner has no friends or family in this county," the judge stated. "And as this is a government felony, she will be remanded to this federal prison until the time of the trial." His gavel hit the wooden block on his desk.

"Your Honor!" Jocelyn said quickly as she rose again.

The judge looked up and after a moment's hesitation, nodded. "Yes?"

"Your Honor, the jail here is used very seldomly and usually for only a night or two. If she is remanded here, that will require a full-time military detachment to guard and care for her. That will cost quite a bit of money and tie up our personnel. I ask that she be released to me, and I will take responsibility for her until the trial."

"You want to do that, counselor?" He seemed amazed at her proposal. So was I.

"Yes, Your Honor," she said. "I need additional help in my household, so she can earn her room and board, and I will be able to keep an eye on her."

"Any objections?" the judge asked the prosecutor.

The public prosecutor looked at me, then back at the judge, and shook his head. "No, Your Honor."

The judge looked at me thoughtfully. "If I agree to this, you will not get into any mischief or cause Counselor Buza any concern. Your actions will reflect on her. She has offered you a great deal, and you will not do anything that will make either her or me regret this decision." His eyes switched from me to her and back. "Do you understand the full impact of this decision?"

"Yes, Your Honor," I responded.

"Then it is the decision of this court to remand the prisoner into the custody of Attorney Jocelyn Buza." His gavel hit the desk block again.

"Thank you, Your Honor," Jocelyn said.

The judge adjourned the proceedings, and everyone started to straighten their papers and files.

"I won't let you down," I said as Jocelyn put her papers back in her briefcase. "You really didn't need to do that."

"Are you complaining?"

"Oh, no, no. That's very generous of you."

"We'll see. Now, what did they take from you?"

"There's an envelope I signed that has the contents of my pockets, my watch, and my rings. My clothes are still in the cell I was in."

Jocelyn beckoned the court clerk. They spoke, and the clerk nodded and left.

"Sit right here until I come back," she said. "If you move, you'll go back to that cell for two months. Do you understand?"

I nodded. "Yes, ma'am."

"I need to speak to the public prosecutor. It shouldn't take long."

I sat back, rather impatiently. I knew I had no way to speed this up, but I wanted to get outside into some air. The closed feeling of the cells seemed to permeate my entire being.

"Chill," I had to keep reminding myself. "Don't cause trouble."

I sat there with my eyes closed until I heard someone. The clerk handed me the envelope with my things and said something. I had no idea what, but I opened the envelope and poured everything out onto the table. It looked all there.

The clerk said something else. When I shook my head, she said "Sign" in German and placed a pen in front of me.

I checked the items off the list and signed the bottom. She countersigned and took the form away. I put my watch and rings back on, and I placed everything else in my pockets.

"Ready?" Jocelyn asked as she walked back to me.

"I still didn't get my clothes."

"I'll pick them up when I'm here again. Let's get something to eat. I'm hungry, and I imagine I ate more than you did for breakfast."

I smiled as she picked up her briefcase and ushered me outside.

CHAPTER FOUR

She took us to a small bistro not unlike the one I'd been in yesterday. Yesterday? All this had happened in twenty-four hours? Unbelievable. Just yesterday morning I was only worried about my belongings. The day before yesterday, I was happily on a train through Austria. My only worries were to inspect new places in Budapest. Now I was unhappily fighting to not go to prison in Rebinia. *What a difference a day makes.*

Jocelyn had asked me question after question about my background, my job, my education, and my life in general. It was easy to talk to her. She seemed really curious and listened very intently. She seemed to know just the right questions, and her smile, when my answer pleased or amused her, was charming.

Her sleek Skoda Octavia was top of the line and had the feel of a sports car. It took us almost a half hour to wind our way to her beautiful estate in the rolling hills. The cruising felt so freeing after last night, I couldn't believe the things I'd taken for granted. Would I ever be this free again? Would I ever be able to think without worrying?

While she drove, she pointed out scenery and talked about her practice. I was beginning to really like her. She seemed open to all kinds of thoughts and asked about life in the United States. She'd been all around the continent, down to several places in Africa, and even to Moscow, but never to the Western Hemisphere.

She drove around a corner. There were hills of grapevines and wonderful-looking grounds that were well-planned and manicured.

We pulled through high brick and iron gates and stopped in front of a large, castle-like building.

I gasped. "This is yours? It's gorgeous."

"It's an old family estate," she answered off-handedly.

I was overwhelmed by the beauty as a stone building, no doubt built hundreds of years ago, came into view. It was carved to perfection, like something out of a King Arthur movie. Of course, in this part of the world, it might have been a Bram Stoker story, but I'd save that judgment until I saw the inside.

As we pulled up to the front door, two young women came running up to us.

"This is Katherine," Jocelyn said. "Anna, see if you can find some clothes for her."

Anna nodded and shook my hand. She and I turned to walk up the long front stairs to the house as the other woman slipped into the car and drove it around the far side of the castle which was where it was probably housed. Anna seemed a few years younger than me and was sandy blond and trim. Her shoulder-length hair bounced along with her.

"Anna," Jocelyn called from behind us.

Anna turned back to her. "Yes, ma'am?"

Jocelyn said something in Rebinian, and she bobbed her head. "And show her to the third bedroom downstairs."

"I understand you only speak German and English," Anna said as we walked into the house. I nodded. "Then we will try to talk German. I think I can find clothes that will fit you. Let's go see."

She led me down a long hallway and through a door to a thin flight of stairs near the back of the castle. On the lower floor was a corridor with several doors along both sides.

"The doors on this side are bedrooms," she said, gesturing to the left. "The other side is storage." She opened the third door on the left. "This will be your room."

I walked in and looked around. The furniture was old but very well taken care of. There was a full-sized bed, a dresser, and a chair. The room was very clean and tidy.

There were small, short windows near the ceiling that showed we were belowground. A low wrought iron fence encircled the house. It curved over the windows to keep people out. The whole house was well fortified. It felt safe, and no one would break in. In light of everything that had happened in the last two days, it also felt confining, but I'd have to put that out of my mind for a while. I had to remind myself that I was free and could walk around...at least for now.

"There are linens and towels in the hall closet," Anna said, pointing down the hallway. I nodded. "How long will you be here?"

I took a deep breath. "One way or another, no longer than two months, I hope."

"That's too bad. I love it here. I've been here for four years."

"What happens here? Are there a lot of people? Are you related?" There were so many questions I wanted to ask, but was now the time? Why was it too bad that I'd only be here two months?

She chuckled. "You'll meet everyone at dinner." Then she turned and looked down the hallway. I knew why I was here, but she puzzled me. She looked like a nice young woman. Was she a housekeeper? An employee? Was this some kind of halfway house or a shelter for homeless or indigent women? She didn't look as if she'd been in trouble or on the street.

"This door"—she said, pointing to a door a few yards past my room on the other side of the hallway—"holds towels and bed sheets. The bathroom is on the left at the end of the hall. If you want to freshen up, I'll have some clothes ready for when you finish."

"That sounds really good. I haven't had a chance to shower today, and last night was not a good night."

"There's a hamper in the bathroom closet if you want your clothes washed. I do them every day."

"I don't want to cause you any work. Can't I do my own?"

"It's no work," she assured me. "We each have chores. Go take your shower, and I'll get you some clothes."

She walked away as I went to get a towel. I guess I'd have to wait until I met the others.

The shower was in an old-fashioned claw-foot tub with a

shower curtain hanging from a circular pipe. A bar of soap waited in the soap dish with a bottle of liquid. It smelled like shampoo.

I adjusted the temperature and stepped in. It felt wonderful to wash. The shower in the hotel the night before last had been quick because I'd been very tired and had to share the bathroom with others. I hadn't showered the next morning because I'd been impatient to see the city.

With everything that had been happening and the stress I'd been under, I was amazed I didn't smell worse. I washed my hair twice and scrubbed my body. I was drying off when there was a knock on the door.

"*Ja?*" I called.

"It's Anna. I have clothes for you."

I wrapped the towel around my body and opened the door. She had an armload of clothes. "These should all fit you. You can wear whatever you like."

"Thank you." I took the pile. I expected her to leave, but she walked in and sat on the closed commode, which seemed strange, but maybe that was the norm here.

"You don't look like you wear skirts, so I only brought you jeans," she said.

"Thank you. I haven't worn a skirt in years."

She watched me as I looked through the clothes. There were two pairs of jeans, several T-shirts, and a light blue men's cotton shirt.

"I'll find a few more shirts for you tomorrow. It's fine to wear T-shirts around the house or out in the garden, but we always dress for dinner," she said.

Really? *I forget that this is Europe and still has the old conventions.* I nodded and shook out a T-shirt. There was no bra, but there were a couple pairs of panties and a few pair of socks.

"I'm sorry they're not new, but they've been bleached."

"They'll be fine," I said.

It didn't look like she was going to leave, so I turned my back to her and stepped into a pair of panties, shed the towel, and slid on a T-shirt. I wasn't used to dressing in front of anyone, but these last two days had been unlike anything I was used to. I pulled on a pair of the jeans.

"Those fit you perfectly," she said. "I knew we were the same size."

"These are yours?" I had noticed she didn't wear a bra, either, but maybe that was the way it was here. I wasn't used to Eastern European customs. I guessed I *could* go without a bra if necessary. I wasn't used to it, but I wasn't that big, either, just a small C cup.

Anna nodded. "I'm sorry they're not the best," she said, nodding to the pile of clothes.

"They're okay. There's no problem." I put on a pair of socks and my shoes.

Anna picked up my old clothes, opened a closet door, and dumped them into the hamper.

"Come," she said. "I'll show you around."

I took the pile of new clothes into my room, then followed her upstairs. The door to the right of the stairs led into the kitchen. There was another woman at the stove, about my age, with dark brown hair. She wore glasses and was an inch or two shorter than me.

Anna introduced her as Lenci. "Do you cook?" Lenci asked me.

"A bit. I'm not great, but I haven't starved." I smiled.

"Can you make American hamburgers?" Anna asked enthusiastically.

"And…I think you call them French fries?" Lenci added.

I nodded. "Those aren't hard."

"I would love to try a real American hamburger," Lenci said. "I've only had one at McDonald's when I was in Pergue."

"I'll be happy to cook some when I get settled here."

"Wonderful." Lenci smiled. "Is there anything you especially like or don't like?"

"There's nothing I don't like, but I've never tasted real Rebinian food."

"You'll get a lot of it here," Lenci assured me.

"Come, I'll show you the rest of the house." Anna pulled me

away. I waved at Lenci as we left. She seemed nice. I looked forward to talking with her.

The rest of the house was phenomenal. The dining room was huge and could probably seat thirty people with enough room for waiters to walk around without bumping into each other.

"This is enormous. How many people actually live here?"

"There are four of us...now five, besides Jocelyn," Anna said. "Emilia handles the garden and winery, Lenci is in charge of the kitchen, I clean and do laundry, and Gabby keeps the truck and cars running and the landscaping trimmed. You saw her when you drove up. Emilia and Gabby are outside, Lenci and me in here. We make a good team."

"It sounds like it." Yes, it sounded like they *were* staff, each with her own job.

She opened the double doors into the living room.

Oh, my God, this really was a castle. The furniture was old but vintage. It must have been made many centuries ago. The heavy drapes looked like velvet. They were pulled aside with sashes to let the light in. There was no dust or grime anywhere. Each room she took me through was as incredible.

"Jocelyn owns all this?" I asked. "Where did she get it?"

"Her great-grandfather was a duke, I believe. She's the only one left in the family, so she's a duchess."

I shook my head as Anna led me up the long circular stairs.

She showed me two of the bedrooms up there. The beds had thick brocade canopies with white gauzy curtains. The armoires, chairs, and small tables were incredibly ornate. It definitely looked like it belonged to royalty.

We didn't go into the two rooms at either end of the hall. "That's Lenci's room," she said, "and the one at the other end is Jocelyn's. No one goes into either one without being invited."

I nodded. "Is Lenci related to Jocelyn?"

"I don't think so," Anna said, "but she's been here forever. Gabby has a room on the top floor, and Emilia and I have rooms near yours."

"This place looks enormous. How many bedrooms are there?"

"Let's see; there are six, no, eight on the top floor, ten on this floor, and ten down on our level."

"How come you and Emilia don't live up here?" I asked.

"We haven't been here that long. Maybe next year."

I frowned. Bedrooms were assigned based on longevity? She looked away and started down the hall toward Jocelyn's room. A door across the hall from Jocelyn's room stood open. Anna peaked inside.

"Hello," she said to whoever was in there. "I was showing Katherine around."

I stepped up to the open door. This room had been made into a very modern office. Everything was sleek white, and the windows had been re-glazed to let in tons of light. It was totally contrary to everything else. One whole side of the room was filled with law books. Jocelyn sat at a desk.

She smiled when she saw me. "Are you getting settled in?"

"I'm trying. This place is beautiful."

"Thank you." She smiled. "I see you've changed out of those jail clothes."

"I tried to wash it all off me."

"I sent a fax to the US embassy in Pergue to see if we can get any information. We should have something back by tomorrow."

I shook my head. "I can't believe this has happened."

"It will get taken care of."

"May I show her the gardens?" Anna asked.

"Not today," Jocelyn said and looked at me. "We need to discuss your boundaries before you go roaming around. We'll do that tomorrow morning. You look like you need a good night's sleep. You should go to bed right after dinner. You look exhausted."

I grinned at her and nodded. "I'm not sure I had any sleep last night at all."

"I imagine you didn't. Last night must have been hard. Did they treat you harshly?"

"Not really, but I was scared out of my mind. I paced back and forth, wall to wall because my mind wouldn't stop. I worried how I was going to prove who I am."

Jocelyn smiled. "Then relax tonight. Things will get better."

"Is that a promise?"

She grinned. "Definitely."

We smiled at each other, and then I turned to follow Anna downstairs. Yes, this would take some getting used to. I'd have to put all my trust in Jocelyn, but whatever was here was way better than where I had been. At least this wasn't jail, even though the lower windows were barred.

CHAPTER FIVE

Anna came and got me for dinner. I had changed into the shirt, and she was wearing a bright floral blouse with a long skirt.

"That's a pretty blouse," I said.

"Isn't it? I love it."

"Do we always dress for dinner?"

"Yes. Jocelyn requires it. I think it's nice. We never used to dress up when I lived at home."

"No. Me either," I said. "I think it's nice, too. Where's home?"

"I grew up in central Austria, but here's home now. Come on, we can't be late."

She led me up to the dining room. Everyone was there except Jocelyn.

"Sit next to me," Lenci said, pointing to the second chair from the front. "Jocelyn will want you close."

"Thanks," I said as I slipped into the chair opposite a pretty young girl, probably Anna's age, with long light brown hair.

Anna sat next to me. She squeezed my hand. "I'm glad you're here," she whispered. She looked across the table. "This is Katherine," she announced. "She's only here for two months." Then she gestured across the table. "That's Gabby and Emilia."

Gabby, a strong-looking butch, said something in Rebinian and held out her hand.

"Katherine speaks German, not Rebinian," Anna said.

"Ah!" She switched to German. "Welcome. I am pleased to meet you."

"Thanks," I said, reaching to shake her hand.

"Are you from Germany?" Emilia asked.

I shook my head. "United States."

"Wow. What brings you here?" Gabby said.

I laughed. "A mistake. I fell asleep on the train and missed my stop."

They all laughed. "Actually, it sounds funny, but I should be in Budapest tonight, working. Now I'm here for a few weeks." I didn't really want to explain it all, but I was saved.

The main door swung open, and Jocelyn walked in. Everyone stood. She had on a beautiful silk dressing gown. Her golden hair was piled on top of her head. She was very elegant. We all turned to her.

"Good evening, girls," she said. "Have you all met Katherine?"

"Yes, ma'am," Gabby answered, then she said something in Rebinian.

Jocelyn turned to Anna and said something else. Anna smiled and cast her eyes down. Jocelyn slid into the seat at the head of the table, and we all sat back down. Maybe one of these days I'd learn a little Rebinian and they wouldn't be speaking around me.

Lenci came in with a platter of breaded meat and set it on the table. Jocelyn nodded, and Emilia served everyone. Lenci returned with a bowl of stewed vegetables and passed them to me. I took some, and we passed them around. I wasn't sure what the custom was, so I sat there watching the others.

When Lenci sat, Jocelyn recited a long, slow speech. I didn't understand it, but the others crossed themselves, so I imagine she had said grace.

Everyone started to eat.

"What do you think of our food?" Lenci asked me after a few minutes.

"It's delicious. Is this lamb?"

She nodded. "You have good taste buds."

"Do you eat lamb in the United States?" Gabby asked.

"Not as much as I'd like. Lamb is a very expensive meat there."

Everyone smiled and nodded. Everyone got off on a discussion about food in different parts of the world, which was interesting, but as I observed each of them, it seemed strange that such a diverse collection of women lived together in harmony. Maybe they knew each other from living together for a few years, but there was something else there that included Jocelyn that bound them together. I'd have to be careful what questions I asked.

It turned into a nice family meal with someone translating for me if I looked like I didn't understand. When Jocelyn had finished, she stood, wished everyone a good night, pointed to Gabby, and walked away.

Anna and Emilia giggled until Gabby cleared her throat and frowned at them.

"Is everyone finished?" Lenci asked.

"Yes, Lenci, delicious as usual," Gabby said as she placed her napkin on her plate. "I hate to eat and run, but I have a meeting to attend." Then she walked out.

Lenci stood, took her own plate and Jocelyn's, and went out. Emilia gathered some other dishes and stood.

"Can I help?" I asked.

"If you want," she said.

I picked up another pile and followed her.

Lenci had the kitchen running smoothly. I washed off the counters and massive stove while she loaded the industrial-sized dishwasher, and Emilia put everything else away. We were done in less than fifteen minutes.

"Thank you for your help, Katherine." Lenci nodded to me.

"I'll help whenever I can."

Well, this didn't seem too bad, but there was still a lot I didn't understand. What was Gabby's business meeting about? Were they all in business together? Or were they all part of Jocelyn's law practice? The more I looked at it, the less it seemed they were Jocelyn's staff. Something more was happening. I could feel it.

I walked out of the back door of the kitchen, and Anna was still waiting at the top of the stairs. I smiled at her.

She grinned. "That was fast."

"I'm amazed," I said, shaking my head. "Lenci has the kitchen running very smoothly. It barely needs staff."

"I know."

"Are you four the only staff here?"

"Yes."

I felt like getting info was harder than getting me out of trouble. We hurried downstairs. "I think everyone likes you. You were very open at dinner."

"Thank you," I said as I entered my room. "I liked everyone, too."

"May I ask you a question?"

I stopped. "Sure. Come on in while I make my bed." Maybe if I answered her questions, she'd answer mine. I picked up the sheets and placed them on the dresser. I shook the bottom sheet out and laid it across the bed.

"Let me help," Anna said as she picked up one corner and stretched it over the edge. With her help, we had the bed made in seconds.

"Phew," I said. "Thank you."

"I think you'll need a blanket, too. I'll get you one." And she was already opening the closet door.

I could only smile as she spread the blanket on the bed and handed me a pillowcase. "Again, thank you. What did you want to ask?" I held the pillow under my chin to put the case on, fluffed it, and placed it at the head of the bed.

Anna hesitated. "You and Jocelyn talked about you being scared and someone treating you harshly. She also spoke of jail clothes. Can I ask what that was? Or do you want to keep that quiet? I can make believe I never heard."

I chuckled as I fell on the bed. "Have a seat. It's a long story."

She sat at the foot of the bed, and I started to tell her about my train ride. When I got to the part about being put in jail, I realized tears were running down my face. Anna was beside me with her arms around me when I finished. I wasn't used to being hugged by strangers, but this felt good at the moment. It was what I needed.

"So I'm in Jocelyn's custody until the trial."

"She'll take care of everything." Anna seemed sure of that. "She's an amazing woman, and we'll all be here for you." She hugged me tightly. "We'll all take care of you. You won't be alone."

"Thank you. I don't usually fall apart like this." I reached for my towel to wipe my face. I still couldn't believe everything that was happening.

"That's okay. You really do need sleep. If you need something during the night, I'm in the next room down the hall across from the linen closet, and Emilia is in the first room by the stairs."

"Thanks again. It does help to feel someone's on my side." Someone who believed what I told them.

She leaned over and kissed me gently on the lips. "Have a good night." She got up and went out into the hall, closing the door behind her.

The small lamp on the dresser had been left on, and it felt safer than the dark, so I left it on as I stripped and settled in to sleep. It was dark outside, but I figured if anyone was outside watching me, at least they couldn't come inside. The moon cast light on the fields of vines behind the house. It did feel safe, a lot safer than where I was last night. My mind was going in a thousand directions again.

What would happen if I tried escape? Where would I go? What would I do? Which way was south? West? I didn't want to get trapped in the mountains, but if I headed southwest, I might be able to get somewhere. But where? I only had a little money. If this was a long-ago war, I could try to find resistance fighters, but it was just me, trying to get out of a mess in Rebinia.

Maybe I could get to Amsterdam. Bob would help. He knew who I was. I'm sure he'd help me. He'd at least call someone.

But Jocelyn would get in trouble for letting me escape. She'd been so nice to me and brought me here to keep me out of jail. Where did my map end up? I had left it with my book back in that little hotel. It was gone by now. I should give it up and put my trust in Jocelyn.

I thought about all that had happened in the last three days, all that might happen in the next two or three months. I didn't want to go to prison for something I hadn't done. I didn't want to go to prison, period. I felt the tears start again. There was only so much that Jocelyn could do.

I must have cried harder than I thought because later that night, Anna crawled into bed with me and held me tightly. I wasn't sure I liked it, but it did feel warm and safe. Being in someone's friendly arms was better than a lot of other options. Her softness filled a place in my soul that needed comfort. The only one that would have felt better, safer, was Jocelyn, but I wasn't even going to go there in my thoughts. No, Jocelyn was out of reach.

Chapter Six

"Jocelyn wants to see you in her office when you finish breakfast," Lenci told Anna when she and I sat down in the morning to eggs and white fish mixed with shredded potatoes.

"Thank you, Lenci," Anna said.

"And she wants to see you, too, Katherine, when she's finished with Anna."

"All right. Thanks." Hopefully, she'd have word about something. At the very least, she'd allow me to go outside to help Emilia or Gabby. I didn't want to hide inside all day, and I figured I should pull my weight. I needed something to keep my mind occupied, to keep me busy while the time passed. There was nothing that I could do today to solve my case, so sitting here and worrying was not helping anything.

Lenci nodded and went back into the kitchen.

"I hope she gives you permission to go outside. The gardens are wonderful," Anna said. "Emilia does such a good job."

"Are all those grapevines part of this place, too?"

"Yes. Emilia works with those. She'll probably bottle five or six hundred bottles. Two years ago, she bottled almost a thousand."

"Wow. Do you keep it all here, or does Jocelyn sell it?"

"Jocelyn will sell a few hundred in the town, but we always keep three hundred or so. We drink almost one a day." Well, there was something here to drown my thoughts in if I went crazy from worrying. That was a perk.

We finished breakfast, and Anna went up to talk to Jocelyn. I helped Lenci clean up.

❖

"You look rested. How do you feel?" Jocelyn asked when I went into her office. She pointed to a chair beside her desk, and I sat.

"I'm doing okay this morning. I guess I really needed to sleep. Have you heard from the embassy?"

"Not yet, but we still have time. You need to relax. I told you to let me worry about it."

"I'm sorry, but I can't be as sure as you. It scares me."

"I understand. I imagine it would scare me, too."

"I want this to go away so I can go home." I sighed.

She nodded. "Unfortunately, that's not in the plans right now. It won't happen for a while, but I'm confident you won't spend any time in prison."

I wanted to be as positive as she was, but I was finding it hard to even think of tomorrow. Should I rethink my escape plan? How far away was Amsterdam?

"Now," she said, "Anna and Emilia want to show you the gardens. You won't try to escape, will you? You won't go wondering off."

Fuck. It always comes back to that. "How could I? I have no money, I don't know where we are, and I'm not even sure which way is Amsterdam. Besides, then I'd get you in trouble."

"Amsterdam? Why Amsterdam?"

"I have a friend there who might be able to help me."

"You should give me his name, then if we can't get info from the government or your parents, I'll contact him."

"I don't even know which way is what. I got so turned around yesterday, I didn't even see which way the sun was setting, and I slept through the sunrise this morning."

"We're not that far from the border, but if you try to run, you'd be running for the rest of your life. I'd be the first to track you down."

"Yes, I figured that would happen. You don't have to worry. I know that if it wasn't for you, I'd be spending the next eight or nine weeks in that cell."

"Yes. Just remember that. Now, do you want to work in the garden with Emilia?"

"Yes, I would. Fresh air is very appealing."

She thought over my answer for a moment. "All right. You may help Emilia. I believe the squash is ready to harvest. Work hard."

I nodded. "Thank you."

She flicked her hand to send me off.

❖

"Hi!" I called to Emilia when I got to the garden. She was on her knees between two rows of butternut squash. "Need any help?"

She sat back on her haunches. "I can always use help, if you don't mind getting dirty."

"Dirt is not a problem," I said as I navigated the rows. "What can I do?"

"If you can take these"—she indicated a pile of squash beside her—"and set them in the wheelbarrow, it would be a big help. I guess, if you want, you could bring the wheelbarrow here, so we won't have to make as many long trips to get to it."

I smiled. "I can do that."

We worked well together. Emilia looked at the squash to see if it was ready to be picked. If it was, it went into a pile that I put in the wheelbarrow, and then I pushed it farther along the row. I also did a little weeding on the plants that weren't ready.

The work wasn't hard, and I found that Emilia had a good sense of humor. While we worked, I helped her with her English, and she taught me some Rebinian.

At lunchtime, Anna brought us sandwiches and bottles of homemade apple juice and sat with us while we ate.

"You look like you got a lot done today," she said.

"It goes a lot faster with two people." Emilia smiled. "Katherine has been a big help. We may get most of the squash picked today."

"Wow. Lenci will be really happy. I can't wait to see what she cooks this year." Anna turned to me. "Lenci loves to experiment. She'll try all kinds of new ways to cook things. They're always phenomenal."

I laughed. "I haven't eaten this well since I left home. I thought my mother was a good cook, but..." I lowered my voice. "I think Lenci's better."

Anna and Emilia laughed. We chatted about almost nothing for a few minutes before I got up the nerve to ask, "Tell me, do you all work for Jocelyn? Are you hired? How did she find you?"

They looked almost frightened before Emilia answered. "I was working with a vintner in Austria, and he recommended me to Jocelyn. It's a great job. I love it here."

"I was recommended by a man from home, and she moved me right here."

"I think we should get back to work," Emilia said. "We should be able to get the squash done today, except for the few that aren't ready yet."

"How much else do we have to do?" I hadn't found out a lot and I wanted to keep them talking, but I couldn't push. Maybe more tomorrow.

Emilia thought for a moment. "The peppers, carrots, and potatoes. We have to cut the herbs, too, and hang them in the cellar to dry. Then in a few weeks, we can start on the grapes."

"I hope you're still here," Anna said. "We have a lot of fun harvesting grapes."

"Fun?"

"Yes, it usually takes us hours to get the juice out of our skin. We walk around all red and purple." They both laughed almost hysterically. "Every year, we have to buy new sheets."

"Are you kidding?"

"You'll find out if you're still here."

"I've heard that you crush the grapes with your feet," I said.

Emilia smiled. "They used to, but we're modernized. We have machines that squeeze the grapes and strain the skins and other things out." She stooped to the squash again. "And we have a machine that bottles it, too."

"Wow. That's really far into the future." I hope they realized I was being facetious.

Anna picked up everything and went back inside with the dirty dishes.

Emilia and I had a good time. We worked until well into the afternoon. As I pushed the wheelbarrow full of produce back to the house, Emilia told me a little about the land in this area and pointed out some features of the terrain in the distance. Yes, maybe I could escape...or at least, it was always an option.

"The winter squash needs to be put in the root cellar," she said as we approached the house. "Come, I'll show you."

She led me to a wooden bulkhead at the side of the house, opened the old door, and flicked on the light. "There are bins for each kind of squash."

I nodded as we carried the produce into the cellar. We almost filled two of the wooden bins. There were shelves along one wall with jars of vegetables that had been canned.

"Lenci does a big job of canning things every fall. There are a lot of things here: fruit, jams, pickles, relishes...all sorts of things."

"Can we bring some in?" I asked. "I'm supposed to make hamburgers tomorrow and pickles and relish go great with them."

"Let's check to see what Lenci already has inside. I can always come out and get what you need tomorrow."

"Thanks."

"No. Thank you for your help."

She hugged me, then stepped back to stare into my eyes. After a few moments, she leaned in and kissed me on the lips. I held back for a moment. Should I kiss her back? Was it an option, or was it expected as part of my stay here? What the hell? Her lips felt soft and warm, and I couldn't come up with one solid reason to turn away.

I couldn't hold back and kissed her. It was a long hot kiss. It was a good kiss, so I let it continue and continue. It was the one thing I'd done lately that I wasn't sorry for. It might be a one-time thing but it felt good.

Finally, Emilia stepped back with a soft smile. "I liked that," she whispered.

"So did I."

We stared at each other for a few minutes in that cool, dank room.

"I guess we need to take the rest inside," she said softly as she ran her hand through my short hair.

I nodded, and we went outside and took armloads of vegetables into the house. Nothing more was said about the kiss.

❖

The dinner routine was the same. It seemed to be a norm. The only one not present was Jocelyn, but she entered a few minutes later in a midnight blue, floor-length gown, her hair and makeup perfect. Talk was warm and friendly.

"I saw you working with Emilia today," she said. "Did you get a lot done?"

"Katherine was a big help," Emilia explained before I had a chance. "We got all the ripe squash picked and stored in the cellar. Katharine is much stronger than me, and I didn't have to struggle with the wheelbarrow, and we could bring it all in at once."

Jocelyn looked at me with a pleased smile on her face. "Thank you, Katherine," she said softly. "Maybe we have found something for you to do."

"She also helped in the kitchen last night," Lenci put in.

Jocelyn smiled wide. "Then you have a lot of things to do."

I nodded. "I enjoyed it." On top of giving me something to do, I'd gotten to chat with Lenci. I learned a lot more from her than any of the others. Lenci was from this area and worked with her mother as a housekeeper. When her mother died, Jocelyn's father hired her to keep house here. That was almost fifteen years ago.

Jocelyn smiled as she continued her meal.

"Can you service cars, too?" Gabby asked.

I shook my head. "The closest I've ever come to fixing a car is to wash it."

Gabby grinned. "Then I'll call you if one gets too dirty."

I looked at Jocelyn when she chuckled to see what she would say, but there was only a happy smile on her face. Did I miss something? Was Jocelyn amused? Intrigued? I had no idea why she had laughed. Maybe one of these days, I'd ask her.

CHAPTER SEVEN

After dinner, I stayed to help Lenci clean up again. I washed all the counters while she loaded the dishes.

"Good job. Thanks," she said.

I smiled. "I'll help whenever I can. I don't have much else to do." Not that I loved housework, but I would be bored otherwise. It would keep me busy and maybe keep my mind off my other problems.

"You helped in the garden today, and I think Gabby was serious about washing the cars." She gave me a big smile and a chuckle. "I'm sure Jocelyn will find lots of things to keep you busy."

I smiled and nodded...unless Jocelyn found out I'd kissed two of the other women here. Would she be angry at me? That was another thing. Jocelyn's women...it was like she had her own harem. I had to shake my head. I couldn't speculate about her having sex with them, though, or any of them being worthy of her. She was so sophisticated. Did she have a thing for younger women? I smiled to myself. *Maybe I should get a harem.*

"Go off and relax," Lenci said. "I think you've done enough for today."

I nodded. "Thanks. Have a good evening."

I walked down the stairs, opened the door to my room, and stopped. Anna and Emilia were both in my room, on my bed, naked. Oh my God. It was like I had imagined them into reality. Was this *my* harem? They smiled as Emilia got off the bed.

"Jocelyn told us that you were unhappy and to be really nice to you, and we couldn't think of a nicer thing," Anna said as Emilia closed the door behind me. Were we doing this in secret? Damn. Of course we were.

"Yes, this is the nicest thing there is," Emilia explained as she pushed me closer to the bed. Were they taking over? Like Hannah?

"Uh," I said, "I've never done a threesome." I'd never imagined it, either. But the idea intrigued me.

"Then tonight's the night to experience something new," Emilia said.

Anna started to unbutton my shirt as Emilia opened my jeans and pushed them over my hips.

"Wait, wait, wait!" I was in shock, standing there, letting them do what they wanted, flashing back to Hannah. I felt a pang of arousal inside my belly but also confusion. Anna and Emilia were at least ten years younger than me. And I had thought I was experienced.

Emilia pushed my shirt over my shoulders and let it fall behind me. No, this was definitely not my imagination. Anna got up on her knees and kissed me as she rubbed my nipples. Emilia was behind me, so I couldn't back up.

"Wow," I gasped as she backed away. What were they going to do to me? Should I put a stop to it? But it felt so good, and I'd been so stressed, and I was getting very turned on. And…and…

Emilia pushed me onto the bed. She pulled my jeans and panties over my feet and threw them to the floor. "You don't need these," she said. But did I? Should I—

Anna rolled over and placed her lips on mine. I felt one of them kneading my breasts. Oh, yes, now that was what I liked. I stopped thinking so much. I tried to reach out, but someone pulled away as the other nibbled my neck and my ear. Anna's kiss was hot with a lot of tongue. I couldn't get my breath. I hadn't been this turned on in quite a while. Was I drowning?

"Want some of this?" Anna asked as she placed her nipple in my mouth. I bit gently and started to suck and lick, taking it between my teeth. I was determined to return the kisses and strokes, but one of them was always there to redirect me. Emilia held my arms over my head as she kissed me, and Anna started to move her mouth down my body.

I flinched as she bit my nipple, but Emilia wouldn't let me move to relieve the feeling. I wanted to be a full partner, and if they were like Hannah, I could get into it.

"Just lie back and let us do the work," Emilia whispered as she claimed my mouth again.

I was lost. This was happening so fast, much faster than I really liked, given my situation. I could feel every movement, but I had no idea whose hands were where, nor what they were doing. The three of us were rolling around like a litter of kittens, hands and mouths everywhere.

Then someone's hand found my center. I gasped as the shock waves filled my body.

"Good?" I heard.

"Oh yes." I wanted to touch them, but I seemed to have lost the ability to move. The feeling in my crotch kept me silent.

Anna licked and kissed all over my body. I was on the edge. Fingers delved into me, and I moaned. I was falling into the darkness and had no way to control myself. It seemed to be going on forever and ever. I was on the precipice, ready to plunge.

"What the hell is going on here?" a voice boomed, and everything stopped. Anna and Emilia sat up quickly.

"I'm sorry, Mistress—" Anna began.

"Quiet!"

I was still in that zone between earth and sky and couldn't have said anything if asked.

"Did I give permission for this?" Jocelyn asked sternly.

"No, Mistress," Anna and Emilia both said softly.

She looked at me, her eyes fiery. "And you seduced two of my girls?" she growled.

"No, ma'am, we—" Emilia started.

"Did I address you?" she interrupted, glaring.

"No, Mistress," Emilia said softly, her eyes down.

Mistress? What was happening here? Had I heard her right?

That sounded as if this was one of those Eastern European BDSM houses. But those weren't real. Those were made-up tales, weren't they?

"Anna, call Gabby and Lenci and have them meet us down here." Anna hurried out of the room. "Pick those clothes up," she ordered Emilia. "We do not live in a pigsty." Emilia scrambled to pick up and fold my clothes. Jocelyn stared into my eyes. "You wanted sex? Then you'll get it and a whole lot more."

"No—" I started, but she held her hand up to stop me.

"Emilia, tell her my rules." Jocelyn turned and walked out. I heard her rushing up the stairs.

Emilia and I stared at each other. "What's happening?" I asked.

She took a deep breath. "This is Mistress Jocelyn's house, and she is in charge. We are her girls, and we love her. She gives us everything we need. We know we'll never want for anything. We never argue with her, and we'd never correct anything she says. We're grateful that she allows us to live here and serve her. There isn't anything any one of us wouldn't do for her. But you don't want to make her angry. We do whatever she requests."

I sat back. So this *was* a harem of sorts. One of those slave dens? A house run by a Master or Mistress where BDSM was practiced regularly? "All of you?"

"Yes, Lenci is second in command. She's first girl. She's been with Mistress Jocelyn for over ten years. Gabby, seven or eight, I think. Anna and I have only been here three or four years. That's why we live down here. You have to prove your worth before you're allowed upstairs."

I'd heard about things like this, but I didn't know anyone who practiced it. Hannah was the closest I'd come, and she just liked to tie me up. But a house where bondage and sadistic sex was practiced? Did it really exist?

"I'm sorry we got you into this, but we both like you, and Anna said you were depressed, and we wanted to make you feel better. Mistress is angry because we're not supposed to be together unless she requests or approves it."

Requests or approves? Oh my God. "What did she mean by 'and a whole lot more'?"

Emilia bit her lip. "I don't really know. We'll find out." She put the pile of clothes she'd just folded into the dresser. Then she reached for my hand and squeezed it. "You'll be fine. You're strong."

"It would be a lot better if I knew what was going to happen." I needed to be prepared, and I definitely wasn't. Should I be scared? How scared? Oh my God. Out of the frying pan...

"I can't tell you because I don't know. Every time it's different, but she seldom calls for everyone, so I have no idea what will happen."

I frowned. What had I gotten into?

"It'll be okay. Don't talk back to her or refuse a command. She knows what's right for us."

"Every time?"

She nodded. "Every time. I've only been here for just over three years, but I've never been happier. It feels very secure here. Let her make decisions for you."

I'd have to think about that. It sounded like I'd be surrendering a lot of my free will, not just being tied up now and then. But then, I'd have to surrender my free will if I went to prison, too.

But sexually? Would I be raped? No, it was Jocelyn. I couldn't imagine her doing something like that.

And I had to admit, I wanted her.

After Hannah, I had seen a notice for a leather group meeting in Seattle, and it had felt interesting. I was curious but was so very afraid to go on my own. I'd missed the things Hannah had made me feel.

Now I had no choice, scared or not. But I had to see what would happen.

CHAPTER EIGHT

Jocelyn appeared in the doorway. She was dressed in black: tight black trousers, a black vest with no shirt, and high black heels. Her blond hair, piled on top of her head, highlighted the entire effect. She looked very intimidating as her eyes roved my body.

Should I say something or remain quiet? Which would make her angrier?

She lifted an eyebrow as she stared at Emilia, who rushed out of the room. I guess that was some kind of signal.

Jocelyn turned and nodded.

Lenci and Gabby walked into the room, took me by my arms, and pulled me out into the hallway. It hit me that I wasn't scared, that I was turned on. I had hesitated too long, and now I didn't have the chance to pull away.

A wide door across from the bottom of the stairs stood open. A false wall had been swung to the side so the door was accessible. They pushed me inside a large room filled with strange furniture. The walls were painted black, but there were spotlights around the room, each focused on one piece of equipment.

I stared with wonder at all the things in the room. I was definitely out of my comfort zone. I didn't have to worry or wonder very long. I tried to hesitate, but they marched me to the center of the room where two heavy chains hung from the ceiling. This wasn't any silk scarf. I started to balk, but Lenci winked, and I relaxed. She shackled the chains around my wrists and drew me up until I was on my toes. I hung there, barely touching the floor.

"Hang on to the chains so your wrists will not be hurt," Lenci whispered. She stooped, and I felt her wrapping something around my ankle. Then she went to the other. My legs spread apart, and I could do nothing to pull them together. I couldn't close my legs to protect myself.

Why the fuck would I want to? Feelings I hadn't experienced since Hannah washed over me.

I looked around as best as I could. Emilia and Anna were on their knees against the side wall. They were staring at the floor, their hands behind their backs. Jocelyn stood in front of me and scanned my body. There was a strange smile on her face. I wanted to stand tall and not look like a wimpy little chicken. "This is sooner than expected, but you *will* enjoy this." It sounded like an order. "Where is your home?"

"I live in Seattle, Washington." I straightened myself proudly. I'd prove I could do whatever this became.

"Then if, with all your heart, you want this to stop, say Seattle, and everything will cease. Seattle will be your safe word. Otherwise, we will continue as I want. The girls know to obey my demands. I am in charge. I decide what happens, and you will obey my wishes without question. Once you say Seattle, you will be returned to your room, and you will never come in here again. In fact, you will be moved to the south wing where you will live until your trial. Do you understand?"

I nodded, although I wasn't sure I did.

"You will say yes, Mistress, or no, Mistress, not just nod your head."

"Yes, Mistress," I said tentatively. It felt almost silly, like role-playing. I giggled.

"Do you find this funny?"

"N...no. I'm nervous."

"As you should be."

It was hard getting used to this, but I had the feeling it might be worth it, just like with Hannah.

"You will not scream, and you will not refuse whatever I tell you to do. This house is a monarchy, and I am the queen. My word is law, especially in this room." She studied me again. "This is new to you, isn't it?"

I must have nodded. She raised an eyebrow. "Y...yes, Mistress," I whispered. "I've only been tied up with silk before."

"It will be good practice for prison."

I had to swallow my gasp. I couldn't read her expression. Finally, she walked around me. I heard something roll across the floor. It sounded like a pile of sticks.

I wasn't ready when the first wallop hit my butt. I swallowed the scream that wanted to escape.

"Good," I heard her say as something smacked me again. I didn't know what she was using, but it was not her hand. It felt flat and hard. Damn, that hurt. She hit me a few more times. My ass stung, but I couldn't stop her, not without using my safe word. But...did I really want this to stop? If it stopped, I'd never know what would happen next.

I might miss something beautiful.

"And that was only the beginning," she whispered in my ear.

I had imagined something like this for years. Well, not exactly like this, but something harder than normal. I had thought it was going to be like the bondage that Hannah had done. Not with chains and paddles.

Gabby came over in front of me, "Welcome to the family," she said as she planted a passionate kiss on my mouth. She ran her hands down my body and up to my breasts. What did family mean? Was this just the beginning?

She looked over my shoulder. "May I?" she asked.

Jocelyn must have nodded because Gabby motioned to someone. I was lifted off the floor until my nipples were level with Gabby's mouth. She ran her hands down my body as she inspected every inch. Did I pass inspection?

She took one of my nipples into her mouth while she squeezed the other. She sucked each forcefully, going back and forth between them.

What a turn-on: suspended in the air, totally helpless, my breasts being fondled forcefully. I had never felt like this before.

I could feel myself getting hotter and hotter. She didn't stop until I moaned. Immediately, Jocelyn's paddle hit my ass. When Gabby bit my nipple, the muscles in my arms spasmed, and I lifted up. Her teeth didn't let go. Pain shot through my body, and I gasped. Did I need to call my safe word?

Gabby stepped back with a laugh. She softly stroked my face.

"Enough?" I heard behind me.

"For this time." Gabby grinned. She looked over to the side, and I was lowered to where I'd been at the beginning. No, I'd gotten this far without my safe word. I could go a little further. She patted my cheek and kissed me again, this time gently.

I felt Jocelyn behind me. She caressed my body. "You like your breasts sucked, don't you?" she whispered.

I started to nod. "Yes, Mistress." I whispered.

"Very nice. I think you'll enjoy this house."

Then Lenci was in front of me, smiling. "I told you that Jocelyn would find other things for you to do." She stared in my eyes and nodded. It felt like a shared secret. Then she took a step back and scanned my body and squeezed my breasts. She looked over my shoulder. "Are you sure we can't keep her longer?"

"Not this time," Jocelyn said.

"That's too bad." Lenci pulled my neck closer, then kissed me. While the kiss was happening, Jocelyn hit my behind three more times. I didn't know whether to respond to the kiss or the strikes, so I closed my eyes and kissed Lenci back.

She ran her hands over my entire body, sometimes so soft it became a tickle, and I squirmed, which caused her to chuckle. When she touched my ass, I flinched.

"Does this hurt?" she asked.

I nodded. I was sorry I had, because her fingers dug into me. She continued until I moaned.

"Do you like pain?" she asked.

I stopped. "I don't...know."

She took her hands back around my hips to hold me steady as Jocelyn's paddle hit my ass again...and again...and again. She ran her hands back around my hips and felt my ass. She chuckled. "Nice and hot." She moved her hands slowly down my side until she got to my hips. Then her thumbs brushed my triangle. She looked into my eyes as she delved farther in.

I gasped as I trembled from her touch.

"Not all of it," I heard behind me as her fingers ran around my clit.

She stopped.

I blinked and stared. I was on the edge, and she had stopped. I needed more.

She pulled me forward and kissed me again, a long, lingering kiss with lots of tongue. I really liked that. She stepped away.

Jocelyn pulled my head back by my hair until tears came to my eyes. "Are you enjoying this?" she whispered.

"I, uh, I don't know."

"Are you ready to use your safe word?"

I didn't know, but if I did, everything would stop. I was curious. I wanted to find out more. "I don't think so," I answered, then added, "Mistress."

I heard her laugh. "Then we'll have to do more until you know for sure."

She wrapped her arms around me and took my breasts roughly. She kneaded them until tears started down my face, and then she worked down my torso. She bit my neck as her fingers found my crotch. "You must have enjoyed it. You're sopping wet," she said as she delved in.

I think I stopped breathing as she explored me. She was slow and gentle but insistent. Good God. The woman was phenomenal. On top of her beauty, she had power and hands of gold. I tried to take a breath, but my chest was locked in a tightness that defied any movement. I had no control of anything. What was this doing to me? Was I falling into a role, letting Jocelyn control my every move?

Soon, I was writhing.

"Don't you dare come until I give you permission," she growled. "If you must, you can beg."

Oh God. I was right on that razor-sharp line between this world and the space that opened into ultimate pleasure. Suspended and not quite anchored to the floor, I flailed as her fingers continued.

"Please," I moaned. I was about to lose it. "Please."

Her finger started to move faster. "No. Hold on to it."

I wasn't sure what I was feeling. I seemed to be getting tighter and tighter, hotter and hotter. I was sweating.

"Ready?"

I tried to catch my breath. "Yes…please."

"Then come for me."

I closed my eyes as my body erupted. I tried to curl into a ball, but my feet were secured to the floor. I pushed back into her as wave after wave overtook me.

I wasn't sure where I was. I opened my eyes when I heard applause.

"Yes." she whispered. "Very nice. You'll do well here."

Her praise warmed my heart. I might have been falling in love…with her or with the situation? It was so much more than anything I'd ever felt with Hannah.

As she stepped back, I heard, "Emilia and Anna. Come here."

When they stood in front of me, she said. "You two started this. You should have some, too."

"Thank you, Mistress," they said.

"May I eat her?" Emilia asked.

"May I have her breasts?"

Jocelyn gave a quick laugh. "Yes."

Emilia knelt, lifted my legs by the bar that held them apart, and placed them over her shoulders. Then all I knew was sensation: rubbing, licking, sucking, slurping. The way my body reacted, I would have never believed I'd come a few minutes ago. I threw my head back and let myself be washed away.

CHAPTER NINE

A nna woke me with a tray of pastries and scrambled eggs.
"Lenci figured you'd be pretty hungry this morning." she
said. "I guess everyone was."

I looked at my watch, then around the room. It was 11:15, and
I was in the bed in my own room.

"How did I get in here?" I asked. I didn't remember walking
back.

"Gabby helped you. Everyone got scared when you zoned out.
I thought we had fucked you to death."

I had to smile at that. That would have been a way to go.

"Lenci had us take you down off the chains for Mistress Jocelyn
to examine. Do you remember that part?"

I thought back, but the last thing I remembered was her arms
around me.

"Mistress said you were fine, but you were really zoned out."
Anna smiled. "You did answer her questions, but I don't know if
you knew what you were saying. You were wonderful."

And if I remembered correctly, everyone was wonderful. Had
all five women made love…no…had they all fucked me last night?

"Is it like that every night?" I took a bite of eggs.

"No, we haven't had everyone there in a long time. It's usually
Mistress or Lenci with one or two of us. Mistress Jocelyn's favorite
is Gabby, I think, but we never feel neglected."

"How did last night start? Did you really come to me on your
own?"

She smiled in embarrassment. "Mistress Jocelyn told me to think of a way she could get you into the dungeon, and we're not supposed to be with each other unless she requests it, so that gave her a reason to punish you."

That was what they called punishment? It was another category altogether.

"Did I have fun?" I still wasn't sure what had happened.

"Everyone thought you were flying so high, we'd never get you back to earth. I don't think I ever witnessed that many pheromones." Her eyes lit up. "You could feel them all over the room. We were all turned on."

"I barely remember anything after a point." Had I been that high? I couldn't remember ever passing out after sex, but I'd never had sex that good before.

"You should go thank Mistress Jocelyn for last night. She's in her office. Kneel in front of her and thank her for the opportunity to please her."

"Kneel?"

"Yes. It shows respect."

Well, damn, I wasn't sure the word was *respect*, but I did have a new appreciation for all Jocelyn could do, and I did respect her control…of all of us.

I went upstairs to her office and knocked on the door. All I had thought about that morning was her. I was amazed at everything that happened but especially her. She had the power and charisma that defied the average. This house, this situation, astounded me. I'd never imagined something like this existing. I'd never imagined someone like Jocelyn existing. Even Hannah paled in comparison.

"Come," I heard, so I opened the door and walked in.

"I came to say thank you for last night," I said as I looked around. Her office hadn't changed into a torture chamber or a Dominatrix Den overnight.

Jocelyn smiled without looking up. "And you're not kneeling? I'm sure Anna told you to kneel."

"I'm sorry. I wasn't sure she was serious." I sank to my knees.

Jocelyn turned toward me. "You enjoyed last night?"

"Yes, I did, very, very much." I had been astounded by it all. I came harder than ever before. "Sex has never taken me that high."

We looked into each other's eyes. "You've never participated in anything like that before, have you?"

I looked at the floor. "Only some light bondage…you know, silk instead of metal. I've heard of other stuff, but I've never done it."

"I thought there were groups in the US who practiced off-stream sex."

"I know there's one in Seattle."

"But you never went?"

I looked down, embarrassed. "I was a chicken. I didn't know what would happen."

"But now you do?"

I looked up and smiled. "I'm sure I haven't seen everything."

"Probably not, but you have your safe word, so you can control it. You must believe that I will not harm you. I will hurt you if pain causes us pleasure, but not if it harms you."

"Yes, Mistress." Harm me? I'd have to think about that. Physically or emotionally? Bruises to the body would heal, but bruises to the mind or heart took a lot longer, if they ever healed. It had taken me a long time to get over Hannah. Which was Jocelyn the worst with?

"All right. Any questions?"

"Does everyone have a safe word?" I asked.

"Not everyone. Lenci is my second in command. We know each other well enough that we can communicate without one. Gabby has one, I think, but she hasn't used it in years. Anna and Emilia are contracted to me, so they each have one. They know what to expect and what the rules are. I would not harm them because they are so new, so young. However, they still have their words in case things get to be too much for them."

"Is it common around here to have a house like this?"

"Not common, no, but there are houses like this from place to place. There used to be more, I think, back in my grandfather's day, but not now. Anything else?"

"Well…" I hesitated. I didn't quite know how to ask this.

"Well what?"

"Is it always so one-sided?"

She laughed loudly. "Do you want to be on the other side?"

"Yes, ma'am. I think I would."

She paused as she studied me. She had a strange look on her face. "You want to be a mistress?"

"I don't know that much about it, but…" I wanted so much to hold Jocelyn and have her come in my arms. "I would like to try giving instead of always receiving."

"And who did you want to fuck?" Her eyes bored into me. Did she suspect? Did she know how I felt? Should I even suggest this?

I bit my lower lip. "You."

She sat back. She looked astounded. "I see. The way I fucked you last night?"

I shook my head. "No, I want to make love to you."

"Not Anna or Emilia? Or Lenci or Gabby?"

I shook my head. "They don't have the power you have."

"Do you want to match my power?"

"No. I'm sure no one can." She was so gorgeous. Did she even realize it? Did she have someone to hold her and love her? Someone besides Lenci or Gabby? Then I confessed, "I want to make love to you before I go to prison." *Yes, please let it be me if anyone.*

"And that will get you through your sentence?"

I laughed. "Probably not, but at least I'll have the memory to take with me." *And maybe you would, too.*

"So if I can't get your crimes expunged, you want me to let you into my bed?"

"No, I want to make love to you whether I go to prison or not." Couldn't she see that? Hadn't anyone ever told her how desirable she was?

She seemed pleased. "We'll see. Now, get off your knees and go help Emilia in the garden."

"Thank you," I said as I got to my feet and turned to leave, but she stopped me.

"What if I wanted you in the dungeon tonight?"

I shrugged and grinned. "I was told you were the queen, and I couldn't say no to you." I doubted I'd ever consider it.

❖

That night, after helping Lenci with the kitchen, I walked downstairs to go to bed. The wall that hid the dungeon door was swung back again, and the door was open, but there was no light inside.

I turned into my room, grabbed my towel, and went into the bathroom to take a shower before I got ready for bed. I had just rinsed when I heard the door open.

It was Gabby. "Step out of the shower. Don't dry off. You're wanted in the dungeon."

I drew back the curtain to see her waiting for me.

"Come on," she said and started down the hall.

I hurried behind her as I slicked my hair. When I walked into the dungeon, Jocelyn was waiting, dressed in her black outfit and heels. They made her at least four inches taller than me. The only other person there was Gabby.

Jocelyn beckoned and pointed to the floor. I sank to my knees at her feet. "Have you changed your mind about what we spoke of this afternoon?"

I shook my head. "No, I haven't." Did she think I hadn't been serious, that I'd change my mind that easily?

She walked around me. "Do you hear this hussy?" she asked Gabby. "She wants to be in my bed."

Gabby chuckled. "Would she survive?"

"I don't know. I may let her try."

"I might surprise you," I said softly, without looking up.

"Are you that sure of yourself?" she asked as she placed a hand on my head.

I paused. Should I say this? Oh, what the hell, what did I have to lose? "Only one way to find out. I haven't had any complaints yet."

Gabby laughed loudly. "I think she's asking for a lot more than she realizes."

"I'm sure she is." She ran her hand down my cheek thoughtfully. After a moment, she said, "Do you remember your safe word?"

"Seattle, Washington, Mistress."

"Maybe you should chain her to the horse."

"It will be my pleasure."

Gabby pulled me to my feet. She led me to a strange piece of furniture, a bench of sorts. The top was covered with padded leather. It was about six inches wide, four feet across, and came to my navel.

Gabby took two pair of handcuffs and put one around each of my wrists. Then she walked around the other side of the apparatus and pulled me over the frame. She locked the cuffs to handles near the floor on that side. I was bent over the horse, my hands couldn't reach the floor, and I couldn't move. She came back around and placed chains around my ankles that were attached to something on the very outer edge of the horse. I was now securely stretched over this bench with my legs spread wide and my ass in the air. And I'd been scared hanging from the ceiling last night? Now my cunt was on display for anyone to see or touch. So far, this was the worst position.

"That's very pretty...so very pretty. Don't you think so, Gabby?"

"Not bad at all," she said.

"What should I do first?"

"Well, she didn't react at all to the paddle last night, so maybe she should be hit harder."

"Like this?" A wooden paddle hit me hard.

"Maybe harder?" I heard a shiver in Gabby's voice.

"Like this?"

I sucked in a lungful of air. It was definitely harder than any of the others. There were three more in rapid succession. The last one brought tears to my eyes. I kept my head down so they wouldn't see, but Jocelyn grabbed my hair and pulled my head up.

"Any reaction?" Now they'd see I was crying, that I wasn't as strong as I wanted them to think.

Gabby leaned down to look into my face. "A couple small tears, but that's all. Oh wait, and she's drooling."

"Let's see what this does," Jocelyn said as she hit my butt even harder. I couldn't control my whimper. It hurt like hell, but maybe I could show them that I was made of something stronger.

"That's much better," Gabby said.

Another hit my butt. I tried to shift my weight to stop some of the sting, but I couldn't move. I was breathing hard. A long silence followed.

It was Jocelyn who finally broke it. "Are you packing?" she asked Gabby.

"Of course."

"Then let's see what she can take."

Gabby moved in back of me, and I heard her moving something around. Before I could take a breath, a large dildo slid into me. I almost screamed. I was gasping. A hand landed on my back as Gabby slowly pushed in and out.

"Hang on to it," Jocelyn said. "Don't let it end too soon."

I wasn't sure who she was talking to.

Gabby kept pumping back and forth. Oh, she was good. I'd been penetrated before but never this way. She seemed to know every special spot and moved just right to touch each of them. The slowness of her strokes almost drove me crazy. I wanted it faster, harder, and even deeper. I felt my head shaking back and forth with each of her strokes. I wanted to push back into her, but I had nothing to push against. She glided slowly. Again and again.

Then she pulled out and stopped. I gasped. My flesh was quivering, searching for the hard rod.

"What's wrong? Are you missing something?" Jocelyn asked.

I took a deep breath. "Yes."

"Do you want more?"

"Yes."

"Please?"

"Yes, please…please…yes." I was quaking. I didn't know what

to do. I hung over the bench for a few minutes. "Please," I begged again. I heard laughter as Gabby started again.

I wanted to let go, but something stopped me. Was this a test? Would failure keep me out of Jocelyn's bed? Could I chance it? I closed my eyes and bore down harder. No, not even this was going to keep me away.

Then Jocelyn was standing at my head. "Enjoying this?" she asked. Her voice sounded huskier than I'd heard before. She stroked my face, running slowly across my lips. As she put her fingers in my mouth, I sucked them. Then she laughed and stepped back. I still was in that zone where I felt no pain and had no doubts. I wanted whatever she deigned to give me. I was flying. I felt like I was soaring over everything. Maybe it was because I'd been half upside down for so long, or it was that my mind was spinning out of control from having been fucked so well for so long, but I was well past caring about what was happening.

After a moment, she stepped up to me again.

"Suck on this." Then her fingers stroked my lips again. I drew them into my mouth and was amazed by the wetness there. The taste was salty but sweet. She was giving me some of herself. I feasted hungrily. As Gabby's strokes became faster and faster and deeper, I sucked harder and harder.

Finally, I heard the sweetest words I'd ever heard. "Come for me."

My body erupted harder than I'd ever felt…harder than I ever imagined. I screamed. My whole body was on fire.

I was suspended somewhere I'd never been before. My muscles twitched, my temperature soaring. My head felt like it was going to explode. I wasn't quite sure where I was.

Finally, as my breath started to even out, I slumped.

Gabby laughed. "I think we finished her."

"Did we?" Jocelyn asked. She massaged my back and butt. "Did we?"

I don't know what possessed me, but I said, "Almost."

Jocelyn burst out laughing. "Oh, you're asking for it, aren't you? I think you're asking for more than you realize."

This time I kept my mouth shut. I might already have said too much.

"Let's leave her here. She'll reconsider it," Gabby said.

"Yes, I think so, too." She patted my butt, and I heard them both walking away.

The lights went off, and the door swung shut.

CHAPTER TEN

I might have fallen asleep or passed out, but the next thing I knew, a cool, wet towel was wiping my face. I opened my eyes and saw Emilia kneeling to release my hands.

"Emilia," I heard Anna say. "Look at how red her butt is. They really tortured her."

"At least they didn't draw blood." She stood, and she and Anna pulled me off the horse and lowered me to the floor.

"Good God," Anna said. "What did they do to you?" She placed the towel on my brow.

"Everything," I whispered. I had trouble getting my voice to work.

They both sat beside me. Anna held a glass of water to my mouth. "I figured you'd need this now."

"Thanks." I gulped the whole glass down.

"When they came out, Mistress told us to give you five minutes, then come in and get you. Are you all right?"

"I think so, but my head is throbbing."

"You were upside down much too long."

"Then let's get you to bed, and I'll get you some aspirin," Anna told me.

They helped me to my feet, and I took a step. Emilia caught my arm. I moaned but caught myself as I started to stumble. Anna caught my other arm, and Emilia's hand was on my back to steady me. My cunt felt bruised. It didn't hurt, but it was damned sore. I felt like it was still full. I'd never felt that before. It felt so stretched that it might take weeks to shrink back to normal size. I almost laughed. Was this what they meant by being fulfilled? Or was that filled full? Was this what mothers felt after giving birth?

"Let us help you." Emilia said. They took my arms around their shoulders and walked me back to my room.

"Does this happen often?" I asked.

"I've never seen it, but I've only been here three and a half years," Emilia answered.

"I don't remember it happening before," Anna added.

They lowered me onto my bed. "Oh God," I moaned when I moved.

"Relax," Emilia said. "Don't try to move." She lifted my feet up.

I could only nod.

"Did Gabby fuck you? I saw she still had her package on."

"Yes," I whispered.

"Wow." Emilia sounded impressed. "Mistress seldom lets her do that. I think she keeps that for herself."

"I would, too, if that were me," I said.

"Is she really good?"

"Yes," I said. "Very good. She knows all the right moves to touch every sensitive spot. It was amazing."

Anna came back into the room and held out a glass of water and two white pills. I hadn't even realized she'd left. I had trouble sitting back up. Emilia had to help me. When I had downed the pills, I fell back against the pillow.

"I brought your jewelry from the bathroom," Anna said, "And I put your clothes in the hamper."

"Thank you. What time is it?" I asked.

"Twelve thirty."

Twelve thirty? I remembered leaving Lenci in the kitchen at nine. I guessed I got more than I imagined.

"Get some sleep," Emilia said "We have to pick peppers tomorrow." She and Anna each gave me a kiss. Then they left, closing the door but leaving the light on.

I closed my eyes. Where was I now? I'd had the best sex of

my life, and I seemed to be falling in love…with Jocelyn? Lenci? Gabby? All of them? At least it was beginning to feel that way. But I was facing a twenty-three-year prison sentence. I hadn't been able to contact anyone, and no one knew where I was. If I didn't go to prison, where would I go? In reality, I'd owe my life to Jocelyn. Would she want me to stay here? Would the others? Could I? Would I?

Did I need this life? Did I want it? This was so new…but also so overwhelming.

Come on, kid. You've only been here four days. We still had six or seven weeks to go. Six or seven *long* weeks. I wanted to get this cleared up now. I hated waiting. A lot could happen in seven weeks. Look what had happened in four days.

My God. My whole world had changed. I used to be that steady world traveler who people looked to when they wanted to plan a successful, happy vacation. Now who was I? On the verge of becoming a sex slave in an Eastern European sado-masochism house? Was I even considering the idea? I had to get past the trial first. Was I putting too much faith in Jocelyn? Too much hope? And why was I even thinking that far ahead?

It would mean leaving so many things behind. I was successful at what I did, and I was happy in my life, or at least I was until I came here and met Jocelyn. The only thing missing in my life was a lover, a solid relationship. I hadn't had one in years. Oh, there had been a few, like Hannah and Jessie, and what was her name? The brunette with that shaggy dog…damn, she must have been very important if I couldn't even remember her name…oh, Jean, yes, Jean. But none of them had lasted very long. Hannah, a month, Jessie almost a year, and Jean…well, that one wasn't my fault. She was the one who cheated while I was away. I hadn't had time for a relationship. Did I now? *Oh, Katherine P. Lowe, get yourself together first before you think of adding another person to your life. Do one thing at a time. One thing.*

❖

"How are you feeling this morning?" Anna asked at breakfast.

"I'm stiff and a little sore, but I feel great," I told her and Emilia.

They laughed. "Don't forget, I need your help in the garden," Emilia said.

"I'll be out in a few minutes," I told her as I finished my breakfast.

She nodded.

"I have to say thank you to Jocelyn."

Emilia and Anna laughed. "I guess you do." Emilia picked up her dishes. "I'll see you outside," she said as she took them into the kitchen.

I looked up. Anna was staring at me across the table. "What are you going to do?" she asked.

"About what?"

"If she gets your prison sentence reduced or thrown out?"

I frowned. "I asked myself that last night. I don't know."

"Don't you want to go home?"

I breathed deeply. "I really don't know. I guess it depends on what happens with my trial."

"I know she'll keep you here if you want."

"That's the problem. I want to stay, but it would mean giving up a lot. I have a good job and a beautiful apartment, and I get paid to travel the world. I liked my life...before I came here."

"Do you have a lover at home?"

I shook my head. "I date a lot, but there's nobody special. I haven't found anyone that feels right."

"I can't imagine leaving here. I know I don't get all her attention, but what I do get is well worth waiting for."

"I know what you mean. I don't know what I'm going to do if I don't go to prison."

"Stay here," she said. "We all love you."

"It's a thought, but what would I add? You all have jobs. What's not taken care of?"

Anna nodded. "I understand." She thought about it for a moment and shrugged. "I'll bring your dishes out if you want to go up there."

"Thanks. I would." I walked slowly up the stairs. It was still a little hard to walk, and I had to decide what I was going to say. I had thought about it for a long time last night. Maybe I shouldn't say anything. I had no idea what she wanted. I walked down the hallway and knocked on her door.

"Come."

I opened the door and took two steps inside. Then I sank to my knees. "Thank you for last night."

She turned in her chair. "Did you enjoy yourself?"

"Very much so."

"I thought so. How do you feel this morning?"

I smiled. "I'm a little sore and stiff, but mentally, I feel wonderful."

Jocelyn chuckled. "I imagine you do." Then she breathed deeply. "All right, to business. I haven't been able to get in touch with anyone in your family. No one answers. Might they be on vacation?"

I thought back. It was September. They might have gone to visit Grandma June for her birthday. "They might be, but my sister should have answered."

Jocelyn shook her head.

Knowing my sister Pamela, she probably took this opportunity to stay at her boyfriend's house, but she still wouldn't have gotten the quality I got last night. I laughed to myself. Or the quantity.

"Did you hear from the embassy?" I asked.

She nodded. "They still say there's no record of you."

I slammed my hand on the floor. "There must be." I leaned my forehead into my palm. I felt like crying.

"We still have time. We'll find something. I won't let you go to prison."

"How can you stop it?"

"There's still no proof that you were the one who put the drugs in your backpack. There's a lot of things that cast a doubt. Trust me."

I nodded, my head still down.

"What are you going to do today?"

"Pick peppers," I said softly.

"Then go help Emilia."

"And I'm also supposed to cook tonight."

"American hamburgers?" When I nodded, her face lit up. "I can't wait."

I nodded again.

"Hey," she said, tapping my shoulder, "I thought I instructed you not to nod."

I took a small breath. "You're right, Mistress. I won't just nod."

"Good. Now, smile. You'll get through this."

"I hope so. Thanks." I got up and went outside to help Emilia.

As I walked out into the garden, Emilia gave me a big wave. "What did she say about last night?" she asked as I stooped to help her gather the peppers.

"Not much. We talked about my situation with the authorities. She said they still can't find any record of me in the US."

"Oh. Katherine, I'm sure she'll find something. She can work miracles."

"I think it will take more than a miracle." I frowned.

"Don't give up hope. We're all here for you."

I nodded as we continued down the row of plants. "Can I ask you a question?" I needed to know more about this place before I made a decision.

"Sure," she answered.

"How did you get into something like this?"

"My father sent me to work for a very sadistic Master. He taught me a lot, but I was always more interested in the other girls in the house. He reprimanded me several times because of that. I'm not sure what happened, but I found myself on a train to here. I guess he had decided I didn't belong there and had made arrangements with Jocelyn."

"And you never had a say in what happened to you?"

"Well, I got him to send me to a lesbian house instead of a regular one. The older generation still adheres to the old customs. It *is* changing. I think this generation is much more aware that women are handling their own lives and how things like sexuality are handled in other western counties. It's quite different." She moved down the row.

"Do you think a life like this will change, too?"

"It probably will, but I'm not sure if it will become more accepted or throw us deeper into hiding." She looked at me. "How is it handled in the US?"

"It still isn't in the mainstream," I answered, "but there are more and more groups in the big cities, so it is becoming more popular. A lot of women still think it's abusive." *Here, this sort of life is in houses out in the countryside. In the west, it's only in big cities.*

"Did you belong to one of those groups?"

I shook my head. "I was scared. I didn't know quite what happened there." There was a moment of silence. I laughed. "There's a store in Seattle that sells whips and chains and all sorts of things like Jocelyn has in the dungeon. I used to go in there to look around, but I only bought one little thing that I used on myself. I guess, if you and Anna hadn't seduced me, I'd still be afraid."

She smiled at me. "Then I'm very glad we did."

"Me, too."

As we worked, Emilia tutored me in how to respond to a mistress and the proper etiquette within the dungeon. "When we're in the dungeon, or discussing it, always refer to her as Mistress. Never as Jocelyn. Besides that, use your best manners, and don't assume you're on the same level as her. She's always above us."

"I think I picked up on that." I smiled. "Does anyone ever get close to her?"

"Lenci and maybe Gabby, but not us. I really can't say for sure."

I frowned. It didn't seem right to me. Yes, I understood the manners and etiquette, but how could Jocelyn keep herself away from everyone? I knew she was a duchess and had probably been brought up to expect people to bow to her. Didn't she want someone to be close? Oh sure, she could have anyone she wanted, but why didn't she? Was she that close to Lenci? It seemed that we were all equally below her. Wasn't she lonely?

From what everyone had been saying, I guessed there would come a time when Jocelyn would have enough of me, and I'd be shuffled back to *every once in a while*. I couldn't expect to be her first choice every day, and I'd have to ask if I wanted anyone else. *So much for sudden desire, for being impulsive.* Could I take that? Did I want it that way?

I'd put up with "every once in a while" in my private life because I had a very active business life, and Amy and I would go out to eat or to the movies together every week or so. There was always something to do, somewhere to go. I wasn't kept in a house that was miles from everything.

But Jocelyn? Wow. What a beautiful lady. The others were cute or nice, but not like her. Of course, I hadn't seen them dressed up with makeup and their hair perfectly coiffed like Jocelyn was every day. No, Jocelyn was perfect. My heart skipped a beat every time I looked at her. And last night, when she put some of herself into my mouth? It was manna from the goddess…unlike any I'd ever tasted. *I could live on that.* But how often did she do that? How long would I have to wait?

No, Katherine, if she gets you freed from all this court bullshit, run home. Right away. This place will drive you insane.

CHAPTER ELEVEN

These are wonderful," Jocelyn said as she chewed her burger. Everyone agreed. I had cooked dinner that night: hamburgers and fries. "They're not officially American. The rolls and cheese are different."

"It's all I could find," Lenci said sadly.

"Actually, these are better," I said. She had bought thick Kaiser rolls and cheddar and mozzarella. Of course, there was no such thing as American cheese in Rebinian grocery stores.

"What did you put in the burgers?" Anna asked.

"Chopped onion, salt and pepper, a little garlic, a little vinegar, and some oatmeal."

"It's very good."

"Sometimes people add pickles, but I like them better without." I'd also had a dish of sliced pickles and bottles of mustard and ketchup, but the Rebinian ketchup was heavier than American, so I wasn't sure how it would work. It turned out that everyone loved them. The fries were also a hit. I had left the peels on them so they were chewier.

"Do you eat these a lot?" Gabby asked. "I think I could do that."

I nodded. "Mostly in the summer for barbecues. The hamburgers are even better cooked over an open flame."

"Well," Jocelyn said, "you can cook these for me anytime you want."

I beamed. At least there was some American tradition that was new to them and exciting. Everyone agreed.

I helped Emilia take the dishes out to the kitchen. When I came back into the dining room to get the last of the dishes, Jocelyn stopped me.

"Are you up for the dungeon again tonight?" she asked.

I took a breath. "Mentally and emotionally, yes, but physically, I'm still a little sore."

"All right," she said, "but I think you'll want to be ready for tomorrow." Then she walked away.

Tomorrow? What was so special about tomorrow? Would I be ready? Could I?

It seemed that my days were planned for me. Work in the garden, help with the dinner dishes, and have sex in the evenings. The daytime chores were easy and gave me something to do. The evenings were, well, they were much more exciting. I looked forward to them. I hadn't had this much sex in years...who was I kidding? Ever. And such *good* sex.

The next evening, I came into the dining room to see Gabby sitting one seat down with an empty seat to the left of Jocelyn.

"We have company tonight?" Anna asked.

Gabby nodded. "Regina will be here."

"Oh, I like Regina," Emilia gushed.

"I do, too," Anna said. Then she turned to me. "I don't think you've met her."

"I don't think so."

"Regina is another Mistress," Emilia said.

"And Jocelyn's best friend," Lenci added.

"Does she have a house like this?" I asked. How many other houses were in this country? Was this an anomaly or the norm?

"I don't think so. She's in the military," Gabby said.

"Oh God." That was just what I needed. I'd seen enough military in the past week. Did I want to see more?

"You'll like her," Anna said. "She's a lot of fun."

"Fun? Didn't I have enough fun this week?"

"One can never have too much fun." Gabby smiled.

I grinned at her. "Really? I had so much fun the night before last that I couldn't have any at all last night."

"Yes. I noticed that." Gabby laughed. "By the way, when a mistress walks into the room, stand until she's taken a seat."

I said, "I can do that." Yes, I could do that, but did I want to? Manners were one thing, and yes, my mother had taught me well, but kowtowing to every person who used the honorific Master or Mistress? Why? *I'm as good as them. I may even be better educated.*

"Is she here yet?" Emilia asked. "I haven't seen her."

"No," Lenci answered, coming out of the kitchen. "Jocelyn went into the city this morning, but she said to hold dinner until they got here. I hope they come soon, or some of the vegetables will be too soggy."

"Is she staying the night? Should I garage her car or leave it out there?"

"I have no idea. You'll have to wait until they get here."

Gabby nodded. Almost at the same time, I heard a buzzer in the front foyer. That meant someone had driven through the gates.

"That's my cue," Gabby said as she got up and ran to the door.

"Okay, girls," Lenci said, "get ready."

It took a few minutes, but as we heard the dining room door open, we stood and turned to face them.

"Good evening, Mistresses," Lenci said as two women entered the room.

I looked past Jocelyn, and my jaw dropped. It was the officer who had searched me and locked me into the cell, the one from the train.

"Oh yes," she said. "It's our little drug dealer. Is she causing any trouble, Jocelyn?" She stared into my eyes.

"Lieutenant," I said as I kept my eyes lowered. I couldn't keep my head up, not because I was honoring her, but I didn't want her to the look in my eyes. I didn't hate her, but I definitely didn't like her. She was a reminder of all the bad things that had happened. I hoped no one would see the disgust in my eyes.

"No trouble," Jocelyn said. "In fact, she's become quite enjoyable."

"Really?" Regina said. "Can I see that?"

Jocelyn looked at me, a question in her eyes. Oh God. I was in a cul-de-sac, and there was no way out. "Certainly, Mistress," I mumbled. I looked into Jocelyn's eyes but not into Regina's.

They laughed as they sat at the table. Then Lenci nodded, and we all sat. I breathed a sigh of relief. I didn't think my legs would have supported me much longer.

Emilia took the bottle of wine from the sideboard and went to pour some into Jocelyn's glass, but she covered it with her hand and gestured to Regina. Emilia bowed her head, turned, and poured a little wine into Regina's glass instead.

After inspecting the wine, Regina took a small sip. "This is very good. From your vineyard?"

"Yes." Jocelyn said. "Emilia has been able to bottle some very fine wine the last two years."

"Very nice, Emilia," Regina said. "Where did you learn?"

"My father was a wine master in Rheingau."

"He taught you well."

"No, ma'am. He would not teach me because I was a girl. I had to spy while he was teaching my brother."

"Then you spied very well." She turned to Jocelyn. "You got a good deal, didn't you?"

"Yes, I rejoice in the day I found Emilia. Actually, all my girls. I seem to have the best house in this valley."

Regina smiled. "Perhaps in the whole republic."

Lenci came in with plates for Jocelyn and Regina, then went back into the kitchen. I got up to help her and returned with Anna's and my plates while Lenci carried Emilia's, Gabby's, and her own. Emilia poured wine for everyone, but when she got to me, I held my hand over my glass.

"You're not drinking tonight, Katherine?" Jocelyn asked.

"No, ma'am, I have the feeling I need to keep my head clear. I'm sure there will be other things to adjust my thinking." Yes, one of the last things I needed was to be even slightly tipsy. With Jocelyn and Regina in the room, I'd need to keep track of everything. I trusted Jocelyn, but I wasn't certain about Regina.

"Yes, she flies quite high," Jocelyn said. "Doesn't she, girls?"

Everyone agreed as Gabby came back into the room, and we all ate.

"Will you be keeping her?" Regina asked.

Jocelyn looked at me and motioned for me to answer.

I glanced at Anna, then back at Regina. "I still need to stand trial, ma'am," I told her. "I haven't made plans beyond that."

"Ah, yes, your trial. I'm sure you'll get what you deserve."

"Thank you," I said. Then I said in a low voice, "I think."

Jocelyn and Regina laughed. They continued talking as they ate; the other girls and I spoke softly to each other, trying not to interrupt. As dinner finished and Jocelyn and Regina were sitting with their wine, I got up to help Lenci. As I reached to take her plate, Jocelyn stopped my hand.

"Shower and be naked in the dungeon at nine thirty."

"Yes, Mistress," I murmured and continued clearing the table. Oh no. I sincerely hoped Jocelyn wasn't planning anything between Regina and me. Well, whatever it was, I'd do it...for Jocelyn, not for Regina.

❖

"Do you know what's going to happen tonight?" Anna asked as she sat with me. I'd taken my shower, but there was still fifteen minutes until my appearance in the dungeon.

"I have no idea, but I fear she's planning on giving me to Regina."

"Yes, I thought that, too. Where do you know her from?"

I shook my head. "She was the one that arrested me and locked me in jail."

"Are you scared?"

"Petrified. I'm scared of everything these days," I admitted. "I used to be so sure of myself. Now I question everything." Where did my self-esteem go?

"You'll get your confidence back. Once your trial is over and you're free, you'll be as good as new."

"I think that needs to be amended to once my trial is over and *if* I'm free."

"Don't lose hope. You'll be fine. Jocelyn won't let you go to prison."

"I keep telling myself that." I looked at my watch on the dresser. "Five minutes to go."

"Are you ready for this?"

"No, but when has that mattered?" Did anything *I* want make a difference? That was the worst part of this. Nothing I wanted, or didn't want, mattered, and I wasn't sure how I felt about that.

Anna hugged me as I got up to go to the dungeon. When I walked in, Jocelyn beckoned and pointed to the floor. I walked over to her and knelt. Behind her, two people lounged against one of the tables. One was Regina, the other…was Lenci.

"You were quite sure of yourself the day before yesterday, and you boasted that you were a good sexual partner. So good that you wanted me to let you make love to me. Well, I realize you're quite capable, but in bed? I guess I need to see it, so this will be your audition. Are you romantic? Adept? Gentle? Insistent? Forceful? Let me see. Make love to Lenci."

I looked up at Lenci and smiled. "With pleasure." Wonderful. Lenci and not Regina? Yes. That I could do.

"There's a bed in that corner," she said, pointing behind her.

I looked to where Regina and Lenci were lounging. Jocelyn flipped switches on a console. The light, focused on the bed, dimmed to a very romantic hue. "Is that all right? Do you need it brighter?"

"No." I had a surge of confidence. "It's fine. I could make love in the dark, if need be. I'm very good by touch." I exceled in Braille sex.

I got to my feet and walked to Lenci. The first thing I did was take her glasses off and set them on the bench. I caressed her face and kissed her gently.

"I hope you don't mind that we have an audience," I whispered. I sure did, but what did it matter? "Make believe they're not there." I gently pulled her into an embrace. "Is there anything you don't like?"

Lenci smiled. "No. Do your best...or worst, as the case may be."

I kissed her as I lowered her onto the bed. I let it grow into a deep, passionate kiss with a lot of tongue as I cradled her face and neck. The bed was a large platform, bigger than a king-sized bed, as long as it was wide. Plenty of room to roll around, not too soft, not too hard...just right.

While I kissed her, I drew her robe off and let it drop behind her. I kissed her neck as her head fell back, giving me the softest, warmest part. I could feel her blood pulsing through the skin beneath my lips. Would Jocelyn taste like this? Would she be this responsive?

I slowly worked my way around her neck, under her chin, under her other ear. I heard her breathing become a little ragged. Oh yes, that was the reception I wanted. I started over her shoulder and continued down her arm, biting, nibbling, and kissing every inch. When I got to her hand, I licked her palm and started to pull her fingers into my mouth. Yes, I was enjoying this, and it felt like she was, too. Lenci had a very good body: small, but firm. Her breasts were plump and her shoulders were strong but not that wide, and she responded to everything I was doing. I fondled her fingers, then started up the inside of her forearm where other veins were pulsing. My slow, warm breath seemed to have a quickening response.

I returned to her neck and kissed and nipped. "You're more beautiful than you usually let people see," I whispered into the space above her ear. "You need to stop hiding in the kitchen."

I licked down her body, stopping at her breasts long enough to coax her nipples to erection. I tongued the crevice beneath her breasts, the fold where her legs met her body, and down behind her knee. I didn't touch where I knew she wanted. I worked my way around the edges. I could feel the heat and smell her arousal. I could feel the twitching of her muscles. Oh, it would be so wonderfully easy to go right to the source, but I didn't. I drew her hands to me, sucking her fingers and massaging them with my tongue.

"Oh, Katherine," she whispered.

I took her mouth with mine, massaging it with my tongue.

I drew us up on our knees where we could hold each other

tightly and caress each other's backs, like I wanted to do to Jocelyn. We remained there, kissing, caressing, touching our breasts together and holding each other until I slowly slipped down between her legs, her beautiful center above my lips.

I was doing what I'd never thought of doing and realized it was what I was meant to do. Lenci was beautiful, responsive, reacting to my every move. I wanted to do my best no matter who was watching, although I hoped Jocelyn was imagining this was her instead of Lenci.

Tightening my hands around her hips. I carefully lowered her onto my face. I took possession of her with my lips and tongue.

"Katherine," she said, sounding out of breath. I sucked her wetness into my mouth until my face was covered with her. She gasped and moaned.

I slowly lowered her back to the bed and knelt between her thighs. I thrust my hand into her center, first two fingers, then three. When I was sure she would accept me, I added the fourth, then the thumb. As my entire hand entered, I curled it into a fist and gently rocked it back and forth within her.

"Oh my God," Lenci almost screamed. "Yes, yes, yes!" Her muscles started to contract, then her whole body erupted, tightened, and her breathing stopped.

She held my head tightly as I moved my hand to her rhythm, and her moisture flowed around my wrist.

Then came a long, soft scream that grew and grew. It climaxed as I withdrew my hand and cradled her close. I could feel her shaking within my arms. All her muscles contracted as she stiffened. I held her closer, and she clung to me.

After the trembling stopped, she cuddled closer, and her breathing started to relax. I kissed her gently on the lips. I lay back and pulled her on top of me. I held her close as we both relaxed and caught our breath. I didn't know how long we lay like that.

"What are you going to do with this one?" I heard. I'd forgotten there were others in the room.

"I think we need to put a stop to it before it spreads. This one could become an epidemic."

Then I heard laughter. "I think it's too late." It was Regina. "Lenci looks like she already has the fever."

Lenci raised herself far enough to look into my eyes. "Indeed," was all she said, then she kissed me gently on the lips.

A few minutes later, I heard a soft voice say, "Come here, baby," and Lenci was lifted from my arms.

I watched as she turned into Jocelyn, who was sitting on the bed a few feet from me. There was silence for a few minutes as Lenci lay with her head against Jocelyn's chest.

Then the silence was broken with, "I've got to have some of that. Jocelyn?"

She seemed to consider the request. Her eyes had a strange look in them. "Enjoy yourself."

Regina laughed. "This is going to be fun. I've been wanting to do this since I saw her on the train. We're so lucky she turned out to be a drug dealer."

I looked over at Jocelyn. We stared into each other's eyes for a moment. All the warmth that I'd shared with Lenci evaporated.

"That hasn't been proven yet," she told Regina without taking her eyes from mine. I wanted to believe she knew I was innocent.

"Well, before she's imprisoned or released, I'm going to take advantage of the situation." She held her hand out. "Come over here." Reluctantly, I slid across the bed to where she was standing and stood up. "May I use the cross?" she asked.

"Of course," I heard Jocelyn say. "I've never denied you anything."

Regina took me by my shoulders and turned me toward a giant X against the side wall. It was over seven feet high. "Pull that out into the middle of the room," she ordered.

I didn't think I could refuse. It was on rollers, so I dragged it from the wall and pushed it into the room. I examined it with a bit of trepidation. It was made of thick lumber, each leg about eight inches wide, two inches thick. There were ties and belts every few inches along each leg, and a giant hinge across the center in the back, so the whole thing could be tilted.

"Come over here," Regina said as she flipped the levers so the cross wouldn't roll away. I walked around in front. "Step up onto the blocks and hang on to those handles." There were ledges at the bottom of the two lower planks. I looked up to see two handles, one on each of the top legs. I stepped onto the ledges and reached up. They were over two feet higher than my head. I stretched up and grabbed them tightly.

Regina took the thick leather cuffs that were chained below the handles and buckled one around each of my wrists. Two more belts about a foot lower, secured my arms.

She clicked the lock off the hinge and slowly tilted the cross a few degrees so I was no longer standing on my toes.

I felt her come around behind me and grab an ankle. It didn't take long before I was strapped across my ankles and knees. She adjusted a wide strap in front of my forehead.

"You're really going to enjoy this," she whispered.

Then she walked away. I heard soft talk between her and Jocelyn, then swishing sounds.

She caressed my shoulder. "Are you ready for this?"

I had to answer. "Would it do any good to say no?"

I heard laughter as lashes struck my back. They forced air from my lungs. It wasn't hard, but it felt as if there were dozens of strands, each striking intensely.

Then another hit, this one from the other side. Another from the right, then one from the left. Pretty soon, they were coming in rapid succession, too close together for her to be using just one flogger.

Every few minutes, she'd stop and walk up behind me to see how I was doing, then she'd start again. My main hope was that Jocelyn was watching. I'd prove my strength for her. I'd show her what I could take. *Watch me, Jocelyn.*

At first, the lash seemed to brush across my back, brushing and sliding. Then they began to strike harder, whipping across me. I closed my eyes and concentrated on the rhythm of the lashes. I'd do this not for Regina, but for anyone else in the room, for Lenci and for Jocelyn. I'd hold on for *them. No one else.*

My head was starting to spin as I slipped into that zone where there was little hurt. There were now thuds across my back, going through my body...through my head. She had created a rhythm lulling me into another space, as if I could escape her just by hiding in my mind.

They continued and continued. Yes, I would endure this. I'd show Regina she couldn't take me down, but the thuds were pushing me further into my void-zone, and I didn't even know what I was thinking...if I was thinking at all. I was standing on a mountaintop, staring out into the clouds.

I heard an ethereal voice say, "Are you ready?"

The next strike was harder than the others. It was a sting instead of a thud. I heard myself cry out softly as laughter erupted behind me. I closed my eyes tightly as more struck. I was somewhere aloft, soaring through the sky. *That's right, Jocelyn. Watch me fly.*

I didn't know she had stopped until Regina lifted my head and turned it. It took me a moment to focus. "She really takes it, doesn't she?" I wasn't sure what she meant.

I felt the cross start to tilt backward until it was flat, and there was none of my weight on the straps. I relaxed onto the wood as the whole world faded away.

CHAPTER TWELVE

W ell?" Jocelyn asked as I walked into her office.
       I sank to my knees. "Thank you."

She turned to me. "You surprised me last night," she said. "Thank you for what you did with Lenci. Sometimes, I neglect her too much. She's been with me for twelve years, and I usually go to the newer ones."

"It was more than a pleasure," I whispered. *Lenci is a treat, but I wish it had been you.*

"Yes," Jocelyn said thoughtfully. "Lenci is very responsive. I should reward her more often."

"It was nice. I wouldn't mind doing it again." *If only Regina hadn't been watching.*

She had a strange look on her face. "Remember the rules. You cannot be intimate with each other without my permission."

"I remember," I assured her. "I think I learned that the first night."

"Yes." She laughed. "I especially remember that night, too." We smiled at each other for a moment. "What did you think of the flogging?"

I had to laugh. "I don't remember most of it. Maybe I blocked it out." *Maybe I blocked out Regina.* "My back is very stiff and sore."

"Let me see. Take your shirt off and turn around."

I gingerly lifted my T-shirt over my head and turned my back to her. I felt her finger running along my shoulders. When she stopped, I turned around to face her as I shrugged my shirt back on.

"Your back is very red and a little bruised in places, but it will heal. It might take a day or two."

I nodded.

"You impressed us last night. Regina was shocked."

"Really? So was I." I grinned, proud of myself.

"If I get your case thrown out, would you want to stay here?" she asked.

I paused. "I don't know. I've thought about it, and it's tempting, but I'm not sure I'm what you want. I seem to say the wrong things."

"And you can't resist talking back."

"No, I can't."

"There's still at least five or six weeks to decide."

I nodded. "Have you heard any more from the embassy or my parents?"

She shook her head. "We've been unable to confirm anything. My secretary has been calling every day. Have you told me the whole truth?"

Why wouldn't I? I had nothing to hide. I nodded. "I'm beginning to lose hope. Maybe I don't really know who I am." *Or who I think I am? Did I have an injury and forgot everything?* No, it didn't feel like it. It felt like I was Katherine P. Lowe from Seattle, Washington, as I'd always been. Why didn't anyone else know it?

"Don't give up. I'll get you through this."

I merely nodded again and took a very deep breath.

"Emilia thinks the grapes are almost ready to be picked. Check with her, and see if she needs help."

"Yes, Mistress," I whispered, got to my feet and left without another word.

❖

Even barely into the second week, the days seemed to drag by. I tried not to count them and trusted that Jocelyn would come up with a solution. I tried to keep a happy face but time after time caught myself frowning.

I went about helping Emilia in the garden and Lenci in the

kitchen. I waited for Jocelyn to tell me what the night would be like. At other times, I worried about what was going to happen and what other things I could do. I knew more about where we were, now. Should I try to escape? What was I waiting around for? *Run, don't run, stay, don't stay.* Were those my only options? Did I want to spend my life here? Having sex whenever someone else felt like it? Sure, I loved sex—from both sides—but there was more to life than that. I was getting itchy to travel again. I wanted to move! I wanted to be sure who I was fucking next.

I heard a knock on my door.

"*Ja?*" I called.

The door opened. Anna. She was naked. "Come on."

"Where?"

"Into the dungeon."

"Don't you ever get tired of it?" It always seemed the same... always someone else's desires.

"No! And tonight is different. Take your clothes off. Come on."

"I haven't showered."

"I don't care. Hurry before she changes her mind." She ran for the dungeon.

I breathed a big sigh and stood to shed my clothes. Then I walked toward the dungeon. I knew I was dragging my feet, but I wasn't excited about anything today. I wasn't sure what was wrong, but I'd fallen into a bad spot. I didn't want to do anything.

Jocelyn was sitting on the edge of the bed. She pointed to the floor, so I went to her and sank to my knees.

"Are you depressed?" she asked.

"Yes, ma'am," I muttered.

"Anna said you were. Why?"

"I think it's the waiting. I don't know what to look forward to, I don't know what's going to happen past tomorrow."

"Do you know what's going to happen tonight?"

I shook my head, then stopped. "No, ma'am."

"You and I are going to be together," Anna crowed enthusiastically.

I looked up at Jocelyn, surprised.

"Don't you want to?" Jocelyn asked with a very concerned expression.

I looked up into Anna's enthusiasm. I had to smile. How could I hurt her feelings? "Yes, I do." I grinned.

Jocelyn looked over at Anna. "Well?"

Anna grabbed my hand and dragged me onto the bed. "I'll make love to you first. Then when you're happier, you can make love to me," she whispered. I had to smile.

"Think so?"

"*Ja.*" She pushed me back and leaned in to give me a kiss. I glanced up to see Jocelyn watching. Anna leaned down to kiss my neck.

I can't do this. I liked Anna, but I didn't want to make love to anyone tonight. More than that, I didn't want anyone to make love to me. I might have even turned Jocelyn down.

No, I'd never be that depressed. Well, this was better than nothing. Wasn't it? At least Jocelyn was watching.

Anna nibbled on my ear. I rolled over and pushed her onto the bed. I looked into her hopeful eyes. She was so positive. Maybe I did need something like this. Maybe her positivity would rub off on me. Damn, my emotions were all over the place.

"Do you know what will make me really happy?"

Anna shook her head.

"You."

I leaned into her and placed a hot, wet kiss on her lips.

As I sat back, I saw the wonder and enthusiasm in her eyes. She pulled me back to her.

"You're a hot little slut." I grinned. "Aren't you?"

She slithered under me. "Of course. But only for you and Jocelyn."

"Really?"

She nodded enthusiastically.

"Think I should believe her?" I called over my shoulder.

There was a moment of silence. "Does it matter?" I heard. "Fuck her. Take what you want."

I grinned. "As you wish, Mistress."

I ran my hand down Anna's chest as she wiggled to get her breast under my hand. I grabbed it roughly and pinched the nipple.

She moaned. "Yes. It's yours tonight, Katherine."

"Good. But I have to share it. You said you were a slut to both of us."

"There's enough for both of you."

"You can do my part, too," I heard. She wasn't into sharing?

I rolled to the side and ran my hand down her stomach, then leaned forward and took one of her nipples between my teeth. I'd never been this rough before, but I was encouraged, both from the woman under me and the woman behind. I bit and sucked and pulled. No part of her chest escaped. I rested my palm on the hair in her little triangle, making my presence known but not touching anything.

I licked down to her navel.

"Please, quickly," she said.

I sat back. "Are you doing this, or am I?" I asked, my voice low.

She looked up at me in surprise. Then she grinned. "You are."

"Then I'll do it the way I want." I heard laughing behind me.

I straddled her, rubbing my wetness onto her tummy, and took her breasts in hand again. I played and teased until she writhed, then I rolled to the side and turned her onto her stomach. I slapped her butt a few times, then said, "On your knees. Don't make me bend down. It hurts my back."

She struggled to her knees. In reward, I pushed two fingers into her and got on my knees between her legs. I smiled. "You are so wet."

"You made me that way."

"Yup. I sure did." I pushed my fingers in as I reached with my other hand to take her nipple. I added a third finger, then worked my hand deeper.

"Oh, I like that," Jocelyn said.

Anna had her head on the bed, and I could feel her rocking back and forth. I kept going, slowly and added the rest of my hand and plunged in deeper. Her head shook.

"That's not too much, is it?" I asked.

She was out of breath. "No." She moaned. "It's wonderful."

"Really." I rolled my fist from one side to the other. I let go of her nipple and put that fist on the bed to give myself more leverage.

Anna's muscles started to tremble.

"What about a threesome?" Lenci asked.

"The more the merrier." I grinned.

I felt hands on my ass as something pressed into me. "Try this, Katherine. See if she can take it."

As she pushed into me again and again, it gave me the rhythm to push into Anna. We rocked back and forth and back and forth.

"Please, Mistress," Anna moaned.

"No, not yet."

I felt an extra nudge as Lenci lurched forward.

"Damn," I heard her exclaim in my ear.

It became a game. I knew from the way she pushed into me that someone was pushing into her, and I pushed into Anna. As Lenci pulled back, I pulled back. Forward. Back. Forward. Back.

I was a cog on the wheel. It went on and on and on.

"Are you ready, Lenci?" Jocelyn's voice was soft and heavy.

"Yes, please," she growled into my ear.

"Katherine?"

"Yes, please," It was almost too hard to understand the question. I reacted with what I thought she wanted to hear.

"Anna?"

"Please!" Anna howled.

"Then come."

The three of us exploded as Jocelyn took a step back.

We were like a pile of newborn puppies as we curled into each other, trying to get our breath. Anna cuddled into me, and Lenci wrapped her arms around us. None of us could stop gasping.

"Are you still depressed, Katherine?" Jocelyn asked as she leaned back against a table.

"I don't think so."

I heard that throaty laughter. "Good."

CHAPTER THIRTEEN

One night, later that week, I was helping clean up the kitchen when Lenci gave me a hug. "Thank you for the other night." She smiled.

"It was an extreme pleasure, Lenci. You were very responsive, very hot."

"Oh, Katherine, it's been a while."

I raised my eyebrows. How could it be a while in this place? How had she been left out? Everyone was getting fucked almost every night. "You were rather hot last night, too."

Lenci nodded. "I usually dominate the other girls. It's been two or three months since anyone's done me."

"Well, maybe while I'm here, I can rectify that." I smiled broadly. Hopefully, Jocelyn would allow it.

"That would be very nice."

"How long have you been with Jocelyn?"

Lenci smiled. "Over twelve years. She had recently gotten out of law school, and I had just learned about sex and this sort of thing." She grinned. "My mother was her father's housekeeper, but as many times as I came to work with her, I never imagined what was in the basement. Then my mother died, and Jocelyn said to give up my house and move in here. I'd never have to worry about paying rent or buying food." She shook her head in wonder. "I was so impressed by her. Here was this duchess who wanted me to live here and serve her. She is only five or six years older than me. But she had a bearing that put her far above." Lenci laughed. "And then she seduced me...and she showed me the basement."

"Was it scary?"

"Petrifying!"

I imagined it was, like it had been for me that first night.

Lenci nodded as she put a cover over a bowl of leftovers and put them in the refrigerator. "Want another cup of coffee?"

"What time is it?"

She looked at her watch. "Eight fifteen. We ate early tonight because Jocelyn was in the city since early this morning."

"Then, yes, I'd love a cup of coffee."

"Have a seat," she said, gesturing toward the small kitchen table. She poured two cups of coffee, added milk to mine and sugar to hers, and brought them back to the table.

"Thanks, hon," I said. "And then what happened?"

"Her father was a very sadistic Master. He's the one who got the dungeon furnished. He had three boys who did all the work here, except the cooking. He never touched me, but he showed Jocelyn how to use all the equipment...on me."

So Jocelyn came by her sadism naturally. Does it ever become abusive? Good God.

"When I started. I was her only girl. She let me play with some girls she brought home, or I helped her set something up. Her father died in a car accident about a year after I moved in. I think the only thing that kept her going was the dungeon...and me."

"That must have been hard on all of you. What happened to the boys?"

"Master left them very generous amounts of money. Jocelyn told them they were welcome to stay, and one did for about a year, but Jocelyn is a lesbian, so he was bored. Then she found a girl, Sophie, and moved her in, and it was the three of us for about two years, but Sophie changed her mind and wanted out. I think Jocelyn had to buy her silence."

"No! That's horrible."

"Yes, this sort of thing is not illegal, but it's never talked about.

It used to be normal, but that was in the old days. Anyway, Sophie wanted to have a one-on-one relationship with a little less pain."

It must have been hard for all of them, but Sophie made her choice, as hard as it was. How hard was it for Jocelyn? Was that her one true love, or was she happy to see her go? "What happened after she left?"

"It was the two of us for about six months. I knew Jocelyn loved me, but one woman will never be enough for her." Lenci laughed to herself. "Hell, or even two or three. She thrives on the assortment. The dungeon gives her energy. You wouldn't believe all she does."

"I think I saw that." Good heavens. It seemed there was no place in Jocelyn's life for me unless I wanted to become part of her harem. Did I want that? I didn't think so...*but this is Jocelyn.*

"And then she met Gabby. She'd been arrested for shoplifting, so Jocelyn posted her bond. Gabby was given a hefty fine, and Jocelyn paid it for her and asked how she wanted to work it off. That was almost seven years ago. She's been here ever since."

"That explains a lot." Yes, it seemed that Jocelyn took advantage of situations. When Lenci had nowhere to go and Gabby needed money, she was right there with the solution to solve their dilemmas. Just like she was with me. Was she an angel of mercy, always there at the right time? Or was she a predator of the devil, there at the point of conflict? I preferred to think of her as an angel, generous to a fault if she could help and someone could give her what she wanted. Was she turned on by the circumstances? Would I be? Was that the right thought, or was I reading more into it than was there?

"What's your background?" she asked.

"Nothing like this," I had to say. "I've always wanted something a little spicier than average, but no one I knew did anything like this." Except Hannah, and it hadn't been like this at all. "It was hard to come out and say hey, I want kinky sex."

Lenci nodded.

"I bought some nipple clamps once, and tried them on myself." Lenci joined my laughter. "I loved them, but I could only do so much. I put them on as I masturbated." I shook my head. "I never went to a meeting. I was shy and frightened. I mean, what if somebody saw me and told my mother?" We both laughed. "Of course, it never dawned on me that if someone saw me, I'd have something on them, too."

We both laughed at the thought.

"So this will give you the background to join a group?" she asked.

I had to laugh. "If I ever get back there. It looks like I'll be in my fifties before I have a chance to see US soil again."

She shook her head. "It sounds like you're giving up."

"I don't know what to think." I felt myself start to tear up. "Jocelyn says that no one can find any record of me. She can't even get hold of my family." I wiped my eyes.

Lenci reached across the table to grab my hands. "Don't you dare give up. It's only been, what? Not even two full weeks? Jocelyn can do miracles. She won't let you go to prison."

My temper erupted. "But what the hell can she do? My backpack had drugs in it, someone stole my passport, and the US embassy says I don't exist."

Lenci gave my hands a squeeze. "We know you exist, and until your court date, that's all that matters."

I grinned sardonically. "I'm not worried about that. I'm worried about *after* the court date." I slammed my hands onto the table. "And I've never cried as much as I have in the past two weeks. I'm not like this. I don't cry over every little thing."

Lenci came around the table and pulled me up into her arms. "Stop worrying. You need something to take your mind off it."

"I did that last night. Then morning came, and all my fears came rushing back."

"Hold on." She went to the phone beside the refrigerator. After a few minutes talking, she turned and held the phone out. It was Jocelyn.

"Lenci tells me you're still depressed. Did last night do nothing for you?"

"Last night did a lot for me, then the morning came."

"Am I going to have to keep you in the dungeon for the next six weeks?"

I smiled. "Well, that would help, but I don't think it's the answer."

"Come on up here and talk to me. Put Lenci back on the phone."

I handed the phone back. She listened to whatever Jocelyn said, then hung up. "She's in her office."

"Thanks." I pulled her into my arms and kissed her.

❖

Jocelyn's office door was open. She had her head down, working. I knocked softly on the jamb. I waited a moment until she finished writing, then put her pen down. She pointed to the floor, and I knelt.

She studied me for a moment. "Talk to me."

"I keep thinking that no one can do anything and that I'm going to go to prison as a Jane Doe."

"Jane Doe?"

I nodded. "That's what they call unidentified women in the US. A man is a John Doe."

"Then maybe we should have told the embassy your name was Jane." She smiled.

"Most of them are dead." I couldn't keep the bitterness from my voice.

She shook her head and looked at me again for a moment. "Why don't you trust me?"

"I really want to trust you, Jocelyn. I do, but I don't think anyone can get me out of this. I don't know why my family isn't answering, and I don't know why the embassy says I don't exist. Maybe I was hypnotized, and that was why I slept so long on the train, or maybe I have a brain injury or tumor and don't remember my real name. Jocelyn, if I do go to prison, what will happen to everything I have in Seattle? How will my family know, or my friends?"

She placed her hands on my shoulders. "I've been working on your defense, and I'm very sure we can get the drug charges thrown out. I'm also working on a way to prove who you are. If need be, someone will fly to Seattle and visit some of your professors."

Yes, that was what I wanted to hear. She was working on something.

"Is Port Angeles far from Seattle?"

"If you go by car, you have to take a ferry across Puget Sound, which takes a half hour," I said. "Then maybe a two-and-a-half, three-hour drive. There's a small airport in Port Angeles, but it only handles small planes. That's about a half-hour flight from SEA-TAC."

"And this see tack is?"

I smiled. "The Seattle-Tacoma International Airport."

She nodded.

"I'm sorry, Jocelyn. I don't know why I doubted you."

"It's normal. It's been eight days, and I didn't tell you what I was doing. I'm sorry."

"That's okay. I'm a natural worrier. I have to plan everything in advance. That's why I freaked out when this started happening. That's why I paced the floor that night. I can travel without worrying because I plan the whole trip and make reservations and decide what I'm doing. I know what's going to happen, and it calms me. I don't know why that is, but it is. I had a notebook in my backpack with names of what I was going to see in Budapest. It was all scheduled by day. The major who arrested me thought it was a list of places I was going to buy or sell drugs."

"All right," Jocelyn said. "I'll tell you what's happening more, and I'll tell you what I'm planning when I plan it. Will that help?"

"Immensely."

She leaned forward and kissed me. "So you'll know what will happen tomorrow, I want you in the dungeon at nine thirty sharp. And bring all your fears so I can beat them out of you."

I had problems swallowing.

"Now, do you want to know what's going to happen tonight?"

I couldn't help shaking my head like a little kid.

"First, you're going to take your clothes off and fold them into a neat pile and leave them at the top of the stairs. Then you're going to walk down that hall and knock on the last door on the right."

"Lenci's room?"

"Yes. And when she answers, tell her that you are her gift from Mistress. Then she can tell you what's going to happen next."

❖

"I'm your gift from Mistress," I said as she opened the door.

She took a step back and held the door. "Did she say what the gift was for?" she asked with a wide smile.

"She said you'd tell me what's going to happen next."

"So if I told you to clean the room and change the bed, you'd do it?"

I couldn't read the look in her eyes, but I felt that wasn't what she wanted. "If that's what you want."

"I'm not sure what I want." She pointed to the floor and said, "Sit."

I sank to the floor.

"You don't seem as depressed as you were."

"No. Jocelyn cleared up some of my fears. She explained what she was doing, and that helped."

"That's good," she said. "We can have a pleasant evening without a lot of tears."

"Of course. I'm always happy when I'm with you." That just came out of my mouth, but it felt true. I could talk with Lenci. It felt like she was a friend.

"Did she tell you to say that?"

I laughed. "Are you asking if I'm sincere?"

"Are you?"

"Very. I enjoy helping in the kitchen, and the few times we were together in the dungeon were very enjoyable. Lenci, I feel like I can talk to you. I don't know what makes Gabby tick, and Anna and Emilia are a bit too flighty. You and Jocelyn are easy to talk to. I'm sorry I've been such a baby these last few days. I feel like you understand. It's comfortable being with you. I can say what I mean. I haven't had to hold anything back."

She looked at me with a funny expression. "Would you like some port?"

"Yes, thank you."

She grinned and pointed to the table under the window. "Pour two." There was a rack with four small glasses and a bottle. I took two glasses, poured the port into them, and handed her one.

She went over to the bed and sat. "Bring yours over here, and sit on the bed." There was a new tone to her orders. It wasn't like Jocelyn's commands. It was a request I wanted to fulfill. She slid back against the ornate headboard and patted a spot next to her, I crawled onto the bed. "Tell me about you."

"Nothing much. I was average in school and got into my share of trouble when I was growing up. My father is a curator of a maritime museum. My mom stays home. I have a younger sister."

"And you grew up in the state of Washington in the United States."

I nodded. "If there's a map around, I'll show you."

"I'm sure there's an atlas down in the library, but it might be rather old. Where is Washington?"

"In the very northwest corner of the country. You can see Canada from where I used to live."

"Then it's pretty cold."

"Sometimes, but we're right on the water, and the Pacific isn't that far away. That sort of moderates it. The summers are great, though. It seldom goes above seventy degrees."

Lenci looked at me with alarm.

"Oh, that's Fahrenheit. It'd be about twenty Celsius."

Lenci smiled. "Yes, much better. Now you write for a magazine."

"I've been a writer for as long as I can remember. I planned to write a great novel. I went to college and got a job with a travel magazine. After four years, I got my own by-line, and now I get paid to travel around the world." It felt strange to say. Was that what I really wanted? Was that what I was missing?

"You're very lucky. Many people never get out of their hometown."

Oh, how true. And many don't ever want to. "Now, what about you?" I asked. "Where's your hometown?"

"Four kilometers from here."

"Really?"

"Yes. I've never traveled very far. Oh, I've been to Pergue, and I accompany Jocelyn whenever she goes to Germany or Austria to buy wine and other supplies. But that's about it."

"Wow," was all I could think to say. "Do you have other family?"

"Well, I have some cousins somewhere, but I haven't talked to them in years."

"I can't imagine that." I had pictured her coming from a large family. "Does Jocelyn have other family?"

"For as long as I remember, it was only Jocelyn and her father."

We talked about our families for a few moments. Then Lenci downed the rest of her port, took my glass, and set it with hers on the night table. "I think we've talked enough. Come here."

She laid me back onto the bed. She took my mouth with hers, and I saw another side of Lenci I had never imagined. My insides started vibrating as she wrapped me in her arms.

CHAPTER FOURTEEN

It was the end of the second week and here I was sitting on a bench in the middle of the dead garden. It seemed like a symbol of my life, of my mood. There were times when I felt like going into my room, curling up in bed and crying myself to death. Anna and Emilia were so cheery it almost made me sick. I couldn't think of anything to smile about.

Everything had been picked from the vegetable patch, and the herbs had been cut from here and were hanging in the root cellar to dry. The flowers were long gone, and Emilia had gathered all the seeds so she could plant again next year. Where would I be next year? Would I be home or in some dank prison? I couldn't even speculate what that would be like. It was too frightening.

I'd finished pulling up the barren plants and readying them to be mulched. The only things still green were the grapevines on the hills. Emilia had been looking at them every day and said they'd be ready by next week.

The last weeks had been the most wonderful and the most horrible days I could remember. Every other day, sometimes every day, Jocelyn would want me in the dungeon, and it was always spectacular. I'd had sex with everyone but her. I figured that was a losing cause. I spent my days worrying and the evenings in the dungeon in heaven.

If anyone could see what I was doing, they'd be shocked, even with my penchant for sexual things. This was far beyond any of my fantasies. Who could have imagined that life could be such a dichotomy of emotions?

I didn't know what to do. I was supposed to fly home next Sunday, but here I was, waiting…in Rebinia. All of my plans were on hold. If Jocelyn couldn't find some way to have the charges thrown out, I'd spend the next ten years or so in prison. If she could have the drug charges removed, I'd still have "entering the country without a passport and refusing to cooperate with federal authorities." And there was still no proof that I was Katherine Lowe from Washington. How did this happen? Because I'd stayed up all night instead of sleeping like I should have? Because it was more important to stay up and drink and laugh with my friends?

Why had I let myself fall asleep on the train? Where had my traveling savvy gone? I knew better. Why hadn't I put my passport in my pocket with the map? Was the map more important than my passport?

I sighed. Hindsight really was twenty-twenty, wasn't it? No sense worrying about it now. I put my head down into my hands, my elbows on my knees. I felt like crying, but I didn't want to. I'd cried more in the past week and a half than in my whole adult life, and it hadn't done any good.

Had I given up too quickly? Why?

Well, why not? I had the feeling that if Jocelyn couldn't find anything, no one could.

I looked around the garden. There was nothing for me to do here. Maybe I should see if Lenci needed help with something.

Lenci…we had had a wonderful time making love through the night. She was less rough than I'd seen before, and the night was gentle, almost loving. I had slept in there, her arms around me. Then the morning came all too soon, and she got up to make breakfast. I'd hurried downstairs, hoping I wouldn't pass anyone, so I could make it look like I'd slept in my own room. I hoped Gabby hadn't seen my pile of clothes when she went up.

And Regina? And the others? Yes, I'd made love to them all, and everyone else had done me. Made love to them all? No, I had simply fucked them, as they had fucked me. The only semblance of love had come from Lenci. Was it all just a game we played?

And Jocelyn? *No, give that up. It's never going to happen.*

Good God. I'd never been this negative. But I'd never been in a situation like this.

I heard someone running up behind me. I turned in time to see Anna approach. "Katherine!"

I stood up quickly. "What?"

"Jocelyn sent me to bring you inside. Regina's here. I think she found something with your name in it."

"Really?" My heart soared. Might it be proof that Katherine P. Lowe really existed?

"Yes, come on." She grabbed my hand. and we raced back to the house.

Anna raced up the stairs with me but held back when I knocked on Jocelyn's office door. "Come," I heard. Anna gave me an encouraging nod.

I opened the door and walked in. Regina was sitting beside Jocelyn's desk. Jocelyn turned toward me.

"Well, Katherine, we may have found something to help you." She slid a copy of my travel magazine across her desk.

"I found your photo on page eighty-six. I also read your article. You're a very fine writer."

Oh God. "Wow. Thank you." Why hadn't I thought of that?

"We're having someone call the magazine to verify that that's really you."

I sank down onto the floor. I was so amazed that my legs wouldn't support me. Tears streamed down my cheeks, and I couldn't control my breath.

"Come here," Jocelyn said, holding her hands out. I slid over to her and got up on my knees. She drew me into her arms and kissed me, long and hard. I could barely breathe when she released me.

I slid back to the floor. We stared into each other's eyes for several moments. I couldn't read hers.

Jocelyn finally turned to Regina. "Are you staying for dinner?"

"Yes. I was going to talk to you about that." She shifted in her chair. Jocelyn looked at her, waiting.

"Will you need Emilia tonight? She promised to tell me about grapes."

"Grapes, Huh?" Jocelyn asked. "Well, she handles grapes very well." She looked at Regina with a knowing smile.

"Well, may I?" Regina asked.

"Help yourself."

"Can I use the dungeon?"

Jocelyn nodded.

"Thank you," she said as she leaned forward and gave Jocelyn a kiss.

Jocelyn turned to me. "What are your plans for tonight?"

"I don't have any."

"You do now."

I couldn't have smiled wider. Someone knew who I was, and Jocelyn wanted me in the dungeon. Could life get better? I felt I could breathe. There was proof of who I was!

❖

I finished helping Lenci in the kitchen and was putting silverware away when she came up behind me and placed her hands on my shoulders. "I heard that Regina found something that identifies you," she said.

I turned. "The magazine I write for. They print my picture with every article. I don't know why I didn't think of it before."

"Then congratulations. Hopefully, this is just a start."

"I sure hope so." I took a deep breath and smiled. "It's the first hope I've had in days."

She gave me a warm hug, then stepped back to look me in the face. "I also understand Jocelyn requested you again tonight."

I nodded.

"Have a wonderful time."

I reached out to embrace her and gave her a long, hard kiss.

She smiled and caressed my face. "Don't keep her waiting," she said, as she pushed me out of the kitchen.

I ran downstairs and grabbed my towel so I could shower. Life finally had a positive note. I looked at my watch. It was 9:10. *Better hurry.* Dungeon time was 9:30. I didn't want to be late for this one.

❖

As I walked out of the shower, naked, Emilia was also coming out of her room.

"Lucky night," I said softly.

She grabbed my hand and gave it a squeeze. "I hope so."

When we came into the dungeon, Regina looked up, then Jocelyn turned. Regina beckoned to Emilia and pointed to the floor. Jocelyn walked over to me. I watched her hand for the sign to kneel, but she didn't give it. She stopped a few feet from me.

"We're going to have to find somewhere more secluded."

I was confused.

She took my hand and led me up the stairs and through the dining room. When we reached the top of the circular staircase, she headed down the hall. She stopped in front of her bedroom door and opened it. Oh God. Her bedroom?

She held her hand out. "Come, show me what you can do."

This was the perfect culmination of this incredible day. I walked in and looked around. There was a king-size bed and beautiful antique furniture. The whole room was elegant. I turned back as I heard the door close.

She smiled. "You said there was something you wanted to do?"

"I thought you forgot," I said softly.

"I remember everything," she countered.

"Good." I pulled her into my arms. "I've never met anyone like you," I whispered. "Not only are you beautiful, but you exude the most power I've ever faced."

"Is that going to stop you?"

"Not at all." I placed my lips on hers and took control. I,

Katherine P. Lowe, was taking charge of the moment with the fabulous Duchess Jocelyn Buza. I don't remember how we got there, but we were on her bed.

She was allowing me to take control.

I couldn't stop kissing her, her lips, her eyes, her ears as I held her tightly, and on to her neck. I unbuttoned her blouse as I stared into her eyes. They shone with a light so soft and steady that I couldn't look away. There was something in those eyes that filled me with hope and a steadfastness I'd never felt before. I sat her up so I could push the shirt off her shoulders. As she took her hands out of the sleeves, I unhooked her bra and pulled it off. She was allowing me to undress her. I'd never imagined this would happen.

When her breasts came into view, I had to touch them, kiss them, suck them. They weren't large, but they were firm. She leaned back and held my shoulders as I kissed and nipped her chest.

"Nice," was all she said.

"And I haven't even gotten to the good parts yet," I whispered.

She pulled me up into her arms and kissed me. As our breasts rubbed together, the kiss became harder, then more frenzied. She was an animal, getting faster and faster. Our teeth clicked together as we tried to swallow each other. I wanted to devour every square centimeter of her. I ravished every inch of her beautiful body with everything I had: my lips, my tongue, my teeth, my hands, and my soul. Nothing stopped me.

She pushed me back down from time to time to do what she wanted, and I tried to match her. While she tried to devour my neck, I undid her slacks. She pulled back to give me room to slide them and her panties over her feet.

While I was still leaning, she pulled me back, pressed me onto the bed, and straddled me. Oh my God. The feel of her heat and wetness on my stomach was extraordinary. I didn't know I could be this turned on. I felt like I was drowning in us.

She surprised me by moving up my body and placing herself directly over my mouth. What a gift. I wrapped my arms around her legs and grasped her hips. She helped me lower her until she was sitting on my tongue. I had never imagined this. I wanted to inhale her entire being, and I think I did. I hadn't ever done it this long. It was like I had a neck and tongue of steel. Nothing stopped me, nothing slowed me down. I licked and sucked on and on.

When she stiffened and trembled, I embraced her tightly as her wetness flowed over my face. When the shaking stopped, I pulled her down into my arms and laid her gently on the bed. Her breathing was so ragged, I almost got scared, but as I held her, she started to relax. When she finally looked at me, my heart almost stopped. I couldn't read the look in her eye. Was it wonder? Irritation? Amazement? Or was it the answer to a challenge? Did she take my lovemaking as a challenge to her dominance? I leaned down to kiss her gently.

She amazed me with her recovery time. I had barely caught my breath when she pinned me to the bed, her on top. "That was fast," I said.

"Yes, I never procrastinate. And this is something I really want to do." She leaned down to kiss me as her hand roamed my body.

Good God, every place she touched became a fire. As she moved, I became wrapped in her essence. I was smoldering, waiting to explode. But it seemed to grow into years and years of waiting... of longing for her to touch me.

Then she touched my center. I was going to explode, but there was more in store. Her fingers entered me and took possession. Time after time, she stroked the right spot, and I was on the edge. How long could I teeter without sliding off? Would I be good enough for her? Was I strong enough?

Then all her fingers slid into me.

I screamed. It was like everything inside me had burst into flames, melting my bones. I could only let my muscles react as they wanted. I could control nothing. Minutes later, I lay there, totally limp.

I felt her draw me into her arms and cradle me. My eyes refocused, and I looked at her. She didn't say anything but looked down my body, nodding as she did. I had to smile.

My first thought, which fell immediately out of my mouth, was "Was it good for you?"

She smiled. "You really can't control your mouth, can you?"

"You seemed to like that a few minutes ago."

"Yes, I did." She kissed me roughly. "There. Will that stop your smart mouth?"

I grinned. "Not if it makes you do something like that."

She slid down and lay beside me. "How did I get you?" she asked.

"I slept through my stop."

"That was rhetorical."

I rolled over, my head on my fist, and looked down at her.

"Was this what you expected?" she asked.

"More than I expected, and yes, we can tell Gabby I did survive."

"Are you sure?" she asked. "I thought this was only half over. The fun part is yet to come."

With that, she sat up and leaned to the top of the bed. She returned with a long metal cord that came across the bed from both sides. The center was held together by handcuffs. She quickly separated them and snapped one onto each of my wrists.

I held my hands up to look at them.

"You didn't think my bedroom would be kink-free, did you?"

I had to laugh. "No. Of course not."

She smiled widely. "Good." She sat up and reached over the foot of the bed to get a cable box with several buttons on it. She sat back and held it up. "Watch." She pressed one button. The cord slowly drew my hands apart until I was stretched wide, then she let go. An evil smile spread across her face.

"Now we will see if you survive." She pressed another button on the box, and the foot board started to rise. With it came an assortment of other chains, whips and clamps. "Let's see how this works." She took two clamps attached to a short chain, then she clamped one to each of my nipples, screwing tighter until they were squeezed almost flat.

I wasn't sure I liked this pain.

Then she took another cord from the foot of the bed, identical to the one that held my hands apart. She attached one cuff to each of my ankles and pressed another button. My legs slowly spread. When she let go, I was stretched wide across her bed.

She stood at the bottom of the bed and assessed me. Without another word, she crawled up onto the bed and sat crossed-legged beside me.

"Now, I can do anything I want to you," she said softly. "Can't I?"

"You always could," I whispered.

She laughed. "That, too, was rhetorical." She picked up the chain between my breasts and slowly pulled. I gasped as pain shot through me. Several times, she pulled it higher and higher, the pain getting worse and worse. Tears came to my eyes.

"Now," she said without stopping, "should I flog you like Regina did, or should I fuck you like Gabby did? Which did you like more?"

"Do I really have a choice?" I asked.

"No. Of course not. I was thinking out loud." She produced a lone clamp attached to a chain. "Where do you suppose I'm going to put this one?"

"Wherever you want."

"Correct." She reached down into my crotch and started exploring. Then I felt the clasp on my clitoris. She took the chain and drew it up my body to link it to the one across my chest. Now there was enough pressure on all three to make it close to unbearable. "Now, don't move." She tickled me, and I flinched, and when the chains didn't stretch, and I gasped.

"That was silly, baby. I told you not to move."

I was panting. I was trying to be still but not accomplishing it. I had to curl into a crunch to relieve some of the pain. Would she ever stop?

Then her fingers delved into me. The world flashed red in front of my eyes, and I screamed. The clip on my clit was released, and her hands were caressing my face.

"Shh, baby," she crooned. "Now that you know the pain, we can get to the pleasure."

She brought my chin up and took my mouth with hers. It was

the longed, hottest kiss I had ever experienced. I couldn't get enough of her, and she didn't stop. It was frustrating not being able to move. I wanted to hold her, caress her, feel her, but my arms were still spread across the bed.

She slid down to explore my crotch again. It felt good this time, and my body responded. Her fingers slid in and out time after time. I was beginning to become crazed. I wanted more. I wanted her. I wanted to be free to hold her. I wanted to touch her. I wanted...

Her whole hand balled into a fist within me.

I was lost. I was floating. I was drowning. I was loving it. I was loving her. Then my body exploded into tiny fragments. It seemed to go on forever. Higher, deeper, stronger. As she removed her hand, I sank back onto the bed, totally drained.

She cradled my face. There was nothing I could say. She leaned down and kissed me gently on the lips. The cords released, and I was able to move my arms around her.

"Did I survive?" I asked.

"Perfectly. You were amazing."

"Not as amazing as you," I countered as I touched her face. She turned her head to kiss my palm.

"I had to work for that." She smiled. "I think you're powerful, too. I can't do that with my other girls. They're not ready for it."

"Not Lenci or Gabby?"

"No, not Lenci, and I don't want to try with Gabby."

"I thought Gabby was powerful."

"She is, from time to time, but I don't want to think of love with Gabby." I couldn't interpret the look in her eyes. She removed all the cuffs, and I could move again. "Are you thirsty? I could use a little wine."

"Wine sounds nice, but I'm already drunk on you."

She chuckled as she got off the bed. "I have a nice bottle in my office." She went across the hall, A few minutes later, she came back with two glasses of deep red liquid. "This is some that Emilia brewed two years ago."

I sat up and took a glass. She crawled onto the bed and sat

down beside me. "Here's to fulfilling your fantasy," she toasted. I clicked glasses with her, and we both took a sip.

"Hopefully, this won't be the only time," I said.

She kissed me gently. "But I can't neglect my other girls."

I chuckled. "My mother taught me to share."

She toasted me, and we both took another gulp. "So, how do you feel about the last two weeks?" she asked.

"That first night, I was scared. I didn't know what was happening. But you guided me through it, and I grew to love it. I loved being in your dungeon...not as much as being in your bed, but it runs a very close second."

She laughed and pulled me close. We drank wine and talked about my experiences until my eyes began to close.

"I guess you really did wear me out," I told her. "I can't keep my eyes open."

"It was my pleasure," she whispered. She hugged me closer as the world faded.

CHAPTER FIFTEEN

I awoke to loud voices across the hall. I got up and went to the door. Jocelyn was yelling at someone in her office.

"That was the worst thing you have ever done. It wasn't a joke. It was illegal. And you brought it to my doorstep?"

"But look how it turned out. Haven't you had a wonderful new adventure?"

"Adventure? That was a kidnapping. You'll be thrown out of the military. Your whole career will be a fiasco. What possessed you? If she presses charges, I'll have to represent her, and you know I'll win. This is the most ludicrous and humiliating thing you've ever done. Why do I welcome you into my house?"

It was Jocelyn and Regina, arguing...about...were they talking about me? Kidnapping? Illegal? Humiliating?

"Because I always help you set the best scenes and bring you incredible new girls."

"Well, this was not one of them."

"You didn't enjoy beating her and fucking her?"

"But now I've got to apologize and get things straightened out. Lord knows how much this is going to cost me. I should take that out of your hide."

"Oh, Joccy...you haven't tried that in years."

Oh my God!

The office door opened, and Jocelyn stepped into the hallway. She was dressed in her long blue robe. Her eyes widened in fear when she saw me. She walked past me into her room. Her face was red. With anger? With embarrassment?

"We need to talk. Come in here, please," she said softly. "Put this on." She handed me a shirt from in her closet.

I looked up as Regina appeared in the office door. I turned back into the room and took the shirt.

"Have a seat," she told me as I covered myself. "And button it up. I can't be serious with you when you're naked, and this discussion will be ultra-serious." I could see the anger in her eyes. It was so very different from earlier.

I sat down on the corner of the bed as I slid the buttons through their holes.

"First of all, Katherine, I must apologize. You have been the victim of a horrendous game my *former* friends have been playing. You are not, nor have you ever been, under arrest for carrying drugs. Lieutenant Benik"—she gestured to Regina—"set that up so you and I would meet, and I would bring you here."

"I knew you'd like each other," Regina threw in.

"But it was still not right!" Jocelyn paced around her bedroom.

"What?" How was I supposed to handle this information?

"I realize all the anguish you've been through, so whatever I can do to try to assuage your suffering, I will do."

"I'm not under arrest? I won't go to prison?" My God! This was all a joke? What was she telling me? This was all bogus?

"No, Katherine. You are a free woman."

What I'd just heard in Jocelyn's office fell totally into place. I looked at Regina. "You did this to me? You thought it was a joke? You were just playing?"

"I'm sorry, Katherine. It went further than I had expected."

"You want me to believe that? These past weeks were a joke? You played a game with me? You knew exactly what you were doing!" My fists clenched. I wanted to punch her.

"Go ahead, if it will help. I probably deserve it," Regina said softly when she saw me fist my hands.

"Probably?" Jocelyn exploded. "There's no *probably* about

this. You deserve whatever Katherine wants to do to you." She turned to me. "I will not stop you if you want to beat the crap out of her. I'll even swear it was self-defense."

"No," I said. "I don't know what I want to do. This whole thing was just an act?" I twirled around to look at Jocelyn. "Everything?" Did I want to hit Jocelyn, too? I'd been raked over the coals? They'd made me think I was going crazy.

She stared into my eyes. "From me or my girls, no. We were not playing a game. It was Regina, Paol, Tomas, and...no, no one from this house was in on this *joke*."

I turned on Regina. "You thought this was funny?"

She looked away.

"You are totally free, Katherine, and you have several options. If you press changes against her and her buddies, they will be put in prison for their crime. At this point, I will gladly represent you, pro bono."

"Wait, wait. Let me get this straight." I was still trying to understand. "This is coming too fast. Slow down."

Jocelyn wiped her face with her hand. "Do you need something to drink or eat? Would that help?"

I nodded as I sat back down. "I need coffee."

"I'll get it," Regina said. She ran down the hall to the stairs.

"Where is all my luggage?"

"Regina has all of your possessions, which she *stole* while you were sleeping on the train and put in the boot of her automobile."

I still couldn't comprehend. "I need to hold them," I decided. Maybe that would make this real for me.

Jocelyn reached for the phone beside the bed and pressed a number. "Lenci, is Regina down there...No, stop her. Send her out to her car to bring Katherine's bags in...Please bring the coffee up here yourself. I think you need to hear this...Just come up, please."

She put the phone back and turned to me. "I don't know how to apologize for this."

I held my hand up. "Let me get my mind around this first. Then we can talk."

She nodded and sank onto the cream-colored bench on the

other side of her bed. A few minutes later, Lenci came in with a tray holding two cups of coffee. I took one and gulped a mouthful.

"What's happening?" Lenci asked. "You never say please."

"Katherine is no longer a prisoner. Regina, Paol, and Tomas were playing a sick game. There were never any drugs, and all of Katherine's possessions are locked in Regina's car."

Lenci's eyes widened. "Oh, Katherine." She wrapped her arms around me. "I'm so sorry." She hugged me tightly. Then she turned to Jocelyn. "She's free to go?"

"She's free to do whatever she wants."

Regina walked down the hall lugging my suitcase and backpack. She set them down at my feet. I wanted to kick her, to hit her over the head with my bags. I had never been this angry at anyone. I picked up my backpack instead and unzipped it. I grabbed my passport and phone and clutched them tightly to my chest. I finally took a deep breath. I looked into Regina's eyes. "I hate you," was my first thought out of my mouth.

Regina nodded, her head down.

"I need to think…alone. I'm going to my room," I said. "I need to get this straight in my head."

"No," Jocelyn said. "Those are servant rooms. You are a guest." She turned to Lenci. "Is the room next door clean?"

"It should be. If not, the room across from me is. That was used just last week." She went out to check.

"Relax. We can talk whenever you're ready."

I nodded and went out into the room where Lenci held the door open for me.

CHAPTER SIXTEEN

What was I going to do? I walked to the window and looked across the front of the house. The lawns were manicured to perfection. Regina's car was parked out front, and the wrought iron gates stood taller than I remembered.

What did I do now? I'd planned to go to Budapest and Krakow, but that was two weeks ago. Did I still want to go? No. I didn't. Not this time.

I paced.

My head was all turned around. I'd had a wonderful two weeks here. I'd experienced what I'd only dreamed of but also dreaded my future. I thought I'd spend the next twenty years in prison, yet I'd allowed myself to be bound in this house because Jocelyn had wanted it. I'd had the best sex and the worst experiences of my life.

I thought back to earlier. Last night? What time was it? The sun was up. The clock on the mantel over the small fireplace said 7:40. Was it right? What did I need to do? I needed to talk to someone. But who?

I looked at the phone. I could text Amy and explain where I'd been, but how did I tell her what had happened here if I wasn't sure myself? I continued to pace.

Good God. I had to get out of here. I wanted to run away, to escape this...but not like before. No. I could stride out the front door without anyone chasing me. Did I want to beat Regina? And Paol? He had been the worst. I couldn't believe how he had treated me. Yes, I could see myself punishing him...*and* Regina.

What was Jocelyn's part in this? Yes, I'd heard her berating Regina for the whole thing, so she hadn't known beforehand? How long had she known? Did I trust that she was without blame?

I suppose I should blame her, too, but that wasn't me. Their *game* was horrifying. It had almost brought me to my knees. I had thought I was going crazy. But I had met Jocelyn and Lenci and the others. Last night was the best thing that had happened. If it hadn't been for Regina, I never would have come here, never would have met them.

And I would never have experienced any of the kinky sexual things I'd always wondered and dreamed about. What a conundrum. *What do I do?* Because Regina and Paol got a big laugh over me, I'd gone through several days of the worst fears of my life…but also, I'd met a group of women who brought my life into perspective. The worst and the best days of my life. *How do I deal with this?* Punish them or reward them?

Over an hour later, there was a knock on the bedroom door. "Come in," I called, and the door opened.

It was Jocelyn. "How are you feeling now?"

"Better. I don't feel like strangling Regina anymore."

Jocelyn smiled. "What do you feel like doing to her?"

I rubbed my eyes as I thought it through. "Nothing. I just need for this to be over."

"You can file charges, you know. You can have her thrown out of the army, put in prison, or you could sue her and make her pay for your time." Jocelyn stood back and let me think about it. "I don't condone what she did."

"But then I would never have met you." And in the long run, I was extremely happy I did.

She nodded.

"If I filed charges, they'd kick her out of the army?"

"Of course. She, Paol, and Tomas would get dishonorable discharges. All of them. Tomas and Paol got off just imagining what Regina and I were doing to you. That was disgusting. I will not be fodder for any man's sexual enjoyment, and neither should you."

"If I pressed charges, it would ruin all their lives."

"They almost ruined yours."

"But they didn't. We found out in time for me to meet my friends and go home."

Jocelyn looked into my eyes.

"Maybe I should make her pay for my trip. I was going to research the small hotels in Budapest and Krakow."

"You would have made a lot of money with those stories?"

"Enough to cover my expenses for this month."

"Then that's what you'll get. I'll make sure of it."

"I was tempted to write a piece about Nové Ville, too, but I didn't have my phone to take pictures."

"Is that what you want to do?"

I had to chuckle. "It's what I would have done before this whole thing started. I'm not sure what I can do now. My whole perspective has changed. I'm not nearly as naïve as I used to be. I'm not as sure what will make people happy or what will make *me* happy."

Jocelyn seemed to consider something. "Tell me what you think of this: you'll explore the city for the rest of this week," she said. "We'll get you settled in a nice hotel in Nové Ville and let you do your writing before you have to meet your friends in Amsterdam. I'll send Gabby and the car so you can get around the whole city."

"That's a good idea, but you don't need to pay for it."

"Yes. Regina, Paol, Tomas, and Jana have to pay. In fact, I'll find everyone who was involved. What they did was not right."

"Jana? Did I meet her?"

Jocelyn smiled. "No, and you won't. She's the secretary at my office in town who was supposed to be making all those calls to the embassy and to your family. I'll find out how Regina got her involved, and then she'll either pay or she's fired."

"No, don't fire her. It was Regina's idea, I'm sure." I was angry enough.

"You should make Regina pay. I can't believe she did that to you. She will occasionally set up something with a new girl or two, but she's never done anything like this before, and it was over the top, even for her."

"Then hold it over her so she doesn't do it again. I've thought about it, but it isn't in me to punish someone for doing something that ultimately brought me happiness, and I am happy that I met you."

"And I am happy I met you. Last night was wonderful. I haven't had anyone make love to me in ages."

I looked at her with my eyes wide, my eyebrows high. Did I hear her right?

"No. My girls please me with what I tell them to do, but no one's made love to me because they wanted to in a long time."

"I'm sure they want to."

"Yes, but I have to direct them."

I shook my head at the thought. Then I said, "If you ever decide to go to the US, I would be honored to host you in Seattle."

"And if you ever want to come back here, this house is always open to you." She drew me into her arms and kissed me.

CHAPTER SEVENTEEN

I stepped off the train in Amsterdam and saw Amy, Paula, and Judy waving to me. It was easy to identify them. Amy was tall and slender, Paula had fuzzy black hair, and Judy was short and a little plump. They were waiting when I came through the gate.

"Katherine! Where have you been?" they asked, their expressions concerned. "What happened?"

I smiled. How should I say this? "I ended up going to Rebinia," I said softly.

"I thought you were going to Budapest." Amy frowned. "We tried calling and texting, we even called the hotel, but they said you weren't registered. Why didn't you call or text so we wouldn't worry?"

I grimaced. "I sort of misplaced my backpack. I'm sorry. I should have called, but my phone was in it, and just about everything I had. I didn't even know the hotel you were staying at."

"But you have it now," Judy said, patting my back where the bag hung.

"I found it right as I was trying to leave. How could I get here if I didn't have my passport?" I said, skirting the real story. God. I had to get them off this. I looked around. "Is there a place near here to get something to eat? I haven't had anything today."

"Yes, there's a sweet little place just across the canal. We went there the first night."

"Then let's go. I'm starved." We started out of the station. "How was Greece?" I asked as we walked along.

"It was wonderful," Amy said.

"Did you stay in Odessa all three weeks?"

"No. Only for a week and a half, then we went down to Athens for a week," Paula said.

"We took a boat tour out to the southern islands," Amy added.

They each had something else to tell me about their trip, but I had a hard time concentrating on what they were saying. I still had Jocelyn rambling around in my head. We entered the small restaurant and took our seats. "What's good here?" I asked, looking through the menu.

"Everything," Paula answered. "I had the lamb chops the other night, and Amy had the white fish."

"I had a lamb flank steak," Judy added. "It was really good."

"I think I'll have the fish. They eat a lot of lamb where I was."

And Lenci cooked it so well. We gave our orders to the waiter and sat back.

"Where were you?" Judy asked. "Your text just said you were all right and that you'd meet us here today."

"And who is Duchess Buza? That was the return name on the ISP address," Amy asked, one eyebrow raised.

I bit my lower lip. I had hoped I wouldn't have to explain, but then, I *had* used Jocelyn's Wi-Fi. "Someone I met there."

"You mean someone you slept with there," Paula accused. They all shared a knowing laugh.

I stopped. "No. I never slept with her." That was the truth. I didn't have to lie. We had never slept.

They looked at me skeptically. "Why? Was she in her eighties?" Judy asked.

"No, in her late thirties, early forties, I think, just a little older than us."

Judy put her hands on the table "You expect us to believe you didn't get laid this trip, when you disappeared for three weeks?"

I had to get them off this until I got my mind settled around what had really happened. "I didn't say I didn't get laid." I grinned apologetically. "I said I didn't sleep with the duchess. Actually, I only slept with one person for one night."

"How did you manage that?" Paula asked. "Were you sick?"

"She was so busy fucking the duchess that there wasn't time to sleep," Amy decided. She grinned at me.

"No," I answered. I laughed. "I wish. She's a classy lady."

"Did you take pictures? What's she like?"

"I really don't want to talk about it right now. When I get a grip on what really happened, I'll tell you." I frowned. *It may take months to figure this out.*

"Did you fall in love?" Amy asked.

"I don't know. I like her a lot."

"When do you see her again?"

"I don't know," I muttered. "Probably never."

"You didn't make plans?" Amy asked.

I shook my head.

Judy laughed. "Are you getting slow in your old age?"

"No. It's complicated."

"Is she married?" Paula asked.

"No, she's not married, but there's someone else." I looked down at my lap.

"Did you fuck both of them?" Judy's eyes got wide.

I didn't answer.

"You did, didn't you?" she asked.

"It doesn't matter," I said softy.

They looked at me strangely.

"Please don't ask," I said, looking at them. "I'm not sure how I feel about the last three weeks." And I didn't want to hash it out in some restaurant when I wasn't sure what had happened. *I may never know.*

Amy patted my hand, then steered the conversation to other things. Our food was delivered, and we ate and talked like old times.

❖

Amy and I walked into the room we'd share at the little hotel. I set my suitcase down and put my backpack on it.

Amy curled up on the bed. "Do you want to talk about it? You look like you've got a lot bottled up in there."

"I don't know where to begin," I whispered.

"Why don't you start by telling me how you got to Rebinia?"

"You'll think I'm crazy."

"Too late. I've thought that for years." She laughed.

I took a deep breath and told her about my train ride and my missing luggage and backpack.

"Good God," she said. "I would have freaked if my passport was missing."

I nodded. "I thought it would be easy to get it replaced. I figured it would take a day or two, but that would give me time to explore the city. It was a beautiful old place. If I'd had my camera, I would have taken pictures and written a piece about it right then. I thought it was wonderful." Then I explained about my meeting with Paol and Regina and the drugs that were found in my backpack.

Her eyes got wider than I'd ever seen. "So you spent the whole night thinking you were going to prison?"

"I sure did. For twenty years. I think I paced all night. The next morning, I met with the lawyer who'd been assigned my case."

"Was he a good lawyer?"

"She. Counselor Jocelyn Buza."

That surprised her even more. "What? The duchess? She was your lawyer?"

I nodded and went on to explain how I was released to her.

"She was a real lawyer?"

I nodded again.

"And a real duchess?"

"You wouldn't believe her property. It was an old castle with beautiful gardens and three large fields of vineyard. The place probably had twenty regular bedrooms and maybe ten or more servants' quarters. Four other women lived there. Lenci ran the house and did the cooking; Anna kept the house clean and did the laundry. Emilia tended the garden, the vineyard and brewed wine, and Gabby kept the lawns and shrubbery trimmed and the cars running."

"Which one was her significant other?"

I smiled. "They all were."

"All of them?"

I nodded. "It turned out that Jocelyn is a sadistic Mistress, and they are her girls. She told me that the property was a monarchy and that she was the queen."

"You're kidding me." She leaned forward quickly.

"Nope."

"Isn't that what you always wanted?"

I took a deep breath and nodded. "That's why I didn't want to tell Paula and Judy."

"It's better that you don't. They wouldn't understand."

"That's what I thought." They wouldn't have understood Hannah. How would they have understood this?

"Did you make love to all of them?"

I took a deep breath. "Almost. I made love to them all but Gabby at least once. Gabby did me, and I made love with Lenci three or four times, and except for one night, it was always under Jocelyn's watchful eye and direction. We weren't supposed to be together unless she approved it."

"What happened that one night?"

"She gave me as a gift to Lenci. I went to her room to spend the night. It turned into a wonderful night of gentle sex."

"I don't understand."

"It took me a while, too."

"Did you ever get to make love to this Jocelyn?"

I smiled. "Once, in her own bed. It was phenomenal."

Amy sat back. "What happened with your prison sentence?"

"It turned out it was all a joke set up by her best friend who thought we should meet."

"*What?*"

"That was my reaction, too."

"You're kidding. How do you feel about it?" she finally asked.

I hesitated for a moment, trying to decide what I wanted to tell her, but tears started rolling down my face. "Oh, Amy," I said as she held me close. "It was the worst and the best time of my life. I'm ecstatic I met Jocelyn and all the things in her house, but I wanted to kill Regina for what she did. My soul felt raped. I can't begin to describe what the threat of prison felt like. But if I hadn't had Jocelyn and the girls, I might have gone insane."

"But you're on the way home now and you're safe again," Amy whispered in my ear as she held me tightly.

I brushed the tears away after a minute and reached for a tissue to blow my nose. "Well, at least I made some money on the deal. Jocelyn made them pay me what I would have made if I'd gone to Budapest and Krakow. In fact, they each paid me what I'd have earned, so I got four times the fee."

"At least you got something." Amy thought it through for a moment. "What did this Jocelyn look like?"

I reached for my phone and brought up a couple pictures I'd taken before I left for Nové Ville.

"She's beautiful!"

"She's a little taller than me. She wears designer clothes, and her makeup is always perfect. She really carries herself like royalty. It was the way she was brought up."

"Are you going back there?"

I took a deep breath. "I don't know."

"You did fall in love, didn't you?"

"I don't know if I fell in love with two or three of them, the situation, or just with her."

"That's quite different, isn't it?"

I could only nod.

Amy slid down onto the floor beside me and wrapped her arms around me. I felt my tears start to fall. "It's okay, Kath. It's all right to love. You can't dodge every bullet."

"I could have stayed there, but I'd only be another of her girls. Yes, I'd be the newest one, so I'd get most of her attention...for a while at least...until she brought the next one home."

"What are the others like?"

"Anna and Emilia were younger, in their early twenties. They are rather naïve but very caring. Anna kept me informed about everything that happened in the house and how to handle it." I switched the phone to pictures of them. "Gabby is butch, the strong type. She is almost thirty, I think. Her lovemaking was utterly fantastic. It took me two days to recover from it."

"Two days?"

"Yes. I've never been that sore or that fulfilled. Lenci is our age or maybe a little younger. We got to be friends. We talked and shared a lot. She'd been there the longest, something like twelve years." I smiled. "She is considered the first girl. Basically, she ran the whole place. I helped her clean the kitchen in the evenings, unless Jocelyn wanted me in her dungeon."

"Her *dungeon*?"

I smiled. "Yup. She has a giant room in the basement furnished with torture devices. Someday, I'll probably look back on it fondly."

"Did you experience all of them?" Amy asked, her eyes wide again.

"Not all," I threw off as if it didn't matter.

Amy studied me. I think she knew I wasn't going to tell her more about it. "I guess I don't have to ask if you had fun."

I smiled to myself. "I had a lot of fun and a lot of terror. I think I went through every emotion there is. Pleasure and pain. Terror and elation."

Amy hugged me tighter. We were silent while I tried to calm down. After a few minutes, she said, "We're going on a tour of the cheese factories tomorrow. Want to come?"

I paused. "I do and I don't."

"I've heard that before. You're coming. Look what happened the last time I let you get away with not going with us."

I tried to smile. "You shouldn't worry about that. It was a once-in-a-lifetime thing. I don't think I'll ever run across a situation like that again."

"If you don't feel you can go with us, then stay here and sleep... but if you can, please come with us. It will put some *normal* back in your life."

CHAPTER EIGHTEEN

Two days later, we boarded the plane to Seattle. I pulled my iPad out of my backpack and started writing. Maybe if I saw my story in writing, I'd get a feeling for what had happened. Drinks had been distributed and a meal served, and the other passengers had sat back to read or sleep or watch a movie. I kept typing away. I guess I worked on it for quite a while.

"What are you writing?" Amy asked from the seat next to me as she paused her movie. "You've been intent on that for the last three hours."

"I'm not sure," I said. "It started as a list of what happened before I could forget, then it turned into an email to Jocelyn, but I'm not sure I'm saying what I mean to say." Things had continued to crowd in on me every few minutes.

"Let me see." She held out her hand, and I passed her my tablet.

Dear Jocelyn,

I sit here winging my way west with as many emotions and questions as I experienced these last weeks. It may take months to sort it all out in my mind and heart.

Please tell Regina that I haven't forgiven her, but I don't hate her anymore. I did when I first found out what she had done, but in thinking back over it, I realize that it was a big part of my growth into accepting my interest in the BDSM community, and I know that if she hadn't set that scene, none of this would have happened. In fact, I'm

I am extremely glad we met, Jocelyn, and I might show up on your doorstep one day. Please remember that if you ever decide to visit the United States, you are extremely welcome to come to Seattle. I would be honored to host you.

If our paths do not cross again, please remember me. You will always hold a special place in my heart.

My love to Lenci, Gabby, Anna, and Emilia, oh, and yes, Regina, too. I will never forget any of them.

Much love to you,

Jane Doe, always known as Katherine P. Lowe

"That's a nice email. What's wrong with it?" she asked.

I shrugged and shook my head. "Did I say too much?" I reached to take the tablet back.

She thought about it. "I don't think so. It's warm and says what you wanted. It says what you meant. If that's the way you feel, you shouldn't try to change it."

I scratched my ear. "You really think so?"

"Just email it when we get home."

I'd been home about two months, but I still hadn't gotten everything straight in my head. I didn't really know what I was thinking, but not a day went by that I didn't think of her. I knew she had the other four, so why would she want me?

I was asked out a couple times, and I'd gone on a few nice dates: movies or dinner. No one made me want to go home with her; it didn't seem right. Had being with Jocelyn spoiled me for everyone else? I didn't have the energy or impetus to go out to parties or dancing.

"You're turning into a nun, Katherine Lowe, and it doesn't look good on you," Amy said one day. We were ambling though the grocery store looking for something she could cook for both of us.

"It isn't what I want to do," I said.

"You were the one who was ready to go to any party. What the hell happened to you in Rebinia? Do you want me to help find you someone to talk to?"

She tossed two steaks into the basket.

I grimaced. "It's all just so boring."

Amy studied me for a moment. "You still think of her, don't you?"

"Who?" I asked, knowing full well who she was talking about.

"Who the hell do you think I'm talking about? Your blessed Jocelyn, who found out her friend played a nasty trick on you and took you to bed as the consolation prize." Amy stood there looking me in the face. "Well, sweetie, you need help. If you don't get it, you have two choices. One, go back there, or two, get over it."

"It isn't that simple," I said softly as I picked up two large potatoes.

"It sure is. Get help or get in touch with her again. If she says get lost, then you'll know. Either way, you'll end up having to go with the flow. What do you want from her?"

I shook my head and shrugged as if I didn't know.

"If she has all those hot chicks living there, then you're going to be somewhere down the line. Is that the way you want to live? To have her look at you maybe once a week if you're lucky? Watch her pay attention to four other women instead of you? To have her send you down the hall to someone else because she couldn't be bothered?"

"She's not like that," I said softly.

"Like hell she isn't. Has she taken the time to write to you, to answer your email? Come on, Kath. If it meant something to her, she would have at least acknowledged you. It doesn't take a lot of time and energy to write something like, 'I'm glad you got home okay.' If you ask me, I think this Jocelyn person got what she wanted from you, and that's all she's ever going to do. Honey, you were taken advantage of. Face it, her best friend slammed you so she could fuck you. I'm sorry if I seem harsh, but you need help getting over this, and it's not something I'm qualified for. I think I've helped as much as I can."

I took a deep breath and sighed. What she said was probably true. I had to stop hanging on to fantasies that would never exist in reality. I did need someone to help me with this.

"You're right," I said.

Amy opened the freezer doors. "Peas, corn, or broccoli?"

"Peas."

"Come with me to the party tomorrow night, and meet someone new." She tossed a bag of frozen peas into the basket.

I had to admit that I needed to do that.

"I'm getting hungry. I always get hungry trying to straighten out your life," Amy told me as she headed for the checkout counter.

I didn't go out because I still thought of last year. I wanted Jocelyn, but I still was wary of anyone, including her. Nothing else seemed to interest me anymore. I did need therapy.

❖

In late December, I was assigned to review a five-day holiday cruise that left out of Fort Lauderdale and stopped in Saint Thomas and San Juan. It was an exciting cruise. Everyone was very upbeat. The food and entertainers were excellent, and the accommodations weren't bad. Of course I had a large room on one of the upper decks, but I made some friends who had rooms lower. A couple times, I flirted with a staff member or someone flirted with me, but I never followed up on it. What was wrong with me? Amy was right. I was turning into a nun.

I loved San Juan, so on the way back, I got off to spend a day or two and flew home from there. It was a nice vacation. It still didn't take my mind off Jocelyn. I imagined what she was doing and who she was doing it with. I was about to drive myself crazy.

"Get over it, fool," I told myself. "Listen to Amy. She's never steered you wrong."

But the entire trip didn't feel right to me. Oh, I was fair in my review. I was very professional, but my mind wasn't there. Oh my God. How did I get over this? Would I have to go back? No. I wouldn't go back. I couldn't put myself through that again. I would *not* put myself somewhere down the line, waiting for someone to decide my fate. No. I would decide my own fate. I would do what I wanted to do, not wait for someone to decide it for me, and I wouldn't let anyone put me in fear again. I would not let someone else sneak up on me and send me into the misery of last year... not even Jocelyn. I was back to doing good work, really serious reviews, back to being Katherine P. Lowe, reviewer extraordinary. My professional life was back on track. My personal life was, well, better than it had been. I had gone to a couple Leather Association meetings and even to a play party. I'd negotiated a couple scenes, but they didn't have the feel I wanted. I was, however, making friends, and I was going out. That part of my life was still dragging, but getting better. Not quickly, but it *was* moving.

❖

The winter holidays passed, and I'd just returned from Baja, where I reviewed a new resort. After Valentine's Day, I only had two assignments until later in the summer. I could take a few months to sit back and get everything straight in my head and find a therapist. Maybe I would go home to my parents' house for a few days. Maybe I would sit on a mountaintop and meditate myself into nirvana. I needed to still my mind and stop the delusions.

Amy was right. I should get my head examined.

The tenth of February saw the opening of a new resort in Mexico, and the publisher wanted to be the first to review it. I spent four days there, inspecting the accommodations and talking to guests and staff. There were a few other reviewers, but none that had the prestige of my magazine. I'd get the first national review.

"What did you think of it?" Amy asked when she picked me up at the airport.

"There were beautiful facilities. Someone dropped a bundle on it. The rooms were fantastic and the amenities top-of-the-line. But it was new, so many staff members weren't trained well, and only half spoke English. They were all very eager to serve, but some things didn't get communicated right. It will be an excellent resort when they get the kinks ironed out. I'll give it a good review." It had thrown me at first when most of the staff did not speak English. My German was better than my Spanish, but it had still brought back memories of last year. Would I ever get past that?

We pulled into the underground parking garage of my apartment building. "Coming up?" I asked. "I must have missed a lot of gossip."

Amy smiled broadly. "You sure did. Our little quartet may finally be a thing of the past."

"What?" I wasn't prepared for that. My first thought was the four at Jocelyn's house, but I quickly realized Amy was referring to our traveling clique.

She nodded as I took my suitcase out of the back seat. We headed to the elevator. "Paula started dating someone right after Christmas, and it looks pretty serious. She didn't tell any of us until a week ago."

Was my whole life changing? If we went traveling again this year, would there just be the three of us? Did I even want to travel? I did enough for my job. Maybe I should stay home for once. "Really? Good for her. Do we know this one?"

"No," Amy said. "It's someone she met at a party, from Olympia. I understand she works for an advertising company."

"Whoa. Is this one of those jobs that depends on who's voted in or out?"

Olympia was the state capital, and some of the population changed every two or four years. It wasn't that far south of Seattle.

It was better than Eastern Europe. *No. Stop it. Don't think like that.* I pressed the elevator button to bring us up to the lobby.

"That I don't know. Judy met her but didn't seem to know too much, either. All she could say was that she's really cute, and they look good together."

"Well, that's something." I stepped off the elevator and walked to the postal boxes. "So is Paula moving to Olympia, or is this girlfriend coming here?"

"They're actually talking about finding a place around Puyallup or Tacoma so neither will have to quit her job."

I glanced at her as I took a stack of letters out of the box. "That's a lot of commuting for both of them. Is this a 'let's see' move? It doesn't sound too serious if neither is willing to give up her job."

"We'll have to wait. I guess the move will be the first of May."

"Okay. I hope it's the real thing. I'd hate to see Paula get hurt again." I sorted through my mail, then lifted my phone as it dinged. "Oh my God!"

"What is it?" Amy asked.

I licked my lips that were suddenly desert-dry. "It's an email from Jocelyn."

"Then let's get you up to your apartment so you can relax to read it."

I breathed deeply and nodded. Amy picked up my suitcase and pressed the button to have the guard let us into the main lobby. I was silent for the elevator ride and stared at my phone. I didn't speak until I slipped the key in my lock.

"I didn't expect her to email me back."

"Then you'll have to open it to see what she says," Amy said. "Do you want to be alone?"

I looked up. "No! What have I ever hidden from you?"

"Not much, I don't think." She chuckled. "Okay, sit down and read. I'll make a pot of coffee."

I nodded as I sat to open the email. It took me a minute to get up the courage. I didn't know why I held back; it was just an email.

Dearest Katherine,

I hope this finds you well and that your life in Seattle is going the way you'd hoped. I would love to hear what you found about the Life there. Please be careful when you play with others, as some sadists, especially new ones, can go beyond your limits without you realizing it.

Life here is the same as always. Everyone is happy. The gardens have been replanted and are growing well. The grape crop last fall was extremely good, and Emilia bottled over seven hundred bottles. It is quite delicious.

I have decided that Lenci needs to see more of the world, so we're planning to visit part of the United States this spring or early summer. Is your offer to see us still valid? Lenci has said many times that she would love to see you again, and so would I. We have missed you a great deal.

Let me know if mid to late May would work for you and what hotel I should book. I so look forward to seeing you again.

The girls send their love.

As always,

Jocelyn

That was it. Short and sweet.

I sat there, staring.

"Well?" Amy walked into the room and handed me a cup of coffee.

"Jocelyn and Lenci are coming here in May," was all I said.

Amy looked skeptical. "Well, at least she wrote to you. Did she say why she was coming?"

I handed her the phone.

"Well, it's to the point," Amy said. "Lenci wants to see you… and, as an afterthought, so does she."

"I thought that, too," I said.

"Would you be happy with Lenci? Maybe she's coming to ask you to come back to her."

I thought for a moment. Lenci? Not Jocelyn? Did I love Lenci? "I like her a lot," I finally said, "and the sex with her was hot. I'm not in love with her. She's sweet, and in the dungeon, she's powerful...not as powerful as Jocelyn. I think it would grow into a good friendship."

"With benefits?"

"With benefits." I smiled.

"Are you excited?" she asked as she sat across from me with her own cup.

"Yes, very, but I'm scared to death, too."

"Why?" she asked.

I shook my head. "I don't know. My stomach just got all fluttery."

Amy stared at me for a minute. "Because you're still in love with Jocelyn, aren't you?"

I sighed and whispered, "Yes."

Amy looked at me seriously. "And it's going to rip your heart out to find that it's Lenci and not Jocelyn, who wants you. Can you live with that?"

"I know, I know. Just get over it," I said.

Amy chewed on her tongue as she studied me. "What are you going to tell her?"

I took a moment. Did I want them to come? Would I be happy with Lenci? Enough to give up what I had here and move there? No, not for Lenci, but if it were Jocelyn? How would I know? "I'll tell her to come. Then I'll know for sure if this is a dead end. At least it will give me time to see how I really feel about her when the threat of prison isn't there."

"And you'll see her in your world as a guest, not a savior."

"I hadn't thought of that."

I'd have to think about that, though. Had I thought of her as a knight in a shining armor, riding in to save me from a fate worse than death?

"I'll suggest a couple hotels or tell her they can stay here." Then the impact of what I'd said hit me. "If they choose to stay here, I'll have to get this place cleaned."

"That won't be hard," Amy said. "We can get Keith's company to come in and do the whole place in less than a day."

Keith's company, which he owned with his husband, was a house-cleaning company, and they did good work. I nodded. "Good idea."

"And if there's anything else that needs to be done, I can tackle it while you're in Brazil. We'll get it done, hon. Don't worry. I'll take care of it."

I had to laugh. "That's what Jocelyn told me when I was obsessing about prison. 'Don't worry, Katherine. Trust me. I'll take care of it.'"

Amy laughed.

Was I expecting that they were coming here just to have sex? *Get your head on straight, Lowe, before they get here.*

"And I'll have to meet them so you'll have an objective, unbiased opinion of the situation."

I grinned. "When have you ever been unbiased?"

"All right. Forget unbiased, but a clear eye would help."

I set my cup down and ran my hands through my hair as I thought about that.

"Don't obsess about it. If they want to stay here, you'll know what's happening from the sleeping arrangements. You'll be certain whether Jocelyn loves you or not. Then you can go on with your life without unanswered questions."

"You're right. I don't think I could live without knowing for certain."

CHAPTER NINETEEN

I couldn't sleep. I had been exhausted when we'd left the restaurant, so Amy had brought me right home, and I was in bed almost before she'd driven away. But the minute my head hit the pillow, I was awake...wide awake.

Why was I trying to sleep? I had work to do. First of all, I had to write back to Jocelyn. And if she was going to visit, I had a lot of things to plan.

In addition, I had to write about Baja, then I was going to Memphis, and then to Rio de Janeiro. All in two months.

Should I tell Jocelyn not to come? My stomach turned sour. Oh God. I wanted to see her again. I wanted to see Lenci. I wanted to see all of them...and I wanted to feel the torture they handed out.

I started hyperventilating.

What was I thinking? What was happening to me? This wasn't the way I was brought up. I was raised to be gentle. But now...was I craving pain? I was hungering for the experiences that Jocelyn had shown me. Did I want the unlimited sexual experiences that I'd known there?

I was taught to be nice to people. Then I ended up in Rebinia.

Come on, fool. I've been told a good sadist will keep pushing almost forever, but when does the attraction to the same masochist fade? Maybe no relationship's sexuality lasts forever. A couple years? Sometimes only a few months? Look what Lenci said about not being touched for a while.

Then I stopped.

Who said Jocelyn and Lenci were coming to have sex? They were coming to see a different part of the world. I'd take them to the Space Needle and maybe whale watching. I'd drive them through the mountains out on the peninsula. We'd ride a ferry. *Get your head on straight. Stop focusing in the sexual part of this. Get real.*

I poured myself a cup of leftover coffee and stuck it in the microwave. I walked into the other bedroom where I had my office and laptop. I took my tablet out of my backpack and opened a file about the Baja resort.

I opened my laptop and set up the beginning of my review.

Then I sat there looking at the screen.

I might have spent as much as an hour thinking.

Finally, I started typing to Jocelyn.

Dearest Jocelyn,

I would be honored to host you and Lenci this May. I'm scheduled to go to Rio the end of April, but I should be back by May tenth at the latest. Then I have about eight weeks free before my next assignment in July. I hope that fits your schedule.

I can recommend several very nice hotels near here. I could also reserve rooms or a suite for you, but I want to offer my apartment to you and Lenci while you are here. I have a very nice two-bedroom place with a full kitchen and laundry facilities. I can sleep on the sofa so neither of you would be discomforted. The arrangements are yours to decide.

Have you decided how long you'll stay? Are there any other places you wish to see while you're here? Do you want to go down the Pacific coast or to California? I think you might like to see the gigantic redwoods. They are the world's tallest trees, and in one place, a tunnel has been carved though the trunk so you can drive through it.

That is the beginning of the California wine country,

too. I know it doesn't compare with European wines, but you might like to try them.

I was disappointed in the Life here. There are many people who regard themselves as "Leather" or "BDSM," but I've found only a few who can afford to live the Life 24 hours a day, 365 days a year. There are some very fine professional dominatrices who find the means. I could be very active in the community here, but I really don't want a string of one-night stands. I fear you've spoiled me.

I can hardly wait to see both of you again.

Love to everyone,

Katherine

I read it through again, then emailed it.

Now I could go to sleep.

❖

Two weeks later, I got an email from Jocelyn.

Dearest Katherine,

Our plans are finally complete. We will arrive at Seattle-Tacoma International Airport on the seventeenth of May. We will depart on June eighteenth. I hope that gives us enough time. I'll leave it to you to decide what we will explore, although Lenci was quite enthused about the redwood trees. I hope we'll get to see where you grew up, too.

Lenci says she would like us to stay at your apartment, but we do not want to cause you any hardship. We can always move to a hotel if we wear out our welcome, or your neighbors complain about our noise.

Travel safely to Rio. We will see you on the seventeenth.

Love, Jocelyn

Arriving on May seventeenth and staying until June eighteenth? That was four and a half weeks. I guessed that would give me more than enough time to see if this was real or simply a fantasy. Had I read more into everyone's reactions and emotions than was really there? Had I wanted her to love me? Of course I did. But was it real? Logical? She had girls who lived there, so maybe they were boring compared to the new girl who no one knew about. It was the novelty factor. Nothing more. And now she could travel halfway around the world and not have to pay for hotel and transportation. They'd also get a free tour guide. And it was going to be the best one ever.

I'd also have plenty of time to get the apartment cleaned after I got back from Rio. I'd make arrangements for Keith and his company to come in on the fifteenth or sixteenth, so it would still be clean when they arrived, and I'd get my car detailed and buy good food and new sheets for both beds and good soaps for the bathrooms. Great. Now I was going to go crazy obsessing about having enough new towels.

I packed my suitcase to go to a new bed-and-breakfast in Memphis. I was glad I only had to stay there three days. Then I'd be home for a week before I left for Rio.

CHAPTER TWENTY

I paced in front of the elevators coming down from the gates. Their plane had landed twenty minutes ago, but by the time everyone got off, went through customs, and could get a shuttle, it would probably be a few more minutes.

I'd bought two sets of new sheets for each bed and washed them so they wouldn't feel new, replaced all the towels, put new lotions and expensive soap in the bathrooms, and organized my closets and dressers so they'd have room to store their stuff. I hoped I hadn't forgotten anything. Keith and his guys had gotten the apartment sparkly clean. I was afraid to use anything for fear of messing it up. In fact, I'd slept on the sofa last night so the bed would be fresh.

Then they stepped off the elevator. God, she was stunning. There was no one in the terminal that could compete with her beauty. Her long blond hair was piled on top of her head. Although she'd been on an airplane for hours, she still looked fresh and nicely coiffed. Her makeup looked freshly done.

"Jocelyn! Lenci!" I called as I ran up to them.

Jocelyn drew me into a tight embrace. She placed a gentle kiss on my lips. "It's good to see you again." Her face and eyes lit up.

I turned to Lenci and gave her a tight hug and a kiss. She, too, looked freshly coiffed and wide awake, despite the long flight. She was pushing the luggage cart that held their suitcases.

"How was your flight?" I asked.

"Long," was all Jocelyn said.

"Amazing," Lenci added.

"This was your first long flight, wasn't it?" I grinned at her as she bobbed her head.

"Just the first." Jocelyn smiled. "I don't know why I let her wait this long."

"How many bags do you have?" I asked, eyeing the suitcases on the luggage cart.

"Just three," Lenci said. "I figured if we needed something warmer or cooler, we could simply buy it here. You said you have laundry facilities, didn't you?"

"Right in my apartment, and there's a dry cleaner on the next corner. I have everything you'll need."

Jocelyn and Lenci looked at each other and smiled. "Have you planned our itinerary?" Jocelyn asked as we started down the corridor toward the exit.

"Some of it," I answered. "I was thinking we should take a few days and drive down the coast. It's absolutely beautiful. We can drive through the redwoods, and that's also wine country, so you can get a taste of California."

"I'd love to taste some. I've heard good things about it, but we've never bought any."

"Of course not. You have your own vineyard. And the German and Austrian wine regions aren't that far away."

Jocelyn grinned. "Yes. I think we're spoiled."

"As you should be." I smiled.

"Are you trying to get on my good side already?"

"I've seen your good side, and I wouldn't mind at all being there again." I smiled to myself, not looking into her eyes. Oh, jeez, I wanted to sweep her into my arms and take her to the floor to ravish her. No, all the denial I'd done in the past was completely erased just by her first short kiss.

"Is your mouth starting already?" Jocelyn asked.

"I guess we'll find out."

She burst out laughing. We continued through the terminal to the exit.

"Do you have a good kitchen?" Lenci asked.

"Not like yours, but it works for me. Of course, I eat out a lot."

"That's too bad." Jocelyn frowned. "Don't you cook for yourself?"

"When I have time, but that's not a lot," I said, embarrassed. "I buy food, and it sits in the refrigerator until I throw it out. I'm not home that often." I turned to Lenci. "If you want to cook, you have free rein in the kitchen. We'll need to go shopping to get what you need. I have the basics. I mainly broil, boil, or fry. I never bake or roast, but I have the pans. I bought them when I moved in there, but I've never used some of them."

Lenci shook her head. "I will see what's there, and then we can get what we need."

"But not tonight," I said. "Unless you're really tired, I'm taking you out. We'll go up to the top of the Space Needle so you can get a panoramic view of the city. It's quite beautiful, and I think everyone should start their visit to Seattle with that view. Then I've made reservations at Candler's. It's one of the best seafood restaurants in the city." Yes, I'd show them the best of my world. This was my turf, not theirs.

Lenci's smile widened. I could tell she wanted to get started right away.

"I made the reservations for seven, so we'll have time to do whatever you need, or if the time change is catching up with you, we can be home early."

"You sound like a wonderful tour guide," Jocelyn said, "but you don't need to spend all your money on us."

"I put away the money I got for a story about Nové Ville, so tonight, we splurge. I've missed you so much." I looked from one to the other. "I want to show you the best of my home country." The language would be foreign to them, and I wouldn't let them get overwhelmed, not like I was those first few days in their country.

They treated me to two of the best smiles I've seen in ages.

"I'll get the car," I said. "I'll meet you right outside that door." I pointed to the exit. "I have a red SUV, a Chevrolet. I'll be right back."

I jogged outside and through the taxi line, onto the walkway, dodging cars that had picked up their passengers. I raced through the parking garage. I'd taken my car to be detailed yesterday so it would shine, inside and out.

As I pulled up to a stop where they were waiting, Jocelyn scanned my car and smiled. I got out and opened the back hatch. "All right," I said to Jocelyn, who got into the passenger seat, "do you want to go to the apartment first to freshen up, or are you hungry? It's almost one o'clock." I jogged around to get into the driver's seat.

"Yes and yes. Let's drop our bags off. We can discuss our hunger after that." I guess Jocelyn took charge no matter where they were, but if she was comfortable, she could be the boss until she was out of her element.

I pulled into the exit lane, drove out of the airport, and finally merged into the traffic going north on I-5.

"Is it always this rushed?" Lenci asked, looking at the traffic ahead.

"This is just the lunch hour. It'll clear up after people go back to work, but morning and evening rush hours can get quite congested." I continued north, pointing out places of interest. "This is where they make Boeing aircraft," I said as we passed the Boeing plant. There was the body of a 747 sitting on the tarmac. I pointed to the Space Needle. "That's where we're going later this afternoon. You can see for miles and miles from up there." I looked into the mirror to see Lenci's wide eyes. "Do you want me to speak German so you won't have to try to translate everything?"

"That would help," she said, "but I do want to speak English while we're here. You may have to help me."

"That's not a problem," I said as I switched to German. "I'll have you sounding like a native in less than a week."

We finally pulled into my parking garage. I jumped out and ran to open Jocelyn's door, then opened the back. Lenci took two suitcases, and I rolled the other toward the elevator.

"This will take us up to the lobby, then we have to change. That's for security reasons. No one can walk into the garage and go right up to the apartments."

I could see Jocelyn assessing everything. I watched her eyes to make sure she was content. This was America, not Rebinia. Things here were different, scarier, but I didn't want her to fear anything. I felt much safer knowing I had this much security around me. My apartment was high enough that it couldn't be reached from the street, and the lower floor was guarded with cameras, special lighting, and locks. It had felt comforting to return here after my Rebinian adventure.

The elevator stopped at the lobby, and we rolled everything off. I walked to the glass doors leading into the main part of the building and slipped my key into the lock. I waved to the camera. I pulled the door open and held it for Jocelyn and Lenci. Then I pressed the call button for the inside elevators. When one dinged its arrival, I stepped up to hold the doors open until Jocelyn and Lenci got on. Then I pressed the button for the fifth floor.

"This is quite an arrangement. Do all apartment buildings have this much security?" Jocelyn asked.

"Not all. Only the newer, more expensive ones," I answered. "We pay enough for it."

When the elevator opened on my floor, I held the doors open until they got out, then I rolled the suitcases to my door and slipped the key into the lock. "My house is your house."

Jocelyn walked in and looked at the light auburn couch and chair, the glass-topped coffee table, the small glass lunch table with four chairs under the front window. There was a small media station with my TV, DVD, and CD player and a few books against the side wall. "This is a sweet little place."

"Thanks." I closed and locked the door. "Let me show you around. You can leave your carry-ons on the couch until later. The kitchen is that way with laundry and storage, and the bedrooms are down this hallway." *Oh yes, definitely the bedrooms.*

Lenci looked around the kitchen with surprised eyes. "This looks nice. The appliances are so new."

"This whole building was built five years ago, so they were only two years old when I moved in."

"You've taken very good care of them."

I smiled at her praise. Little did she know how seldom I used everything.

I brought the suitcases as I led them to the main bedroom with its queen-sized bed and private bath and then showed them the second bedroom, which had a double bed. I pointed out the bathroom in the hall. They admired the artwork on the walls. Jocelyn walked back into the main bedroom and looked out the window.

"What do you want to do first?" I asked as I stood just inside the door. My heart skipped a beat at the sight of her standing in my bedroom. I had pictured her there so many times. She turned and thought for a moment, then beckoned to me. I walked to her, and she wrapped her arms around me and planted her lips on mine. After a very long, hard kiss, she stepped back and looked into my eyes.

"I missed you," she whispered.

"We all did," I heard Lenci say behind me.

"I missed you, too," I said, looking into Jocelyn's eyes. "All of you."

"How far away is the Space Needle?" Jocelyn asked.

"Only about twenty minutes. You'll probably want to look around from up there for at least an hour."

"And how far to the restaurant?"

"Depending on traffic, a half hour, forty-five minutes." I smiled.

She looked at the clock on the table beside the bed. "So we need to leave here by four thirty to get to the restaurant in time."

"About that," I agreed. "Are you hungry now?"

"Very."

The look in Jocelyn's eyes almost frightened me. It was sharp and determined. She was scanning my body. My insides started to clench, and my panties grew wet.

She shot a look at Lenci, who said, "I'll go look at your kitchen."

Jocelyn started unbuttoning my shirt. "I'm assuming you want this as much as I."

I didn't make a move to stop her. Was I falling back into the Mistress-submissive role already? Had I ever gotten out of it? Was this the way I wanted our relationship to be? Did I have a choice?

She got three buttons undone, then said, "You finish that." She reached to unbutton and unzip my jeans. She pushed them and my panties to the floor. It felt different being naked in my own room in front of her, but I didn't want to stop her. I wanted her so badly, and I wanted her to want me.

"I don't remember you being this slow." She chuckled. She reached to undo the last button that I was fumbling with, and she pushed my shirt over my shoulders so it dropped behind me.

"You never saw me take my clothes off. I was always naked."

She smiled and pushed me onto the bed. "I like you that way." She kicked off her heels and lowered herself on top of me. As she kissed me, her hands roved my body.

I kissed her back. Yes, this was what I remembered. This was the Jocelyn I'd dreamed about.

She sat back and took off her blouse. I reached around her to unhook her skirt. "No, baby," she said as she took my wrists and placed my hands above my head. "I'll do you first."

She put her hand around my throat, not that tightly, but I could feel it. Then she leaned in and kissed me again. Did I want this? Should I call my safe word?

Then I didn't know what my reaction was, but it felt wonderful. I melted into her kiss. It was so forceful and rough. I could feel her heat throughout my entire body. Oh God. Her hand around my throat made me feel vulnerable but safe, as though she owned me. I wanted to turn myself inside out. I was ready to give her anything she wanted…everything I had. *Yes, Jocelyn, despite everything, I am still yours.*

Then she pulled back and stood. She shed her skirt, hose, and garter belt. She was more beautiful than I remembered.

"You are so exquisite," I whispered.

She got onto the bed and took my breasts and squeezed. She took one into her mouth and sucked hard. I started to squirm until she clenched my other nipple between her fingers. I wanted to hold her, to hug her tighter, and I started to reach for her.

"Don't touch," she said. "Reach up and grasp the headboard."

I stretched up, but when I did, she increased the pressure on my nipples. I moaned loudly.

"Shh, baby. It's been months, hasn't it?"

"Too long," was all I could say.

"Yes," she agreed as her hand roamed my body.

I wanted her to touch me. I wanted to touch her. I didn't want to hold the headboard. I wanted to hold her. I must have reached toward her because she whispered, "I thought I told you not to move."

I closed my eyes as I gripped the headboard.

"Do you have any toys?" she asked.

"Just one dildo."

She chuckled. "We'll have to get you more. But we can do without today." She took one of my nipples between her teeth as her hand dived into me. Every muscle in my body went into spasm. It took every bit of what little control I had to keep from screaming.

"I need to hold you," I whispered through my teeth.

"Not yet, baby."

One hand tightened around my throat, then let go as she moved farther down my body. Each of her touches made me quiver. "She is touching me" went through my head. Then her hand delved into my center again.

I was lost. I didn't know where I was, and if someone had asked me my name, I couldn't have told them. It was continuing on and on and on, I didn't know what planet I was on.

Then the most beautiful voice I'd ever heard said, "Come for me now."

I could feel the explosion start right below my belly, and then it spread like an atom bomb. I curled into a small ball, covered with sparkling light. Then there was another explosion. As it started to ebb, I rocked back and forth.

I finally felt myself breathing and opened my eyes. I was wrapped in Jocelyn's arms. I smiled up at her. "Wow," was all I could say.

She stroked my cheek as she held me close. Then she called, "Lenci?"

"Coming," we heard from the living room. A moment later, Lenci leaned into the room.

"Do I smell coffee?" Jocelyn asked.

"Yes, ma'am. For both of you?"

"And bring one for yourself, too. And is there anything for a snack?"

Lenci nodded.

"Come on in and sit with us."

Lenci grinned and left for the kitchen.

"How do you feel?" Jocelyn asked.

"Blown away," I said as I rubbed my eyes with the heels of my hands. "I thought that last time was good, but this was even better." Yes, after all these months, my feelings hadn't faded, not one bit. *Admit it, Kath, you're seriously hooked.*

Jocelyn squeezed my shoulders. "I found your spot to really turn you on." She smiled.

"Every place you touch me turns me on."

"But this is the best, I think." She wrapped her hand around my throat.

"Oh God." I sighed. My head zoned into another dimension as soon as her hand touched my neck.

Jocelyn leaned forward to look into my eyes. "Was it good for you?"

We both broke out into laughter.

Lenci walked into the room with a tray of coffee and a plate with cheese, crackers, and apple slices. I sat up as she handed me one cup and another to Jocelyn. Lenci crawled onto the foot of the bed as we each took a sip. I reached for a piece of cheese and a slice of apple.

"Oh. This is very good coffee," Jocelyn said.

"Seattle is the coffee capital of the US," I said proudly. "One day we'll go to one of the coffee houses downtown where they have baristas."

"What are baristas?" Lenci asked.

"People who know how to make special coffees like cappuccinos, lattes, espressos, macchiatos and and are experts at serving them. You'll see. You'll love it. They can flavor the coffee any way you want, and then they use the cream to make designs and pictures on the top. Sometimes, I hate to drink it and destroy the piece of art."

Jocelyn smiled. "I'd like to see that."

"Me either." Lenci smiled, trying her English.

"Me, too," I corrected. "I'm sorry we ignored you on your first day here."

Lenci smiled widely. "I was prepared for it. I even brought a book to read."

I looked up at Jocelyn. "That was planned?"

She smiled into her coffee, then turned her head to look at me. "Yes, it was."

"Did you plan time for me to make love to you?" I asked. *You had better, or you might see a dominant part of me that may shock you.*

She looked over at the clock. "Not until later."

I grinned as Lenci chuckled. The warmth between us felt just like it had in Europe.

"Oh, I'm sorry," Lenci said, "but I was hungry. I ate some cheese and a slice of your bread. It was very good."

I looked over at the clock. "It's almost too late to go to the Space Needle. By the time we got showered and dressed, we'd have to rush, and I don't want to rush you on your vacation. We have almost five weeks to do everything. We can go tomorrow."

"That's fine with me," Jocelyn said.

Lenci nodded. "Did you make plans for tomorrow?"

"Only one if we can get up early."

"How early?" Lenci asked.

"Well, I'd like to get some fish and seafood for the next few days. There's a wonderful place that gets it in fresh every morning, but you have to get there by seven a.m. to get the choice pieces. I think you'll like it there. They make a big show of it. It's fun to watch."

"Then we'll be ready to go."

"We can go to the Space Needle tomorrow afternoon, then," I said. "I think you'll need to relax for a day or two." And a little time for me to process all the feelings this had raised. I definitely was not over Jocelyn Buza, but how much of her sadism could I accept?

CHAPTER TWENTY-ONE

We got to the restaurant before seven. We'd taken our time showering, dressing, and getting ready. I sure hoped they liked this place. In my opinion, it served the freshest seafood in the Northwest, and I wanted them to start their visit tasting true Washington food.

"Party of three for Lowe," I announced to the host when we walked in.

"Right this way, Ms Lowe." He picked up three menus and led us to a table on the outer patio. "Might we get you something to start?" he asked.

I looked at Jocelyn. "Do you want a drink or just wine?" I asked.

"I'd like the wine."

"A bottle of Riesling, Washington State? And six Treasure Cove oysters." I hope at least one of them was adventurous enough to try the dish.

He bowed his head and walked away.

"You'll have to explain what each of these dishes are. I have no idea what to order," Jocelyn said as she scanned the menu.

"Are you very hungry?" I asked.

"This is our first night here, so I guess we could eat quite a bit. We missed lunch. Dinner and breakfast on an airplane are never really filling."

Lenci nodded.

"Then I would suggest Caesar salad to begin, and then the Chandler's crab platter for the two of you, and I'll get the scallops so you can taste them."

Jocelyn nodded. "That sounds good."

"I've only had the crabmeat in the can. This must be very different," Lenci said.

"Very. Fresh crab right out of the water is always much tastier."

"Tastier?" Lenci asked.

Jocelyn translated, and Lenci nodded. Then Lenci continued to read the menu. "Crab ice cream?" she asked. "Am I translating that right?"

I nodded. "Gelato made with clam stock, whiskey, and honey. We can try one later."

Lenci's eyes were like a kid's on Christmas morning.

"You amaze me." Jocelyn grinned after we ordered. "I never realized you were so worldly, but I shouldn't be surprised. You *have* traveled quite a bit." I loved the look in her eyes.

Lenci peered into the plate of oysters. "Are those alive?" she asked.

I smiled. "Yes. That's a delicacy." I reached for one and squeezed some lemon onto it. "The secret is to swallow it. Let it sit in your mouth a moment so you can taste it. Then let it slide down. You shouldn't chew."

I slid the oyster into my mouth and swallowed.

"I'll try one," Jocelyn said as she squeezed the lemon and poured it into her mouth. I saw her taste it for a moment, then she swallowed it right down. "Interesting taste," she said.

Lenci looked skeptical but tried one, too. "Different," was her comment.

"They're supposed to be an aphrodisiac." I grinned.

Jocelyn laughed loudly. "That's something none of us need."

"A what?" Lenci asked.

"They are supposed to increase your sexual desire," Jocelyn explained.

Lenci inhaled quickly. "No, we don't need them. We'd all go crazy."

"But it never hurts," I said as I swallowed another.

"No, it doesn't." She swallowed her second.

"Then I guess I need to keep up with you two." Lenci smiled as she reached for the last.

The waiter brought the bottle of wine and showed me the label. It was from a Columbia Valley winery. When I nodded, he uncorked it.

I remembered the time Jocelyn had refused to test the wine in favor of Regina. I held my hand over my glass with my index finger extended to signal him to wait. "Do you want the honor?" I asked Jocelyn.

"No. I enjoy watching you."

I took my hand away and allowed him to pour a little. I picked up the glass by the stem and swirled the wine around to see how it clung to the glass. I smelled it. Then I took a sip and swirled it around in my mouth.

"Nice herbal…sweet." I nodded, and he poured some into each of our glasses, then nestled the bottle in a bucket of ice. "To a wonderful holiday," I toasted.

"And new adventures," Jocelyn added.

We clinked glasses and took a sip. I watched their expressions, hoping they enjoyed this.

"That is nice," Jocelyn said. "Very interesting."

I smiled. "I'm glad you like it."

"Yes. It's a little fruitier than ours, but it has a rather woody aftertaste."

"We don't have the history that Europe does, but we're trying."

"The scenery is beautiful," Jocelyn said after we'd started on the salads. "Is this Puget Sound?"

I was pleased she liked it. "No, this is Lake Union. You saw part of Puget Sound from the highway. I'll show you more tomorrow. I have a map if you want to see where everything is." I should have brought it with us. This would have been the perfect time to do my tour-guide thing.

They continued on their salads, each asking questions about the city and admiring the view. I was happy that they thought Seattle was beautiful. It *was* my hometown.

A waiter placed a large platter of crab between Jocelyn and Lenci with a plate of grilled vegetables in an orzo salad for each of them. In front of me he placed a plate of scallops with a mushroom puree. Jocelyn and Lenci watched, their eyes wide at the food. They seemed overwhelmed.

The waiter set small ramekins beside the crab platter. "If you wish any more of them, please let me know."

I shook my head, thanked him, and he walked away.

"I'm not sure what to do with all this," Jocelyn admitted. Her eyes went from one dish to the next in wonder.

I took the shell cracker and showed them how to open the crab. "You can eat the meat the way it is or dip it in the sauces. This is one of those entrees you can eat with your fingers." We settled in. I shared my scallops with them and showed them how to eat each piece of crab. They had a lot of fun and laughed as much as they ate. I breathed a sigh of relief that they enjoyed it.

When it was finished, we were all stuffed, but the thought of crab ice cream intrigued Lenci so much, we had to order dessert, too. I ordered the key lime pie and Jocelyn ordered crème brûlée. We each tasted everyone else's, and we decided the crab ice cream was "interesting." We ended with espresso. It was a successful first meal.

❖

I looked across the bed at the brilliant blond hair draped over the next pillow. She had allowed me to make love to her and then the time-change and excitement of the day had taken its toll. I was definitely head over heels about her. What was I going to do about it? Probably nothing. I didn't want to go back to the same circumstances as last year. I'd been burned, and it had taken me months to even *start* to get over it.

Regina's little scam had left me feeling used and abused. I'd been tricked. I'd been scared for my life. Even when I got back home, I was shell-shocked, and I hadn't trusted anyone. It had taken me months to get back into the groove of doing my job correctly. I questioned my own sanity, my own abilities.

In my heart, I wanted to be with Jocelyn, but I didn't want to stand in line. I wanted a relationship like everyone else seemed to have: one-on-one, with no waiting in line or hoping it was my turn. It didn't matter if she had others as long as I knew I was her priority. I doubted Jocelyn would go for that, though. Lenci had said she thrived on the assortment.

Maybe that was what I should do. If I went to more leather meetings, maybe I'd meet someone comparable. *No, there is no one comparable to her.* When I was in her castle, she'd told me that I had switched with Anna. Maybe that was what my problem was at those leather parties, I'd only been looking for a new Mistress. No one could replace Jocelyn. Why had I even tried? What I needed was my own girl. Maybe that was where I should be. But could I do that? Could I always be in control the way *she* was? Did I even want that? I guessed time would tell. For the next four weeks, I'd just have to take advantage of what I could to get the most from her and Lenci. I could make up my mind and restart my real life once they went back home.

I woke them the next morning at six a.m. I had made love to Jocelyn when we got home, but when she fell asleep, I crawled into bed with Lenci. Of course, I had gotten Jocelyn's permission first. I should have been exhausted, but I was so excited they were here that I could barely sleep. I was ready to go.

"I suggest you wear flats today," I said.

"I hate wearing flats," Jocelyn said.

I had to smile at that. Jocelyn was dressed in tight, camel-colored slacks and a beautiful peach blouse. Her canvas wedges looked great with it. There was no way she could hide her royalty.

"Don't worry. You'll always be larger than life," I told her.

She shook her head. "All right. Tell us about this place," she said as we got into my car.

I laughed. "You'll have to see it to believe it. Don't be surprised by anything you see. Basically, it's a fish market."

"Do they sell scallops?" Lenci asked.

"It depends on what's caught today. They have almost everything."

"This is a lot more exciting than even Pergue," Lenci said.

"You've got to get out more." I laughed, thinking of all the places in the world I'd been. It was sad that she hadn't seen much of what I had.

"She will," Jocelyn declared.

As luck would have it, I found a parking space right on Pike Place. We only had to walk downhill one block. I could smell the fish before we ever walked inside. The inside was just as noisy and crazy as it always was.

"Watch that fishmonger," I said, pointing to one of the men behind the hardwood chopping tables.

"Monger?" Lenci asked me.

"A fish butcher. He skins, cleans, bones, and filets anything you want."

"One king salmon," he yelled. And a twenty-five-pound fish sailed across the room, right into his arms. He slammed it onto a table and chopped its head off.

Another one yelled "Copper River," and a twenty-pound fish flew across the room.

"How do they do that?" Lenci asked, her eyes wide as she watched the salmon being tossed around the room.

"Practice." I laughed.

We took one step closer to the table. "What do you want, young lady?" the man asked Lenci.

"Three pounds of scallops and a whole Copper River salmon," she said as I'd taught her.

"What? I can't hear you," he yelled. "There's too much noise back here."

I pushed her. "Say it louder."

She repeated it.

"Louder," he yelled again.

She laughed and yelled it again.

"Is that a Russian accent?" he asked.

"We're Rebinian," she told him. "The language is like Czech."

"We don't take checks. Cash or credit cards only."

It took Lenci a moment to realize why I was laughing. When she realized, she laughed too.

"We're from Rebinia," Lenci explained.

"And that's like Czechoslovakia?" he asked.

"No, those are all different counties now: the Slovak and the Czech Republics. Rebinia is a different country."

"When did that happen?" he asked.

"In 1993, I believe."

"Probably just a way to earn map makers more money. Now, what kind of fish did you want?"

"Tell him again." I whispered.

"Three pounds of scallops, and a whole Copper River salmon," she said loudly.

"You don't have to yell at me," he said, and then he turned and yelled to one of the guys at the back, and a large salmon flew across the room. He slammed it onto the counter and turned to one of the assistants, who ran off. "I bet you want it filleted," he stated, smiling at the look on her face as she stared at the twenty-pound fish.

I nodded to her. "Yes, please," she said.

"Well, you should have said that first. Now I've got to pick that sucker up again. Give me a hand." He winked at me.

I saw the look on her face, so I helped her pass the fish back. He handed us a few paper towels to wipe our hands.

He laughed as he slit the fish up the dorsal and removed all the organs. In less than five minutes, he had it scaled, filleted, and wrapped. He printed *CRS* on the front with a giant heart. Then he wrapped up the scallops the young assistant had brought him. "Do you want anything else?"

"Not today," I said.

"Then get out of here. You can pay over there." He pointed to the front. "Next."

Jocelyn had stepped back and was laughing at us. "He'd make a good Master, wouldn't he?"

Lenci and I laughed as we took the packages to the front of the market.

A young woman stood behind the cash register. I placed the two packages up on the counter. "You're the one Sam gave a hard time to?" she asked.

I pointed to Lenci.

"Thanks for being a good sport." She smiled. "You get a ten percent discount. Do you want anything else?"

"One of the chef's aprons," I said. She took a package from the shelf behind her and placed it on the counter. She rang up the sale and accepted my credit card, then placed everything into a shopping bag. "The apron is for you," I told Lenci. "So you'll remember this place."

She gave me a hug. "I don't think I'll ever forget it." I was glad to provide her with something to bring back a memory of her trip. I felt she'd been forgotten, that Jocelyn had traveled, but Lenci hadn't.

"Was that a good price for salmon?" Jocelyn asked as she looked at the sales slip.

"It sure was." I smiled. "This puppy was swimming in the river less than twenty-four hours ago."

"Do you know how to cook it?" she asked.

"Yes. There are lots of different ways."

"Do we have all the groceries we need?" Lenci asked.

"Why don't we check the rest of the market, and you can see if there's anything else you want."

Lenci's eyes lit up as we walked around the kiosks. I smiled as I walked beside Jocelyn, following. She ended up buying some herbs, a pound of sweet peas, three sweet potatoes, tomatoes, and a head of romaine lettuce.

"Is that all you need?" I asked.

"We may need flour and baking powder," she said.

"That's up to you," I said. "We can go shopping this afternoon. Let's get these puppies into the refrigerator first."

"Puppies? Why do you call them puppies?" Lenci asked. "These are fish."

"In America, almost anything can be a puppy."

Lenci giggled. "Puppies! I like that."

❖

After sorting, cutting, and rewrapping the salmon into meal-sized packages and putting all but one in the freezer, we got to the Space Needle just after noon. Both Jocelyn's and Lenci's eyes were wide as they looked out over Seattle.

"In which direction did you used to live?" Jocelyn asked. I walked around the disc and pointed down the Strait of Juan de Fuqua.

"West from here," I told her.

"And that's Canada?" she asked, pointing north.

"No, those are US islands. Canada is farther north and west." I motioned to a map on the wall and pointed out some places.

"Are those the ferries you were telling us about?" Lenci asked, peering at the ships crossing Puget Sound.

"Yes. They each hold about two hundred cars and maybe two thousand passengers. Big trucks use the ferries, too, because it's cheaper than driving all the way to Tacoma to get to a bridge and then driving back."

Jocelyn smiled. "I'd love to ride the ferries."

"We'll take one when we go out to where my parents live and probably when we go to California," I said.

We walked halfway around the disk. "Those look like massive houses," Lenci said, pointing to Queen Anne Hill.

"Yes. That's where the rich folks live." I turned to Jocelyn. "That's where you'd live if you lived here."

She nodded thoughtfully. We walked around and around the disk, me answering all their questions.

It was almost three before we got back on the elevator to go back down to my car. I was tired, but seeing the smiles on their faces made everything worthwhile.

CHAPTER TWENTY-TWO

A nything else you want to see today?" I asked.

"Yes. Where is that store that sells the whips and floggers?"

"Not far away," I said. "Is that where you want to go?"

"Yes, it is. We've got to get you more toys."

I frowned. "Maybe I shouldn't have told you about it," I said softly. But I had bragged about the store, so of course she'd want to go there.

"But you did, baby." She grinned as she kissed my lips.

Me and my big mouth. Maybe she wouldn't want anything... who was I kidding? I did want to show her the store, but I was afraid of what she'd find there. We drove down Eleventh, and I found a parking space in the same block as the store. Inside, her eyes lit up like a kid in a candy store.

"Oh yes." She sighed. "I'm going to look around." She walked away.

"I don't like the look on her face," Lenci whispered.

"I'm sorry I told her."

"She probably would have found it anyway. She has a nose for these types of places."

She patted me sympathetically on the shoulder and walked away to look around. I shook my head. When would I learn to stop talking? I didn't have to tell her about this store. But I never could keep my mouth shut. Maybe it was because I was so quiet as a child—now all those words I never used were spewing out of me. Well, Jocelyn was happy. I guess that was what really mattered. *Remember: Be the perfect host. They'll be gone next month.*

I looked around the store. Jocelyn was talking to one of the salesmen. I had to take a deep breath. She was so gorgeous…and I had made love to her last night. How had I gotten this blessed? *Yes, make the most of this month.*

I wandered around. I was looking through a table of sale items when I felt a hand on my shoulder. "Hey, Katherine. I haven't seen you around lately."

"Hi, Vi. I've been traveling a lot." Violet was one of the first to befriend me when I started attending the meetings and play parties. We had negotiated a couple flogging scenes, but her flogging didn't feel right. Something was missing. I couldn't get my endorphins going.

"Lucky. You didn't miss much. It's been quiet since the beginning of April." We shared some gossip and talked about almost nothing for a few minutes. "Oh!" she finally said. "Did you see that beautiful blond trying all those floggers? I was listening when she asked Rob a couple questions. She has a wonderful Russian accent. With all she's buying, she must be very rich."

I smiled. "Her accent's not Russian. She's from Rebinia. She's a duchess and very sadistic," I bragged.

"You know her?"

I nodded with a big smile. "She's the Duchess Jocelyn Buza. I was initially trained in her house."

"Her house? Were there others there, too?" Vi's eyebrows rose in amazement.

"There were five of us." I motioned over to Lenci. "That's her First girl. They're visiting for a month."

Vi looked from Lenci to Jocelyn in wonder. "I've heard about those Eastern European houses," she said, "but I always thought they were someone's wishful thinking."

"No, hon, they're real. In many ways, I still consider her my Mistress."

Vi seemed quite disturbed by that news. "You should have told me about her before we negotiated."

"It was okay," I assured her. "There's no contract between us, and she was halfway around the world."

"Holy cow." She looked back at Jocelyn for a minute. "There's a play party at the Station next weekend. Do you think she'd want to come?"

"I'll ask, but we may be in California next week. She wants to see the coast. And she wants to try the wines to see how they compare to her vineyard."

Vi looked amazed.

"Would you like to be introduced to her?"

"God, no." Vi sighed. "I'm intimidated by her all the way across the store. I'd probably trip over my own tongue."

Lenci walked over. "Did you find anything? I know she found a lot."

I sighed. "Let's hope she bought them to use on the others."

Lenci grimaced. "I heard your name mentioned a few times. I think she found you some restraints. She was rather upset that you had none in your apartment."

"Well, whatever she wants," I had to say. I looked at Vi and shook my head. Then I introduced them. "Violet, this is Lenci," I said, then to Lenci, I explained, "Mistress Violet was at those meetings I went to."

Violet held her hand out, and they shook.

"Very pleased to meet you, Mistress Violet," Lenci said, looking at the floor. Then she turned to me. "Did I say that right?"

"Perfect."

"Yes, you speak very well, Lenci," Violet said as she smiled. "But we don't have to be so formal in public. You can call me Vi."

"Thank you. Katherine is teaching me English," she explained.

"You do well. I love your accent."

"Thank you."

"Have you been with your Mistress long?" Violet asked.

"I've been with Jocelyn thirteen years next month," Lenci said. "Katherine is the newest member of the house. I wish she didn't have to come back here, though. Everyone misses her. We had such a good time together."

"And you came back here?" Vi asked in awe.

I shrugged. "I have a job and an apartment. I couldn't just leave them."

"Katherine!" The sound interrupted our conversation.

I looked up to see Jocelyn waving me over.

"Gotta go. See you later, Vi." I patted her arm, then went over.

"Have you ever used one of these?" She was holding up a large dildo attached to a harness.

"No, I haven't." I couldn't imagine what my face was like. I'd never imagined myself on the giving side of one of those.

"Then you will learn."

"I don't think I'd ever be as good as Gabby."

"No, very few are. But you will practice."

I looked at my crotch. I couldn't imagine a dick sticking out of there. I almost laughed but held it in. "If that's what you want," I said softly. Jocelyn patted my cheek and went on to look at something else. Well, this would be different. I'd never thought of myself as butch, but it seemed that was what Jocelyn wanted, so... I looked over to Lenci and Vi, who were watching me and laughing. Yes, I guessed it was funny.

"Oh my God," I thought as I looked at the tall stack of things on the counter that Jocelyn was buying. She might have been spending a mint. She'd need another suitcase to get all that back home.

❖

I looked at the sales slip sticking out of the bags. Jocelyn had spent almost four thousand dollars. She had all her treasures laid out on the bed. There were two matched sets of floggers. They looked top-of-the-line. Much better made and with better materials than the ones that cost one hundred and fifty dollars. There was a new harness and dildo for Gabby. I gasped. It looked a whole lot bigger than the one Gabby had used with me. There were also bondage straps, a hooded mask, and several wooden paddles. One had holes all along one edge of it.

"That one will hurt," Lenci whispered. "With all those holes, there's no way that the air will slow it down."

There was also a large pump-bottle of lube. Like that was going to help. Oh, why did I tell her about that store? There was a large package of quilted beige denim. "What's that?" I asked.

Lenci picked it up and turned it over to read the writing on the bottom. She looked at me, her eyes wide. "It says 'suspension straitjacket,'" she whispered.

"Good God. Who's that for?"

"Whoever deserves it," Jocelyn said as she walked into the bedroom. "I really like that one. There are rings attached so you can hang someone right side up or upside down. I think it's one of the best bondage devices I've seen." She smirked. "Do we have plans for tomorrow?"

"I hadn't made any," I said. "Whatever you and Lenci want to do." Then it hit me. I'd just given Jocelyn permission to use her new toys. Hopefully she wouldn't want to use all of them on me. "Why did I say that?"

"Because you haven't learned to control your mouth." Jocelyn assessed the situation. "That's all right. I think we'll find something to do."

I flashed back to some of the pain I'd felt at her place. Yes, I could do that again if that was what she wanted. I could do *anything*, if Jocelyn wanted. I looked to Lenci. "I think we need to go shopping for whatever you need in the kitchen." I looked at Jocelyn. "Do you want to come, too?"

"Is there anything special about your market?"

I shook my head.

"Then I'll stay here and look at my new toys."

Yes. If that makes you happy, enjoy all of them.

The look in her eyes as she surveyed her purchases was what I enjoyed seeing. She was happy, and that was what I wanted. If I could keep her happy for the next four weeks, I could look back on this as a triumph in my life.

CHAPTER TWENTY-THREE

Dinner was completed, the dishes were in the dishwasher, and the stove and counters were clean.

"That was wonderful, Lenci," I told her. "I'll have you cooking like a real northwesterner before you go back." She'd broiled scallops with mushrooms and onions as an appetizer, then baked salmon with bread crumbs, spices, and a mustard glaze with rice and sweet peas.

"I was amazed what the mustard did for the fish. I'd never thought of that," she told me.

"Yes, I love it. I use mustard a lot, strong mustard, a dark brown or Dijon." I hung the dish towel on the oven rail and started back into the living room. Now what would happen? I hadn't planned anything.

Jocelyn was sitting on the couch, a strange smile on her face. It was ten o'clock already. "This has been a fantastic day. Thank you, Katherine."

I smiled back at her.

"Excellent meal, Lenci," she continued.

"Thank you. Is there anything else I can get you? Would you like some port or more coffee?"

Something in my stomach tightened when Lenci said that. Why? What would Jocelyn want? Had she planned something?

"No drinks," Jocelyn said. "I had enough wine with dinner, but there is something else I'm hungry for." She smiled. "Katherine, take your clothes off."

Well, that answered that. I turned to go back into the bedroom, but she stopped me.

"No. Right here. I want to watch. Lenci, you may sit and watch, too." She looked over at me. "Seduce us."

Seduce them? Oh my. How did I do that? Just by taking my clothes off? I'd never been one to be a sexy dancer...but stripping?

Jocelyn nodded. "Yes. Slow and sexy. It'll be well worth it for you."

How did I start? I kicked my shoes off, and I brought my leg up and slowly pulled off my sock. Then I did the other. I started to unbutton my shirt. I did it slowly, staring into Jocelyn's eyes. I undid my jeans and lowered the zipper, but I didn't push them down. I knew that slow was sexy and didn't try to show too much all at once. I was glad I hadn't worn a bra today. It felt like I should have some stripper music. The silence felt deadly. But... *Here goes.*

I pushed my jeans down slowly and coyly turned to the side as I bent, keeping my knees straight to push the jeans to the floor. As I turned, I smiled at Jocelyn and stepped slowly out. Jocelyn raised an eyebrow and smiled. Her look like that always got me wet, and today was no different.

Shirt or panties next? I decided panties. Leave the shirt on for a while. I slowly pushed them to the floor.

Jocelyn had a strange look in her eyes. She stood and pointed to the floor. Exactly like at her place, I knelt in front of her. My heart almost stopped. What was she planning? Whatever it was, when she pointed, I knew it was something I was going to enjoy, no matter how torturous it became.

"What do you think, Lenci?" she asked.

Lenci said something in Rebinian. Uh-oh. She always slipped back into Rebinian when she was flustered or nervous. Jocelyn replied in kind.

Damn. It didn't bode well for me. I continued to stare into Jocelyn's eyes. She hadn't taken her eyes from mine, either. The smile on her face made me nervous. We'd left her alone with all her new toys for several hours this afternoon. Was that smart?

"Lenci, there is a pile of red straps on the bed table. Get them for me."

Lenci ran into the bedroom. She came back and handed them to Jocelyn. They were made of a flat braided polypropylene. They wouldn't break.

"Now take her shirt off." The shirt was off my shoulders and down my arms in seconds. Jocelyn took one strap and held it out. "Put your hands up."

I raised my hands over my head, and she wrapped a band, about an inch and a half wide, around my wrist. It fastened with Velcro. Then the second one was around my other wrist. The long straps, made of the same material, fell to the ground around me. I looked at them carefully. They were indeed unbreakable, not like the silk scarves Hannah had used.

She picked them up and headed for the bedroom, leading me. She pulled me to the bathroom door. There was a hook with a large ring over the door near the hinges that hadn't been there before.

"Your store had some wonderful inventions to make any room into a dungeon. People here are very inventive." She threaded the straps through the ring. She pulled them up until I was at my full height, face-first against the door, my hands high above me. She took the ends of the strands and wrapped them around the hook and knotted them tightly.

"There you go," she whispered as she walked behind me, her body pressing me into the door. "I suppose the curtains should be closed so someone doesn't see." She motioned to Lenci to close the blinds. "Now I get to try some of my new toys."

I heard her walk away and open a drawer. "Are you ready?"

"Would it do any good to say no?"

She laughed, and the flogger thudded across my back. Then it fell again, and again, and again. Lenci whispered in Rebinian. Jocelyn responded.

"I don't understand what you're saying," I said softly.

"You don't need to. Lenci was complimenting my work." Two more lashes struck. They were harder than when Regina had flogged me, but that was understandable. Jocelyn was more forceful. "Are you leaning into the door?" she asked.

I looked down. "Yes, ma'am."

"We'll have to do something about that, too." She turned me around. "I don't think you'll want to lean into the door with these." She placed big metal clamps to my nipples. The pain shot through me as she tightened the screws. Oh, my God. I hadn't felt this much pain since last year.

"See?" She turned me back around and pushed. Pain traveled through my entire body as I pushed into the door. I had to grit my teeth to keep from screaming. I struggled to get my knees to support me. "Will your neighbors hear if you scream?"

"I don't know. But the bathroom and kitchen are on one side, the other bedroom and the closet on the other. The carpet in here is rather thick. I've never heard anything from upstairs."

"Good." She flogged me several more times. I straightened to keep from leaning on the door. It was hard. When I'd been flogged before, I was leaning against that wooden cross and could relax my muscles to absorb some of the sting. Now I couldn't, and I felt every single lash. I wasn't sure I could keep this up. Maybe I should call my safe word.

I lost my balance on the last and fell into the door. I couldn't begin to describe the pain that shot through me. Could I get to that place where I felt none?

Then she stopped and walked to the dresser. Without warning, a hard sting struck my ass, and I had to concentrate to not scream or lean into the door. The *whap* was a lot harder than the ones in her dungeon. Yes, I thought, the paddle with the holes. Air did not soften the blow. I leaned my head on the door so I could lever myself away from it.

The paddle struck again and again. I lost count as my mind zoned into the void. I could hear them talking, but I couldn't even tell what language they were speaking. I wanted to say something, but what was it? What did I need to say?

Lenci's arm came around my midriff as Jocelyn reached to

undo the Velcro tabs. Lenci pulled me back against her, holding me securely. Jocelyn unscrewed the clamps on my nipples. As the blood rushed back into the crushed skin, I screamed. I'd never felt pain like that. Then I was lying on the floor in Jocelyn's arms, tears running down my face. I was gasping. She was holding me tightly.

"Shh," she crooned to me as she held me tight. "That one's over. You're all right."

The echo of the pain still streaked through my body. I wasn't sure where I was or what had just happened. I lay in Jocelyn's arms as tears streaked my face. "You've made me very happy tonight," she said softly. "You've grown in your tolerance and forgot the pain. I'm very proud of you."

"It was for you," I said.

"I know." Her arms tightened around me.

❖

I woke up later that evening. I was in bed, lying facedown. It was still dark out, but I heard voices in the living room.

I started to push up, but there was still a lot of pain in my back and butt. I moved slowly and got to my feet. It took a minute to get my balance. I went into the living room. The clock on the living room wall said 3:45.

"How do you feel?" Jocelyn asked.

"Physically, I'm stiff and sore." It hurt like hell, but I was proud that I'd lasted through it. I'd almost called my safe word, but in the end, I hadn't. What did that say about me? Had I lasted for myself or to make Jocelyn proud? Wasn't that the same thing? *Not sure I want to do that again.*

"Turn around and let me see."

As I did, I heard Lenci gasp. "Yes," said Jocelyn, "your back is bright red, but there is no blood. Your ass has nice little white circles on it."

I turned back around with a deep sigh.

"Those white circles are so nice. I may be able to form designs if I handle it right." She and Lenci smiled. I didn't.

"How did you feel emotionally?"

"Were you happy with your new toys?" I countered.

"Very much."

"Then, emotionally, I'm fine."

Jocelyn and Lenci laughed. "Are you sure you don't want to come back with us?" Lenci asked.

Was that the answer? It was Lenci who asked, not Jocelyn. "I'd love to, but I have to work to pay the rent."

Lenci nodded. "Well, there's always the future. Have you decided what we'll do next?"

"Tomorrow I may have to rest. We can do something that's not on my back or butt." I sighed. That left a hell of a lot of other tortures.

"Well, we'll see. I may dream of a new torture." Jocelyn laughed. "I've been thinking about that store all evening."

"Whatever you want," I said. "We've still got four weeks." *If I survive that long. I might have to call a stop to all of this if it gets too bad.*

"Then I'd like to see where you grew up," Jocelyn decided.

"All right. We can go the day after tomorrow."

"And take the ferry?" Lenci asked hopefully.

I nodded. "And take the ferry."

CHAPTER TWENTY-FOUR

My back was still sore and stiff the next morning. I'd slept in the other bedroom while Lenci slept with Jocelyn. I took a shower but couldn't turn my back to the spray. I ended up putting on a very loose, soft cotton shirt and not tucking it in to my jeans. I would have to get Lenci to smooth lotion across my back.

When I walked into the living room, Jocelyn was sitting at the table drinking coffee. Wonderful smells coming from the kitchen told me Lenci was cooking breakfast. I looked at the clock. It was almost noon. So Lenci was cooking brunch.

"How are you today?" Jocelyn asked as I carefully sat on a chair.

"Stiff and a little sore on my left cheek."

"Let me see," she ordered.

I stood and dropped my jeans, then I took my shirt off.

"Oh yes. You're very bruised. You have a deep purple line there on the left. I'm very sorry. I'll have to adjust the use of that paddle. It feels the same, but it looks like it's a lot more biting. Your back is glowing, but that will go away today." She studied me thoughtfully. "I'm sorry your bottom was harmed so badly."

"I guess that's one of the dangers of this. I'll think of you every time I sit down." Then I smiled. "At least it's where no one but you and Lenci will see it."

"Yes, and Lenci will have to give you a massage."

Lenci came in with two plates of brunch but almost dropped

them when she saw my butt. She placed the dishes carefully on the table. "Oh, Katherine. That looks so painful."

"Yes. You will have to give her a massage today. We can't go visit her parents if she can't sit right."

Lenci nodded and went back into the kitchen to get her own plate. I pulled my jeans up and put my shirt back on. Then we all sat down to eat. Jocelyn was still scowling.

"What's wrong?" Lenci asked.

"I don't like harming any of you. Hurting, yes, but harming, no," she muttered.

"It will heal. It's not permanent," I told her. It was good to know she cared about going too far, but it still didn't stop the pain.

"But it could have been." Her frown grew deeper. "If there had been a break in the skin, you would have been scarred. That is never right. That bruise is very alarming."

"But it's not where anyone can see it," I said.

"*I'll* see it. It's an occasion that none of us should be reminded of."

I looked at my plate. Lenci had cut a sirloin steak into thin strips and fried them with eggs and shredded potatoes. It was too good a meal to be spoiled by something I considered trivial. Well, maybe not really trivial, but all the words in the world wouldn't make it go away. It did feel better when Jocelyn expressed regret. "This is a great brunch," I said. "I never cook like this. I never even think of it. A hot brunch for me is instant oatmeal."

Lenci laughed. "Then I'm going to have to teach you before we go back."

"Do you have that much time?" I asked, grinning.

"You sell yourself short, Katherine," Jocelyn said. "I think you can do anything you try. You're a bright woman."

"Well, that may be the thing. I've never cared what I make myself. I review what others have cooked."

"We can change that." Jocelyn looked at me with determination in her eyes.

"Of course." I was going to say, "Of course, Mistress," but for the first time in a very long time, I thought before I spoke. I wasn't in the mood to cause any rift in our plans. We ate the rest of the brunch in silence.

❖

The next morning, I was a lot better, but even if I hadn't been, I was not going to tell Jocelyn. I wasn't ready to face that again. I knew she'd been right, but she'd made too big a deal about it. The skin wasn't broken, and Lenci's massage had relaxed the muscles. My back had already returned to its normal color. I merely wanted it all to disappear. Jocelyn had expressed regret, Lenci had massaged me, and I wanted to go on to other things. I didn't want to waste our precious time on something that would fade away.

I called my mom first. "I'm bringing some friends out to see Port Angeles," I told her. "They're two of the women I met in Europe last year. From Rebinia."

"So far away from home."

I chuckled. "Yes, they're staying four weeks so they get their money's worth."

"Do you want to have a barbecue?" she asked.

"That would be very nice." She was always ready to have a barbecue. I knew she'd start making potato salad as soon as we hung up.

"Chicken, hamburgers, or steak?" she asked.

I could almost hear the gears in her head grinding away. Mom loved to entertain. "Let's have chicken and burgers."

"All right. I'm pretty sure we have everything we'll need. Do they write stories and reviews like you?" she asked.

"No. Jocelyn is a lawyer, and Lenci is her roommate." I figured Mom would be happy with that.

"Well, bring them out. I'm sure we can make them comfortable. Will you be staying the night?"

"Don't worry about that. If we do, we can check into the Holiday Inn."

"All right, if you think that's okay. That is an extra expense. We could find space here."

"That's all right, Mom. Jocelyn is very leery about putting people out. She'd be more comfortable in the hotel." I hadn't told my parents anything about my trip to Europe last year. It was better Mom didn't know. She worried enough about my travels. I did show her my photos and my reviews, but that was it.

She had never wanted to travel, had no desire to see another part of the world. It had been hard enough to get her on an airplane to visit her sister in Michigan...especially when it was within driving distance, but Dad had insisted, and I'd kept telling her how wonderful it was to see the mountains from above, so she'd finally given in. She'd said it was "okay," but I doubted she'd do it again without a major reason.

We spoke about our adventures so far, especially those at Pike Place Market, then Mom said, "I'm glad they're having a good time. Is this their first visit to the US?"

"Yes, for both of them. Lenci seldom travels, and Jocelyn has never been to the Americas, north or south."

"Then we'll have to make tonight special for them."

"Thanks, Mom."

"All right, I'll expect you this afternoon."

"Love you."

Jocelyn was standing there when I hung up.

"Mom's excited we're coming. She's fixing a barbecue. Now you can taste what real American hamburgers and barbecued chicken tastes like."

"It sounds wonderful, but I don't want to inconvenience her."

"She's be more inconvenienced if we didn't stay for dinner. She wanted to know if we were going to stay overnight, but I told her you'd be more comfortable staying in a hotel. If we stayed there, Mom would put you and Lenci in my old room, and I'd have to bunk with my sister."

"Yes. A hotel sounds better."

"Oh, and she asked what you and Lenci did for a living. I said that you were a lawyer and that Lenci was your roommate. It was easier than trying to explain."

Jocelyn seemed to think that was fine. "When do we leave?"

"As soon as you're ready. I thought we could get coffee and pastries aboard the ferry. It's not the very best food, but it is an experience."

Jocelyn smiled. "Then we'll have an experience." She turned as Lenci walked into the room. "Are you ready to have an experience?"

"Katherine hasn't failed us yet."

Yes, *an experience*. I'd have one, too. I'd brought a couple women I was dating out to visit my folks but had never talked of sex around them. Those had been day trips, so the idea of sleeping together had never come up. Now I'd bring two women, and I was sleeping with both of them. I'd never had to lie to my parents, but my folks didn't need to know everything. No, Jocelyn and Lenci were two women I met last summer. We'd rent a suite at a hotel in Port Townsend, and Mom and Dad would never suspect.

❖

We were in the third row of cars to board the ferry for Bainbridge, so we were near the front on the side. As soon as we parked and set the brakes, we got out and took the elevator to the upper deck. They were amazed by the ferry. We got glazed donuts and large cups of coffee. We then went out onto the front deck to enjoy the scenery.

"This place is beautiful!" Lenci cried, looking over the water. "Is a ferry like a subway or bus route?"

I nodded. "There are many people who want to live over here on the peninsula who have jobs in the city and travel this every day. Some park their cars at the terminal and walk on. Then they catch a bus, take a taxi, or have a coworker pick them up to get to work when they get to the other side."

Jocelyn smiled. "This is definitely an experience I haven't had."

"I like this ferry. Sometimes, I think people take the beauty of this place for granted."

"Yes, a lot of people lose touch with what they have around them."

I agreed. "If you think this is pretty, wait until we go up into the mountains."

Jocelyn looked up at the mountains that rose from the center of the peninsula. "I thought you said your hometown was at sea level."

"It is, but this peninsula is mostly mountains in the middle. I'll have to get a map so I can show you."

"I'm so glad you brought me here," Lenci told Jocelyn in German.

"I'm glad you're both here," I had to add.

Jocelyn simply smiled as she watched the water. I couldn't picture her or Lenci living here. It was so far removed from the castle outside Nové Ville. This was a jeans and sweatshirt place, not silk and high heels, unless a person was going into the city to do more than shop. Life here was very laid back. Jocelyn's Leather House would have to be hidden.

CHAPTER TWENTY-FIVE

When we got off in Bainbridge, I headed for Sequim, the fastest growing city on the peninsula, where whole neighborhoods of new houses were springing up overnight. I pulled into the parking lot of a cute little sandwich shop that would be great for lunch. It was located in an old church and was run by women. They had wonderful sandwiches and always had pies or pastries for dessert. Their hot mint chocolate and the ginger-spiced cider were absolutely fabulous.

Jocelyn and Lenci were amazed and very pleased by it. When we stopped to buy a map on the main street, I pointed out snow-capped Mount Baker in the distance on the northern part of the state.

"That's a volcano," I said. "It's been dormant for centuries. There are a lot of volcanoes up and down the coast."

"And no one's afraid they'll erupt?" Jocelyn asked.

"They've been sleeping for years and years. Mt. St. Helens down near the Oregon border erupted back in 1980. Some heard the blast as far out as here. They couldn't get some of the people who lived there to leave, although they knew a week in advance that it was going to blow."

"Were they all killed?"

I nodded.

Lenci frowned, crossed herself, and bowed her head.

Jocelyn and Lenci wanted to stop every few miles to look

around or go window-shopping. I was pleased by the happy looks in their eyes. They were amazed by almost everything, and they loved all the public art.

I took them up to Hurricane Ridge, the top of one of the mountains in the center of the peninsula. As we stood at one of the scenic plaques to view the vista, a young deer came up behind the sign and looked at us before starting to graze right there. There were also three deer romping in the parking lot and footpaths.

"They're not afraid of people?" Lenci asked. There were about a dozen other tourists around, looking at the beautiful sights and enjoying the air and flora.

"No, this is a federal park, so there's no hunting. They've never known fear up here. They're protected." Both Lenci and Jocelyn shook their heads in wonder.

It would have been nice if I'd gotten to go hiking in the republic near the castle with Jocelyn. The scenery and flora must be beautiful. The way her face relaxed when we were away from people pleased me. She looked younger and, of course, more beautiful.

It took another twenty minutes to get to Port Angeles. Before we got there, I had to tell them, "I never told my folks what happened last summer. My mother would not have been able to handle it. She worries enough when I travel. She's a homebody, doesn't like to travel except by car."

"She's never been on a plane?" Jocelyn asked.

"Just once to go see my aunt. She wanted to drive, but it would have taken much too long, so Dad and I got her on a plane. She didn't like it."

"Then how did you get the wanderlust?"

"I seldom did what my parents told me. I wanted to see everything I'd read about. Oh, and don't talk about sex in front of my mother."

"She won't talk about sex?" Lenci asked, quite surprised.

"Oh, she'll talk about it, but not in relation to her daughters. I think she's convinced herself that we're both still virgins. It was hard enough convincing her I'm a lesbian."

Jocelyn smiled. "But they accept it?"

"Yes. I convinced them that there was no alternative. When the state approved same-sex marriage, my parents saw that it wasn't as outrageous as they thought. Washington is probably one of the more progressive states in the union."

When we got to my family's home, Mom and Dad greeted them warmly. We were all ushered into the backyard where picnic tables sat atop a bricked patio. Dad already had the grill fired up.

"What can I get you to drink?" Mom asked as we all sat down to watch Dad. "We have beer, sodas, or coffee or tea, either hot or iced." Mom had gone out of her way for this.

"Is it local beer?" Jocelyn asked.

"We try not to drink mass-produced beers. Frank likes Blue Moon from Colorado. They have different brews for every season. Right now, they have Valencia Grove Amber. That's one of Katherine's favorites."

"Then I'd like to try that," Jocelyn said.

Lenci smiled. "Me, too."

"Coming right up," Mom said as she went back into the house.

"This is a beautiful place to live, Mr. Lowe," Jocelyn said to Dad as he flipped some chicken parts.

"It's a modest little town." He smiled. "But we like it here. This is a great place to raise kids. It's not as busy as Seattle or some of those other places on the other side of the sound. You don't have children, do you?"

Jocelyn shook her head. "No."

"Are you like Katherine?"

"In a lot of ways," she answered as she smiled at me. He nodded. I shook my head. Dad always asked the most inappropriate questions.

"Where's Pam today?" I asked about my sister, trying to change the subject before he asked any more.

"I don't know." He frowned. "I think she went out with her friends last night. She'll be back here sometime."

"My little sister is a party animal," I explained.

"Party animal?" Lenci asked.

"Yes, she goes out with her friends more than I ever did. She loves to dance and hang out."

Dad nodded. "Yes. Katherine was the quiet one."

Jocelyn and Lenci looked at me with laughter in their eyes. "Was she always like that?" Jocelyn asked.

"Yes. All she wanted to do was read and write. We thought we had spawned a bookworm."

"Dad!" I frowned.

He laughed.

"What does spawn mean?" Lenci asked.

Jocelyn answered with the Rebinian translation.

Lenci's eyes widened. "Oh!" I was pleased that her English was coming along. Very few words needed to be explained.

Mom came out of the house pulling a wheeled crate of bottles and ice and set it at the end of the picnic table. "I didn't know if you wanted glasses," she said. "We always drink right from the bottle."

"Bottles are fine," Jocelyn told her. "I'm happy to learn how Americans do things." I was amazed at the smile on her face.

I reached into the bucket and took out a beer, unscrewed the cap, and handed it to her. I did the same for Lenci and myself. Dad took one, too. He held it up to us. "Welcome to Port Angeles, Washington," he said, then took a swig.

We all toasted and took a gulp of the beer. "Oh. This is nice," Jocelyn said. "I'm so used to drinking the dark German beers, but this is substantial without getting heavy. I like it a lot."

Lenci agreed.

"The chicken's almost done," Dad announced.

"I'll be right back." Mom set her beer down and turned to go back into the house.

"Can I help?" I asked.

"Sure."

"I'll help, too," Lenci offered as she started to stand up.

"No." Mom looked scandalized. "You're a guest. Katherine can help me." She went back into the house. I winked at Lenci and followed Mom. When we got into the house, she said, "They're very nice, but they seem so different."

"It's the way they were raised. That part of Europe still has the *old ways*. Jocelyn's father was a duke. Lenci's mom was a housekeeper."

"Oh my. But they get along?"

"Of course, Mom."

"Are they a couple?"

How should I phrase this? "They've been friends for fifteen years. They live in the same house."

Mom grimaced. "I should have given Jocelyn a glass for her beer."

"No. Don't worry. She's trying all the American things while she's here. I think she finds the old European ways rather stuffy." I wasn't sure if that was true, but I had to settle Mom. She'd worry all day that she'd embarrassed me.

"I'll put out real plates, not the paper ones, and real silverware." She reached into the cabinet. "I'm glad I didn't set the table before you got here." Mom busied herself getting everything ready. "She must think this house is rather low class."

"Not at all, Mom. Please don't worry. You know I'd never bring anyone out here to embarrass you in front of them."

"If you think that's all right."

"Yes, I do. Please stop worrying." I was glad I'd never told her about my travels. Oh, I had sent postcards and showed them pictures, but there were some things I only told Pam about. I hated keeping anything from them, but there were some things, like my stay in Rebinia, they'd never understand. I was coming out with a large bowl of potato salad when I heard a car in the driveway.

"Ah! The prodigal daughter returns." Dad laughed. "She has a nose for food," he explained to Jocelyn and Lenci. "She always shows up exactly when it's ready."

Mom was behind me with a bowl of green salad. "I guess I need another setting."

"Kath!" I heard as my sister walked around the house. "I thought that was your car." I hugged her, then turned to introduce Jocelyn and Lenci.

"I love meeting Kath's friends," she told them. "She always

meets the most interesting people." Pam looked at me and winked. I'd have to call and explain to her soon. Pam was one person I told everything to. We kept a lot of secrets from Mom. I knew she'd want to talk.

Jocelyn asked Pamela a few questions, and they got into quite a conversation about popular music in Eastern Europe as Mom and I set the table and Dad placed platters of chicken and burgers in the center. Lenci looked around the table with questions in her eyes. Besides the platters, there were dishes of tomato slices, red onion slices, lettuce leaves, and cheese. I think she was overwhelmed.

"Let me help you." I fixed cheeseburgers for her and Jocelyn, then sat back with my own.

Mom sat down, picked up her beer, and reached for a chicken thigh. She used her fork to pick it up and glanced at me. I had to laugh. If Jocelyn hadn't been there, she would have used her fingers. I made sure the salads were passed around and everyone had enough beer. We all sat down and started to eat.

"Are you going to take them out to the coast?" Mom asked.

"Next week," I said. "Lenci wants to see the redwoods."

"This is your first visit to the United States, isn't it?" Mom asked.

"I've never been outside Europe," she answered. "This has been a treat."

"I've never been to the Western Hemisphere, either, but we will definitely come back," Jocelyn said. "This state is beautiful. We should have come here years ago."

"How did you meet Katherine?" Dad asked.

"I misplaced my passport, and Jocelyn helped me find it," I interrupted before she could answer. That was all Mom and Dad needed to know.

"Then thank you for taking care of my daughter," Mom said.

"It was our pleasure." Jocelyn glanced at me with a knowing smile.

I saw Lenci inspecting the brick and iron barbecue pit. "This looks wonderful," she said. "Was it hard to build?"

"No," Dad said. "The only hard thing was getting the grilling shelf made, but if you have good welders where you live, it shouldn't be that hard."

Lenci whirled to look at Jocelyn. "I bet Gabby could build one."

Jocelyn smiled. "If that's what you want. We'll take pictures so she can start planning."

"Gabby does the mechanical and physical work around Jocelyn's house," I explained quickly.

Jocelyn handed Lenci her phone, and Lenci started snapping pictures to bring home with her. Gabby would have a major project this summer.

"We'll get all the dishes cleaned up, Mom, just sit and relax. You've done enough for today," Pam said as she started to pile dishes to take back into the house. She looked at me and motioned to help her. We both went back into the house.

"All right," Pam started, "Who are you sleeping with?"

"Did I say I was sleeping with them?" I asked.

"Come on, Kath. I know you. You can't hide it. Tell me it's Jocelyn."

I smiled and nodded. I started to put the dishes in the dishwasher as Pam covered the leftovers and placed them in the refrigerator. "Why would it be Jocelyn and not Lenci?"

Pam stared at me in that I-know-everything look. "Because that's who I'd pick if I were gay."

"You'll never be gay. Besides, you have to have kids to keep the family going."

Pam stuck her tongue out at me. "She was the one who saved you last year, too, wasn't she?" I had told Pam everything about last year. "And she came all the way here to see you? It must be serious."

"I doubt it. Lenci asked if I wanted to go back, but Jocelyn hasn't said a word."

"And if she does?"

"How could I? I have bills to pay, I can't just pick up and leave. I have an apartment and a job."

"But if she asked?"

"She won't."

"You're positive?"

I nodded. "I'll just take advantage of the few weeks they're here."

"Then you *are* fucking them both?"

"Yes, now get off it, and don't you dare say anything in front of Mom and Dad, or I'll spill some things I know about you!"

Pam laughed. "I know more that you've done. I know more that you've done," she sang in a childish way.

"So? Shut up about it. You know how Mom is." I gave her a sisterly push as we went back outside laughing. Now, if Pam could just keep her mouth shut, this would be a good visit.

❖

It was almost ten o'clock before we checked into the Holiday Inn. They didn't have a suite available, so we got two adjoining rooms.

"I really enjoyed your family," Jocelyn said.

"I could tell they liked you, too. I'm glad you had a good time."

"I really did. This was been quite an education. You look like your father."

"I'm not as tall, and my beard isn't as thick." I didn't crack a smile.

They laughed. "I had a very good time," Lenci said. "But your sister is nothing like you."

"Well, we have one thing in common," I admitted. "She likes to fuck around, too, except she does it with men."

"Does your mother know that?" Jocelyn asked as we sat in one of the rooms.

"She must, but she won't discuss it. America was built on that Puritan ethic that you don't talk about those things. Before nineteen sixty, you didn't do those things outside marriage unless you were a slut. Most of the last generation still thinks that way."

I turned the television on to check out the late-night news and tomorrow's weather and give us time to relax and digest our barbecue.

What a day this has been. I'd never been this nervous bringing anyone out to my folks' place. Why? Because I wanted them to like one another? Of course. Because it was so different from Rebinia? From Jocelyn's? Or was it because the only thing I'd been thinking of was sex? Yes, all I could think of was making love to Jocelyn. I was obsessed.

When I turned it off at the end of the newscast, Lenci stood. "I'd better go to bed. I'm still so full, I need to lie down." She went into the adjoining room, leaving the connecting door open.

Jocelyn got a very sadistic look on her face, "Take your clothes off," she told me as she rummaged through the few pieces she'd packed.

I gladly removed my clothes, but then she handed me the harness. I sucked on my lower lip as I looked at it. Jocelyn helped me as I fumbled to get it on. She checked the buckles to make sure I had it on tight. I looked down at myself...and the hard phallus sticking out in front of me. I didn't know whether to laugh or be horrified. If Jocelyn wanted me to wear it, she must want to experience it.

Jocelyn laughed softly. "Lenci thinks she's full? Well, go fill her even more." She pushed me to the other bedroom. Lenci and not Jocelyn? Well, okay. Lenci was good, and it would be practice for when Jocelyn wanted it.

CHAPTER TWENTY-SIX

The next day, Amy called around two o'clock to see how I was doing. We'd just gotten back from the peninsula. I'd driven slowly enough that everyone could see what they wanted. "How's it going?" Amy asked.

"Wonderful. Absolutely wonderful."

"Are you in love?"

"Totally."

"Then I'm going to have to meet them," Amy said. "Want to meet at that coffee shop on Pike this afternoon?"

"Let me ask." I held my hand over the phone and turned to Jocelyn. "My best friend Amy wants to meet you. Do you want to go for coffee this afternoon?"

"It sounds good to me."

"It's a date," I told Amy. "Four o'clock?"

"I'll be there."

I turned back to Jocelyn as I clicked off.

"Does she know about us?" she asked.

I nodded. "I tell Amy everything. She doesn't always understand it, but she accepts me."

"She's not kinky, too?" Jocelyn asked.

"No. She doesn't see the attraction, but she's willing to let me talk about it. We tried making love once, but we weren't on the same wavelength, so we decided to remain close friends."

"Then I'll enjoy meeting her." I sure hoped they'd get along. I knew Amy was trying to protect me, but this was something I had to decide for myself.

When we got to the coffee shop, Amy was sitting at a table near the back. She waved as we went over to sit with her. "You have to be Jocelyn," she said, holding out her hand. "And Lenci?" They all shook hands. "Katherine has been bragging about meeting you since we came back last fall." It was nice of Amy to say I'd been bragging and not moaning or complaining.

Jocelyn smiled. "We've been missing her. Everyone wants her to come back."

Amy chuckled. "She told me about the trick your friend played on her. I would have freaked out on you."

"Freaked out?" Lenci asked.

"Gone crazy," I translated. Lenci nodded her understanding.

"I wish she hadn't done it, but at least we got to meet."

"I understand Kath had a good time, though," Amy said.

"We all did." Lenci smiled.

"I'm going to get coffees." When I came back with two cups and set them in front of Jocelyn and Lenci. They stared into them. The cream, when it was poured in, had created the picture of a rose.

"This is beautiful. How do they do it?" Jocelyn asked.

"It's all in the way they pour the cream," Amy said. "When we order the next one, you can go over and watch, if you want."

Lenci's eyes lit up. "I'd like to see it."

I sat back as I sipped my coffee, ate my scone, and watched to see how Amy related to them. They talked about where Amy worked and all the travels we'd done together. Yes, we'd traveled all over the globe, but our foursome was now a thing of the past. Did all good things have to end? Maybe it *was* time for me to think about turning over a new page in my life. Who knew what would happen next?

When Jocelyn and Lenci went to the counter to order more coffee and watch the barista, Amy turned to me. "Okay, they get my vote," she said. "I can see what you were thinking. Jocelyn's stunning. Have you slept with both of them here?"

I nodded. "It's about even."

"Have they asked you to go back?"

"Lenci asked."

Amy studied me with her eyebrows raised.

I sighed. "Jocelyn hasn't said a word."

"Then that's your answer. Lenci. Only occasionally Jocelyn," she reminded me.

I nodded.

"Have you decided how you can live with that?"

I shook my head. "I'm not sure I want to."

"Are you even thinking of going back?"

"I don't know how I'd do it. There's still so much to do here. I still have to travel and write. I still have payments on my car. I have to pay the rent."

"It sounds like you're making excuses. What do you want?"

"I want what's never going to happen. I want her to love me." Yes, I wanted to be her love, *her number one love*, beside her in life, not behind or below. But that would never happen, and not in line with Lenci, Gabby, Anna, or Emilia. I could never compete with any of them.

"Then, Katherine, if you even consider going back, even for a short stay, you're going to have to refocus. Lenci has to be your first priority, and if you want to be with Jocelyn, it has to be on her terms, not yours."

I sighed. "I know." That was the one thing I was sure of.

CHAPTER TWENTY-SEVEN

The next two weeks flew by. We did everything I could think of. We spent a full week driving down the coast so we wouldn't feel rushed if we wanted to stop at one of the scenic overlooks or visit places like the Sea Lion Caves in Oregon or the souvenir shop inside one of the redwoods. They were amazed when we stopped at an Oregon beach that had a lock box at the edge of the road for people to put money in to pay for parking.

They took their shoes off, and we went walking on the beach. They were astounded by the force of the waves as they hit the rock. They couldn't believe the power of the surf. We also spent extra time exploring the trees. We stopped at several wineries. Jocelyn bought several bottles to take back to the apartment. I don't think I ever saw either of them smile as big as they did on this trip.

We also checked into a pricey hotel. The rooms were beautiful, but I had a problem spending that much money. I could have paid a month's rent with what Jocelyn paid for just one night. I felt like I should pay at least part of it. Jocelyn had let me buy some of the food along the way and most of the gas, but it wasn't fair. I was showing off *my country*. I should be paying more. I was working. I had money, too. I could at least pay my share.

The next morning, while we were sitting in the hotel restaurant having breakfast, I felt Jocelyn studying me. "Is something wrong?" I asked.

"No," she finally said, "I was thinking."

Lenci looked at both of us. "Are you?" she asked Jocelyn.

Jocelyn sighed. "Yes. I believe so."

I looked from one to the other a couple times. "Did I miss something?"

"No," Jocelyn said softly. "You haven't missed anything." I felt a glitch in my breathing. What was she thinking about? Did she not like this hotel or this whole region? Was she bored of the trip? I was about to ask but Lenci noticed something in the vineyard on the next hill, and we got into a discussion about the California wine country.

The ride home was leisurely, and I took some inland roads instead of riding back up the coast. They always found somewhere they wanted to stop. "This has been wonderful," Lenci told me.

"And this country is so beautiful," Jocelyn added. "I'm totally amazed."

"Then you're going to have to come here more often." I didn't want to think of what it would be like when they went back. It was too hard to think about.

"Oh yes," Lenci said enthusiastically.

"Yes, I think we will," Jocelyn said. "We'll have to find a good reason."

"Well, to visit me," I suggested. "Isn't that a good enough excuse?"

"Definitely," Lenci agreed. Jocelyn nodded. Maybe this *wasn't* going to turn into a once-in-a-while thing. No one had mentioned me going home with them, and I knew they wouldn't stay here permanently. I hadn't really considered what would happen next, or how I'd go back to being here alone again.

Lenci was extremely excited when we went whale watching a few days later. We started out on San Juan Island and took a tour boat. Before an hour was up, we spotted a whale. We got to watch the whole pod for almost another hour. Some swam so close to the boat, I really got a feel for how big they were. When one slapped the water near us, we were all drenched. The entire boatload of tourists laughed as they wiped water from their faces and camera lenses. The tour company was prepared, though, and had hand towels ready.

We spent a day going shopping for souvenirs for the other three girls. Yes, the other girls were still there…as they'd always be. Why was I even thinking about going back with them? There'd always be others, and I'd just be one in the crowd. I wasn't a crowd-type person.

We roamed around Seattle for an afternoon until we realized we were all hungry. "I know this is a seafood state, but I haven't had a good steak in ages," Jocelyn said. And so, we bought steaks to take back to the apartment.

When we finished dinner that night, Lenci fell back onto the couch with a big sigh. "What an incredible three weeks."

"Yes. Thank you, Katherine, for a marvelous time. I haven't had this much fun in…since last September." Jocelyn smiled.

My heart soared under her praise. "We still have fifteen more days. Is there anything else you want to see or do?"

"There are a lot more things I want to do. We'll have to make the most of those two weeks." She took my hand and led me into the bedroom. "Naked. On the bed. On your back."

I shed my clothes and lay down on the bed. I'd miss her authority. I was getting used to her. I was getting used to the sex, too, even when it was painful. At least her hands were there to comfort me, to touch me, to hold me.

She picked up the strap that she'd wound between the box spring and frame. She buckled one side around my wrist and did the same with the other. She also fastened another set to my ankles. Then she adjusted the lengths until I was spread wide. I'd miss this most of all. Of course, I wouldn't tell her, but being controlled felt like she'd made a nest for me to rest in, a nest where she could touch me without restraint, where I couldn't think of pushing her hands away.

She stood at the foot of the bed. I couldn't read her expression. She took her own clothes off, then got on the bed and straddled my stomach. I could feel her heat and the wetness that had already started. Oh, she was so gorgeous. There wasn't a thing about her body that I'd change. It turned me on more than anything else. My one desire was to reach up and touch her.

Her hands started down my body. I lay there, letting the feel of her touch bring feelings into my heart, which ran through me from head to toe. Each touch felt like millions of volts surging through me. The feel of her always made me weak. I lay there, spread out on the bed, letting her handle me whichever way she wanted, and that was the way I needed.

Her fingernails streaked down my sides just hard enough for me to know they were there. Then it turned to feather-like touches. I couldn't help but squirm as the tickling became torture: movement that I had no control of. Looking into her eyes, I could see her studying my movements. She was smiling. It made me grin, too. I saw her admire what she saw.

"I like it when you squirm. It's very sexy. It makes me want to do a lot of other things to you."

"Like what?" I asked, knowing that that was probably the wrong thing to ask, but it would lead to other touches, other ways of handling me. It would lengthen our time together.

She slid off my belly to kneel between my legs. "Like this." She traced the edges of my crotch, stopping shy of my clit, my gateway into the next world. She teased and teased until I writhed again. There was a strange, evil look in her eyes. There was more joy in her touches. Should I be concerned, or just relax and enjoy it as she was?

She flicked my clit now and then. I jumped. It continued on and on. Oh, this was torture, too. I wanted her to touch me, to really touch me, but she continued.

Then one finger entered me, exploring the entrance, slowly, gently. "Do you want more than this?" she asked.

"Please," was all I could say.

"What if I don't want to do it?"

My mind was swirling with need. "Then you won't," I gasped.

Good God, could I continue like this without exploding? How long could I balance just inside the edge? I needed her to touch me. I needed her to touch me hard. I inhaled deeply.

"What would you give me in return?" she asked.

"Anything. Whatever you want."

"What if I wanted this?" She squeezed and rubbed my clit.

"It's yours." There was nothing I wouldn't give her. It felt freeing to recognize that. Yes, I could give her what she wanted, and that was what I had wanted all along.

"What if I wanted more of this?" she asked as she slid more fingers inside me.

I almost screamed but swallowed it before it came out of my mouth. "You'd take it."

She laughed. "Like this?" She slid her whole hand inside.

"Yes!" I said, barely short of a scream.

She left her hand there as she touched my nipples. I didn't think I could take much more stimulation. I zoned into another realm. I didn't know where or who I was, and I didn't care. Then those magic words came, and I exploded.

She leaned to the side and unbuckled the straps around my ankles and wrists. I lay there, not moving a muscle, and she sat on the edge of the bed.

"You'd give me anything I asked for, wouldn't you?" she asked thoughtfully.

I nodded. "Of course."

"Why?"

I took a deep breath. Could I say the truth? I hesitated, then said, "Because I hope that one of these days, you'll let me make love to you again, real love, even stronger than that night in your room. You'd let me ravish you until you experienced the feeling that I just had."

"Is that what you really want?"

"Didn't I please you that time?"

She kissed me. "You please me a lot…every time."

I smiled up at her.

"Now you want to make love to me?" She got off the bed and

reached into her travel bag. She pulled out the dildo and harness. "Put this on," she said. I sat up, and she helped me into it. She smiled. "Now, just lie on the bed and let me do the work."

We made hot, rough love for hours. It was after midnight when we at last let go of each other and rolled away, I had found that I could do almost all Gabby did. I'd finally experienced what made her tick.

"Wow," was the first thing I said.

"Exactly," she said as she reached to hold me in her arms.

We lay there for a few minutes, cuddling each other. "Lenci? Are you still up?" she called.

There was no answer. I looked at the clock. "She's fast asleep," I said. "It's way past her bedtime. I hope she wasn't angry that we ignored her."

"No. She knows that my time with you is my time with you. We'll make it up to her."

Yes, Lenci would always be there. She was the buffer when the world got too intense. Why was I thinking of going back with them? That wasn't an offering. *They don't need me.*

"Are you hungry or thirsty?" I was trying to get myself back into the real world. I had to break myself out of this before these thoughts got out of hand.

She smiled. "Some red wine would be nice."

I winked. "I think there's still some of the pinot noir we had with dinner. We didn't finish the second bottle…unless Lenci finished it." I got up and went out to the kitchen.

We lounged on the bed with glasses of wine. "Is your magazine based in Seattle?" she asked.

"No. The main office is in San Francisco. I get my assignments by email. I send my writing back that way, too. In fact, I've never met my editors. I talk to the department head or senior editor from time to time on the telephone, but other than that, I'm on my own."

"Then you can work from almost anywhere."

"As long as there's an internet connection." *Good God, please don't bring this up. When you leave and I'm alone, I'll always remember this conversation.*

"Let me ask you another question," Jocelyn said. "If you weren't working for them, what would you be doing?"

Crying for you. "Well, I went to college to write fiction. Then I realized I had to pay the rent. I started working on a novel years ago, but I seldom have time for it anymore." I chuckled.

Jocelyn turned us to face each other. "Then move in with us. I have internet at my office in town. I'm sure I could get it out to the estate. Come back with us."

Oh my God! That was what I'd been dreaming of. *Could I? Should I?*

"It is so tempting. I missed you."

"All of us?"

"Well…you, especially. I'll never meet another woman like you." *No, there isn't anyone as beautiful, with so much power…that makes me love her.*

She laughed. "And I don't think there's another like you, either." She paused. "You challenge me. I've never had to work this hard." She watched me as if to see how I was taking every word, then she said, "You know you aren't a submissive, but you are a masochist. You proved that when you let me hurt you."

"Is that good or bad?" A masochist? Yes, I guess I was, because I craved the way she touched me, even with all the pain. I wouldn't take that from anyone else. *Yes, Jocelyn, I'm yours.*

"It depends on the situation. A true sadist like me loves a good masochist, but if you're with someone else, you have to be careful. Don't forget to use your safe word because a sadist could take advantage of you. You could be in trouble before you know it, and some, especially new sadists, don't know when to stop." She looked down with a deep scowl. "I hate the thought of you being in a situation like that."

I had to smile. It sounded like a warning. "You don't need to worry. I don't think there's anyone out there that I'd bottom for the way I do with you. I can't imagine anyone hurting me the way you do." Yes, her pain was exquisite. It sent me into that void zone where nothing mattered, nothing really hurt, because it came from her.

Jocelyn's face lit up. "That's a relief."

"You know, I tried playing with some of the women here, but none of them had the power you do. I couldn't get the pheromones going the way I did in your dungeon." I'd never really gotten them going with Regina, either.

"You certainly got them roaring with me."

I nodded. "Are the others in your house submissive or masochistic?"

"Girls like Anna and Emilia have to be submissive because they need guidance. It will be that way in all aspects of their lives. Not that they're unintelligent, just inexperienced."

"I think I knew that on some level."

"Lenci can be sadistic if she's in the mood or a very passionate bottom...when she's in the mood." She chuckled. "Gabby is on the edge of all those things. She can be submissive, but she's good as an aggressor and a bit of a sadist, as I think you saw that those first two nights in the dungeon. What you didn't see was her masochism, which can be quite hard. I have to watch myself with her because she will not use her safe word, no matter how rough it gets. I'm the one that has to stop it."

I nodded as I let it roll around my mind. "Yes, she's very good."

"Lenci is my second in command, in many ways. She tells me what I need to do because she's very good at analyzing. She was the one who thought you'd be good there. She didn't want me to send you back, especially after she got you into bed."

I smiled.

"Now, you could be submissive if you could control your mouth. I thought you were until I let you do Anna. I was amazed when you told her that you were in charge and you'd do it the way you wanted."

I laughed. "You know, I was depressed that night, and when she came into my room to get me, I didn't want to go. I especially didn't want to be fucked."

"You were quite inventive to get out of it." Jocelyn was silent for a moment. "You'll have to be honest with me about that. If you come back with us and you get into that mood again, and you probably will if you get homesick or tired of us, you must tell me right away. You can't let it fester, or we'll have problems. If you feel that way, we'll be able talk about it and find a way to deal with it." I could hear her brain churning. She sighed. "When we were in my room, I was taken aback when you said you wanted to make love to me. No one's ever said that to me before."

I frowned. "No one? You're the most desirable woman I know. Everyone should want to make love to you. I can't imagine anyone *not* wanting to. You could have your pick of anyone you wanted." I looked at her in awe. I couldn't understand what she was saying. It was beyond what I thought. How could that be? She was stunning.

"But not in Rebinia, and especially not in older times. I'm a duchess. I'm a landowner. I'm above the average. People at my level, especially with an education, are put up on pedestals. I'm unobtainable. When I was younger and my father was still alive, other dukes and high-ranking nobles would petition my father for my hand for their favorite son. I was a much sought-after prize. Seventy-five or a hundred years ago, I'd have been given to the son of another nobleman or ceded to a higher family as a concubine or second wife for my father's benefit. Women were nothing more than chattel."

"That's terrible."

"That's the way Eastern Europe used to be. It has changed but not as fast as the west."

I shook my head, not understanding that culture. "That must have been horrible."

"That's all right. I'm a lesbian and a Mistress, so I can pick who I want."

"That's good."

"Then you came along."

I looked up quickly. She was watching me. Her eyes were flashing with something I couldn't identify.

"When you walked into my office and told me you wanted to be on the other side and that you wanted to make love to me, I didn't know what to do with you." She had a small grin. "I'm a Mistress, and I'm supposed to make those decisions, and I always have, but then, someone was telling me what she wanted. I didn't know how I should handle it."

"I'm sorry," I murmured.

She smiled. "Regina was no help. She told me I had to make the decision all by myself." She laughed, and I joined her tentatively. "I'm a lawyer, Katherine. I have to be on top of everything. I have to know what to do, but in your situation, I was floundering." There was a look on her face I'd never seen before. She looked uncertain, lost. She studied me for a few minutes. "Then came that night, and I thought, what the hell, why not? I didn't expect you to be like that. I thought it was just bravado on your part. I didn't expect you to be that good...or that desirable. I confessed that to Regina the next morning, and that's when she told me what she'd done. She started out so proud that I could keep you without any worries."

That started to squeeze my heart.

"It totally blew my mind. I knew you'd been tricked, and I had to let you leave. There was no way I could keep you there once we knew the truth."

"I know. I was confused, too. I had to get away, but I wanted to stay with you."

"Katherine," she said softy. "I'm going to tell you something, and I'm not telling you to sway your decision." I looked into her eyes. "It's something that I've never told another person."

I waited.

"I've tried to deny it, but I can't. These last few weeks have made it perfectly clear to me." She hesitated. "I'm in love with you."

I couldn't believe what I had heard. She was in love with me? I couldn't have heard her right. She'd never say that. No, because I wanted it too much. "Are you serious?"

"Perfectly," she sighed. Her frown didn't fade as she looked away. "I've tried to talk myself out of it, but every time you say something silly or make a comment that throws me, I don't know how to handle it. I don't know how to handle you. There's no way I can keep from loving you."

I bounced up onto my knees. "I've loved you from that very

first night in your dungeon, but I didn't think I'd ever live up to your standards."

She held my face between her hands. "You've surpassed them. Everyone else has stepped back to see what I wanted. You let me know what you wanted. You've taken every torture I handed out and came up smiling. I didn't know what to do with you. I've never met a masochist like you. I knew that, after what Regina had done, I had to make you go home. I was afraid to let you stay. Lenci told me I was a fool and a coward, that I didn't deserve you."

I leaned forward and kissed her very gently. "I didn't think I'd ever see you again. I've only been with one other woman since you, and that was for one night only. I'm not sure why I went home with her. I shouldn't have. I didn't want to be with anyone but you. The others Masters and Mistresses beat their submissives, but there was no real joy behind their swings. It looked like they were merely playacting. Some were just showing off. It seemed they were afraid to really hurt anyone. They weren't real to me. I wish I had never gone because it made me miss you more and more. There were some who were serious, but they didn't have your power. Some were so sadistic, it looked like they didn't care if they harmed anyone. I couldn't see myself responding to them. Maybe it was that I didn't love them like I love you, but I didn't want to do it with anyone else. I didn't want to love anyone else. I couldn't see giving myself to anyone but you."

"That's why we came to visit," she said. "This winter was the most depressing time I've ever had. Nothing seemed to interest me. I was probably in the dungeon once a week, if that. Finally, Lenci persuaded me to write you. I had to see you again to find out if this was real."

Had I heard her correctly? "I was depressed this winter, too. Amy told me I was turning into a nun because I didn't go out like I used to. She said that I should give up my desires and go on to someone else. I missed you so very much. I didn't want my love for you to be a delusion. But when I got your email, I was confused. I almost told you not to come."

"Why was that?" She frowned, concerned.

"Because your emails sounded like you were only coming because of Lenci. *She* wanted to see me, *she* wanted to see the redwoods, and *she* wanted to stay here. I love Lenci to pieces but not like I love you."

Jocelyn took a deep breath. "That was my fault," she said. "I was a coward. I couldn't take the chance that you didn't feel the same way. I hesitated for weeks. I was afraid you couldn't love me…and if you ever tell anyone about that, I will…no. I *won't* beat you for weeks."

We both laughed, but I felt a little sad. I didn't want Jocelyn to doubt my love or her own desirability. She couldn't be insecure. She had to be strong. Would my mission, my reason in life be to love her so she wouldn't doubt that part of her?

"What does all this mean?" I asked.

"Either you're going to have to move back with me, or we'll be spending all my money on airfare."

I smiled and reached to hug her. She tightened her arms around me and started a very passionate kiss. I couldn't breathe, but it didn't matter. She was kissing me. My heart was soaring higher than it had ever been.

Then we made love again. Not the sadistic love with bondage and pain that we'd had earlier, but hot, searing, passionate, and romantic love. No dominance, no pain, just pleasure. It was that one time where we put our other proclivities aside and brought only love to each other.

We fell asleep in each other's arms, content that we'd shared that one delightful moment.

Chapter Twenty-eight

Lenci was in the kitchen cooking breakfast when I woke up in the morning.

"Good morning," she said. "You look bright and cheery today."

"Good morning." I was almost embarrassed by what must have been a goofy smile on my face. I wanted to shout that Jocelyn loved me, but that would have to be her announcement, and I suspected Lenci already knew. I looked in the baking pan. "Kolaches? Have you been cooking all night?"

"No. I went to bed early, so I was up early. I'm going to feed you well. I'll make extra to put in the freezer. I can't leave you with just the food *you* cook." She laughed. Her English had become very good in the last month.

"You don't think I can cook well?"

"Not as well as me." She grinned.

"No one can cook as well as you." I wanted to laugh. It was amazing what a good mood I was in.

"If I had more time, I'd teach you."

"What would you think if she came back with us?" I heard behind me. I felt Jocelyn's hands on my shoulders. *What a wonderful thing to feel the first thing in the morning.* I reached up to lay my hands on hers. I wished I hadn't put a shirt on so I could feel her touch my skin.

"I'd love it!" Lenci said.

"We'll have to talk about it," I said softly.

"You'd really consider it?" Lenci was amazed.

I turned and looked at Jocelyn. "We'll talk."

Seeing her in her long robe this early in the day made me want to tear it from her body. How in love with her I was. But moving to Rebinia? Could I do that? Should I? My heart wanted to, but my head had its doubts.

Jocelyn frowned and squeezed my shoulders. "Yes. Is there coffee ready?" she asked.

Lenci poured a mug and handed it to Jocelyn, who turned back into the living room. Lenci poured a mug for me. "Sit down at the table," she said. "Breakfast is almost ready."

I went into the living room and sat at the little table. Jocelyn was there with her coffee. She squeezed my hand. "You look worried. What's wrong?" she asked.

"What would the others say?" I asked. "How would it affect Anna, Gabby, and Emilia? It would throw the balance off. And what's my family going to say?"

"You could have your own room, if you want, so you could write without being disturbed."

"It isn't where I sleep or work or even whom I sleep *with*. It would be my role there."

"You could have any of us," Lenci said as she brought a plate of kolaches out. "You could be First girl."

I shook my head. "No. That's your place."

"That's all right," she answered. "Jocelyn and I have talked about it. It's okay with me."

"But it's not okay with me," I stated firmly. No, if I was going to be there, I'd have to make my own space, not fit into someone else's. Jocelyn put her hand on mine.

Lenci stopped to think about it. "Then you could be Mistress, too. The other girls would love that. They all know you have almost the same power as Jocelyn." Then she lowered her voice. "And more power than Regina ever had." Then she smiled. "You wouldn't have to submit to any of us."

I still was not convinced. We ate slowly, considering.

"You must be whomever you want." Jocelyn squeezed my forearm and gave me a reassuring look. "We can get you a new girl all your own, if you want. You'd only have to be below me."

I grinned. "You know I want to be below you...or is that beneath you?"

Jocelyn chuckled. "Then come back with us."

"It may take a while to get everything squared away. I've got to call my magazine, get out of my lease on this place, and decide what I'm going to do with my furniture and my car and what I want to take with me. This is so sudden."

"Do you want me to leave Lenci here to help you?"

"Yes, I can help," Lenci said.

I shook my head. "I need to think this through. I need to go for a drive."

"Do you need to be alone?"

"Yes, and I need to talk with Amy."

"Then go," Jocelyn said. "We need to get this settled so we can make plans." She took a breath. "We'll be here."

I kissed Lenci, and Jocelyn gave me a hug and a long hard kiss. I grabbed my backpack, smiled at both of them, and walked out the door.

❖

Oh my God, I thought as I backed out of my parking space and headed to the exit. This had thrown me. I never expected to hear her say she loved me.

I'd had another storm of emotions last night, even more than when I was worrying about prison. I'd be halfway across the globe. Yes, I traveled a lot, but I always had my home to come back to. Now I'd make Europe my home? What would my role be? I couldn't just sit around the house all day. I'd need something to do, a reason to be. I'd have Jocelyn and Lenci but not Amy or Pam...or my mother and father. And I wouldn't be around for them. What if something happened and it took me two days to get home, not two hours? I never worried about that when I was traveling. Why was it coming up now?

How I loved this woman. She was everything I'd ever dreamed of. She was everything I'd ever wanted. And on top of that, she wanted me.

But...she lived in Rebinia, thousands of miles from here. It wasn't like being two hours away from home. It wasn't like I knew a hundred people I could party with. I knew Lenci, Anna, Gabby, and Emilia, all of whom would be my family. I would get to meet others. Yes, I'd made a lot of friends on my travels. Most hadn't lasted that long, but I'd kept the ones I'd met close by.

I'd have the time and place to work on my book, to research, to read. Jocelyn had promised me that. And, I laughed to myself, I could have sex or spend time in the dungeon whenever I wanted.

It was really the perfect situation: I'd be with my lover and have close friends all around me, have a time and place to do all the writing I wanted, and I wouldn't have to worry about paying rent. How could I pass that up?

But this wasn't like I could just pack a suitcase and leave. I'd have to get rid of everything. Well, at least find places for everything. I'd have to call the magazine and see if I could work from there with the time difference, see if I could get out of my lease, sell my car and furniture...and...oh my God, how could I do all that in less than two weeks?

Was I obsessing? Damn right I was. Who wouldn't be? Was I worrying for nothing? Did I have to go back when they did? After driving around for almost an hour, I took out my phone and dialed Amy at work. "Can you get out for a while?" I asked. "I need to talk to someone."

"Why? What happened?"

I took a deep breath. "Jocelyn said she loves me."

There was a pause. "Oh, boy. And you need to talk about it. Yes, I can meet you in a half hour at the café on the corner."

❖

"You want me to decide what you should do?" Amy looked at me across the table. "This is what you wanted for the last eight or nine months, isn't it?"

"Yes, but I wasn't expecting it."

"So? That didn't bother you when you were in Rebinia...or did you expect that to happen?"

"No, I didn't. But this is a big step. How do I tell Mom?"

Amy put her hand on mine. "Yes, this is a big step, but if you get upset or disappointed, you can always come home. If she kicks you out, you've still got me and your family."

"But what do I do with my furniture and stuff?"

"Is that all you're worried about?"

I scowled.

"You asked for my help. I can't make the final decision. That's something you have to do yourself, but I will help. Decide what you want to take with you and what you need to bring to your parents' house. I'll handle the rest. Don't let silly possessions ruin your future. That's not smart."

I still thought about it.

"In fact, I'll buy your bed and couch. I've was thinking of buying new ones anyway. Your TV is newer and bigger than mine, too. I'll give you good money for them."

When I didn't answer, she turned me to face her. "How have you felt since you came back from Rebinia? Longing? Unhappy? Bored? Depressed? *Horny?*"

I had to agree she was right.

"Now you can rectify all that, and you're chickening out? Katherine Lowe! Stop being a fool. Go with her. I've never seen you this happy. Your face lights up when she walks into the room. You've been glowing since she got here."

"Maybe I should wait a month and get everything taken care of."

She laughed at me. "Maybe you should go get your head examined."

I took a long deep breath.

"If you waited to go later, would you change your mind?"

"No." The idea turned my stomach. "No, I want to go. I want to be with Jocelyn. She said last night that if I didn't, we'd be spending all our money on airfare."

"Okay," she said. "I'll be over tomorrow to help you decide what to sell, store, or take. You're usually up by nine, aren't you?"

"But you have to work tomorrow," I said.

"Let's get your priorities in order. Which is more important? You getting ready to go live with Jocelyn or me taking a sick day? Besides, I want to know what Jocelyn's intentions are. I can't let you go out to explore the world without knowing you're doing the right thing. First and foremost, you have to call your publisher and see if you can work from Europe. Then you have to call your leasing company and see how you can get out of your lease. Now, go home and decide what you want to keep. I'll be over at nine in the morning. Tell Jocelyn that if she wants you to go home with her, she has you for tonight only. Then she has to stop all the fucking until you get everything taken care of."

I had to laugh at that. Like that was ever going to happen. I studied Amy. She was the best friend I ever had. I had relied on her for a heap of decisions. Was I going to rely on Jocelyn now?

"You always help me put things in perspective," I said to her. "How will I get along without you?"

"I wonder that, too. Jocelyn is in for more than she realizes." She stood up and went back to work.

❖

The next morning, Amy showed up at nine. She took charge right away.

"I want you to go through all your clothes and put them in four piles. One that you want to take with you, one that you want to give away, one that has things your sister might want or you need to keep in storage, and the fourth you can sell, either online or at a consignment store. I don't think you need to take more than one box. I'm going into the city to get boxes and supplies. If you get tired and want to take a break, call your publisher or your landlord.

Jocelyn, don't let her get away with taking things that she can get there. See you all in a little while."

She left. The three of us stared at each other.

"Are you sure she's not kinky? She'd make a wonderful Domina," Jocelyn asked as she broke into laughter.

Lenci frowned. "I got the feeling that if our chores aren't done when she comes back, she's going to spank us all."

"She's as far from kink as you can get," I said. "She won't spank us, but why take the chance?" I opened the bottom drawer in the second bedroom and started pulling things out.

By the time Amy got back, we had the beginnings of four good piles. That dresser was empty, and we had made a good start on the bedroom closet. She had a large stack of folded shipping boxes, some newspaper, rolls of tape, and a box of trash bags. "I'm impressed," she said. "I didn't think Katherine would get that far. Were you in charge?" she asked Jocelyn.

"Of course." She nodded.

Amy stepped forward to give her a hug. "Thank you. I'm hopeful about this. Do you know what a burden you're taking off my shoulders?"

Jocelyn studied Amy for a moment. "I'm sorry to take your best friend away, but I won't let her forget you, and I won't treat her badly."

"I know, but it's still a loss. I think I depended on her asking my opinions as much as she did."

Jocelyn hugged her. My heart swelled when I realized what I was giving up in exchange for what I was getting. I'd forgotten how much Amy meant to me.

By four o'clock we had eight boxes filled: four to give away, one for taking, two for going to Mom's, and one to sell. The second trash bag was already half-full. We hadn't even started on the kitchen or the main bedroom.

"I didn't realize you had so much shit, Katherine Lowe," Amy said, hands on her hips as she shook her head. "When do you leave?" she asked Jocelyn.

"A week from Wednesday," Jocelyn answered. "I have a trial

starting on July sixth. I've got to get back. That only leaves me ten days to make sure everything and everyone is prepared."

I frowned as I looked around. "That only leaves us a week and a half to get packed and bring everything out to Mom's." I frowned. "I don't think I can do it." I felt like crying. *I'll never get this all done.* It was useless to try. Now that I had the chance of a lifetime, I was mired down by all the things I thought I needed.

Jocelyn put her arms around me. "We can try. I want you with me. I don't like you being eighty-five hundred kilometers away."

I laid my head on her shoulder. "I want to be with you, too."

Amy looked at all of us. "I think we need something to eat. It sounds like we're all running on empty."

"I'll make dinner," Lenci said, standing. "We still have the ham steaks and all those brussels sprouts. How does that sound?"

"It sounds wonderful," Jocelyn said. "That is what we all need."

❖

"How long do you think it will take?" Lenci asked after we'd eaten.

"Without going completely crazy, we can get it done," Amy answered.

I frowned. "There's still so much to do."

"No," Amy said. "I can take care of getting things sold or brought to charity. After you've left, we can have Keith's boys come in and clean. They'll also help move the furniture out."

"When can you get out of your lease?" Jocelyn asked.

"I told them I'd probably be out by early July."

"We can be done by the end of June." Then Amy turned to Jocelyn. "You know I don't understand any of this, but if Katherine is happy, and it works for you two...or you three...or however many people live there, I'm all for it. I want Kath to be happy. I kind of love this idiot."

"You're a very good friend, Amy. You'll have to come visit us soon. I know you don't like some of the things that happen in my house, but if you come to visit, we'll curtail it while you're there."

"Yes," I said.

"Yes, please come visit," Lenci said. "If you come during the fall, you can see the grape harvest and wine making. Actually, everyone's so busy during that time, there's no time or energy to play in the dungeon."

Amy smiled. "I would like to see your house. Katherine has told me so much about it, and I would like to see your dungeon. I can't imagine the things Katherine talked about. I'm not sure I'd want to see it being used, but I would like to see the equipment."

Jocelyn smiled and hugged her. "We'll provide a special tour just for you."

Then Amy turned to me. "I'm thinking of bringing Judy to help tomorrow. Can we keep the BDSM out of the conversation?"

"Of course." I smiled. Then I explained to Jocelyn and Lenci, "Judy was another of the friends we used to travel with, but she's quite adamant about sadomasochism. She hates it."

"I don't think she's ever actually seen it. None of us have," Amy added. "The only way I know something about it is because of Kath."

"We understand. There are certain factions at home that frown on it, too. The girls are very good at keeping quiet about it when there is company."

It was still a hidden life, but at least everyone in the house was in agreement. Maybe someday…

CHAPTER TWENTY-NINE

The next morning, Amy and Judy showed up in time for breakfast. "Nice to meet you, Jocelyn," Judy said, shaking hands. "I can see why Katherine wouldn't tell us anything about you. She was hoarding you for herself."

Jocelyn laughed that deep throaty laugh I loved so much. "My big mistake with Katherine was to let her go home."

Judy laughed. "Yes, she's been miserable this winter. I expect it would have been a lot cheaper, too."

"But then we'd never have gotten to see your gorgeous country." Lenci threw in as she placed dishes of kolaches on the table. Everyone reached for one.

"These are delicious," Judy exclaimed as she took a second bite.

"Yes, Lenci is the best cook I ever met," Amy added. "I really don't want her to go home."

I smiled at Lenci. I had the feeling something might be happening there. "Lenci would keep you fed well, but there would be at least a half dozen people in Rebinia who would hate you for taking her away." I had to kid them.

"Food isn't the only thing I handle well." Lenci smirked.

"No, it isn't." Jocelyn grinned over at me.

Judy shook her head as she bit into her kolache and sipped her coffee. She drew me aside about two hours later as we were taking trash out. "I like them both," she said. "Did you come between them?"

"No. Jocelyn was pretty single before I met her. Lenci has been her best friend for years." That was what Jocelyn decided we should say if anyone asked.

"Have you slept with both of them?"

"Judy!" I smiled at her. "I don't sleep with everyone. I love Jocelyn."

"She's quite something, isn't she? I'm very happy for you. Will this take you off the market, or will you be traveling around?"

"I'll still be traveling, but I have no reason to look for anyone else," I said firmly. "She's everything I've ever wanted." *No matter who I have to share with.*

Judy hugged me. "I'm so happy for you. Please keep in touch with us. Paula is in Puyallup, and you're in Rebinia. It won't be the same."

"You and Amy will have to travel without us. Maybe you'll find others to travel with you, or maybe Paula will still go with you and bring Kelly."

"It still won't be the same," she said as she hugged me. "We won't have anyone to worry about. No one will ever replace you."

"Is that good or bad?"

"Neither. But you are a singular character. I'll miss you."

I reached out to hug her. "I'll miss you, too. We've done so many things together. I will miss that."

And so for the weekend, the five of us worked our asses off to get everything sorted and ready to go to the correct places. After that, Amy and Judy were back every day after work.

A week later, everything was packed and had been shipped or taken to Amy's apartment. She'd have a yard sale after we left, then take the rest to a charity. Amy assured me that all my other stuff would either be sold or given away. Some of the furniture was already taken. The only things still in the apartment were my queen-size bed that Amy would take—and for which I wouldn't accept her money—and the other bedroom set that she would see sold. We still had my dishes and pans for the yard sale or to be given away.

Jocelyn had paid off the eight-hundred-dollar remainder of

my car loan and an ad had been prepared to go online. Amy would handle its sale. I signed the title.

Jocelyn had called Gabby and the girls, who were to clean and prepare the bedroom next to hers. "Katherine will be coming back with us," she said. "She'll be your new Mistress." I could hear cheering through the phone. "There will also be two boxes coming by post that are hers. Just leave them up in her room. And another box of my stuff that should be placed in the dungeon."

She was asked a question.

"Yes, we land in Pergue at ten a.m. on Thursday morning. Bring the van. There will be three of us and our luggage." She had also booked and paid for a third business-class ticket to match hers and Lenci's. She said a few more things to whoever was on the line, then clicked off and turned to me. "Everyone's very excited you're coming with us. I expect there will be a big party to welcome you home."

"In the dungeon?" I smiled.

Her face lit up. "Wherever it starts, I'm sure we'll end up there at some point."

And I was returning as a Mistress. I had some say in what happened. If I wanted, I could have any of them. It would take some getting used to.

I didn't need to check any luggage because we'd shipped all of the clothes I was keeping: my winter jacket, my underwear, three pairs of jeans, two pair of dress slacks, and a few other miscellaneous things. A second box had been shipped with my writing materials, other clothing and shoes and boots. I'd carry what little jewelry I wasn't putting in storage, one change of clothes, my laptop, tablet, and my Kindle so I could read and write on the ten-hour flight.

On Monday, Jocelyn and I again drove out to Port Angeles with my car packed. Amy followed us in her car, also full of boxes. Lenci was her passenger. I had called and told Mom what I was doing. It was a call I dreaded making.

"Mom, I have news," I started. "I'm going back to Rebinia with Jocelyn."

There was silence on the other end. "For how long?"

"Forever. I'm in love, Mom. And she loves me."

"Oh, Katherine, I'm happy for you, darling, but that's so far away."

"I know. But I want to be with her. I love her."

"Isn't this sudden?"

"No, Mom. I fell in love with her when I was there last fall. This winter was horrible for both of us. We were both so depressed. That's why she came here last month, so we could find out if we were really in love."

"And you're sure? That's so far."

"Mom, I travel that far all the time. I'll be back from time to time. I'll miss you and Dad and Pam, too. Think of it as an extra-long review I'm doing."

"I suppose." I heard the sadness in her voice.

"You'll probably hear from me more often than from here in Seattle. I'll call at least once a month, if not sooner. And you can call me. I'll be emailing Pam, so I'll send pictures. You can send me some, too."

"Still, pictures aren't like holding you."

"No. I know I haven't been the best, most attentive daughter, but I hope you know how much I love you."

"We do, dear, but thinking of you so far away…"

"It's not really that far anymore. I know you hate plane rides, but you can get there in twelve hours, which seems like a lot, but you can sleep most of the way."

"I could never sleep on a plane. I'd be too nervous."

"Then you can finish a whole book. You're always saying you never have time to read."

"Well, you can come home, too."

"Yes, I will. I love you and Dad, but I love Jocelyn, too. I have to be with her."

"I'll try to understand, dear. I do want you to be happy. Now if I could just get your sister to settle down."

"She will eventually"

"I hope so. Jocelyn lives in a big house?"

"Yes. There are at least a dozen bedrooms."

"My heavens. And Lenci lives there, too?"

"She has for the last thirteen years. Lenci loves to cook, so that's what she contributes to the household. Jocelyn has other help who'll be around, too. Anna cleans the house and does laundry, Emilia is the gardener, and we told you Gabby does the mechanical work and takes care of the cars." I had to tell her something so she wouldn't be surprised or confused if their names were brought up.

"Then Jocelyn is rich?"

"She's well off, but she works hard, too. I told you, she's a duchess, but that really doesn't mean that much anymore. She's very down to earth."

"Yes, I liked them both when they were here. What will you contribute to the household?"

"I'll still be doing my reviews, but I don't think as many, and if, or when, I finish my book, I'll try to get it published. I'll be holding my own. I don't want her to pay for everything while I sit back watching TV! We'll be fine."

The call lasted over an hour.

"I'm afraid of what Dad's going to say. He worries about me all the time," I told Jocelyn afterward as we drove along.

"I'll make sure they both know you'll be well taken care of," Jocelyn said.

I smiled. "You're going to take care of me?"

"Oh, yes," she said, not making eye contact. "Am I going to take good care of you!"

I glanced over at her. "I can't wait." *No, I want Jocelyn to take care of me as I'll take care of her. All our needs will be met.*

When we got to my parents' house, my mom asked, "What are you going to do there?" as we sat in the backyard over coffee.

"I'm going to write my novel. I've been wanting to do it, but something always came up."

"She'll have her own study," Jocelyn said, "so she can work uninterrupted."

"And someone will bring food to her if she's in the middle of a thought," Lenci added, "and doesn't want to come down for dinner."

"But you have enough money?" Mom asked.

"I have my savings, and I got quite a bit from selling my furniture, so I'm okay for a while. The magazine said I could review a lot of places in Europe, Asia, and even Africa. They're excited to have someone in that part of the world who knows American tastes. In fact, I have an assignment to check out some places in Norway."

"She won't need money for rent or food, and we have someone who can drive her wherever she needs to go. My house is so big that she won't be disturbed, but there'll always be someone around, so she won't get lonely."

I smirked. "You could fit our whole house into her living room."

"It's not that big," Jocelyn protested.

Lenci laughed. "You haven't tried to vacuum it."

Jocelyn shook her head. "I'll make sure Katherine will never want for anything," she told Mom, trying to change the subject. "I have my office in the city, but I also work from home a lot."

"That's very generous of you, Jocelyn, but you shouldn't work so hard."

"I only work when I want." Jocelyn grinned. "I have money my father left me."

"She's a duchess," Amy added.

"Yes, Katherine told me. I'm very sorry I had you drink beer from a bottle." Mom's eyes were wide.

"Please don't feel bad. I came to the US to do American things."

"That's very nice of you to forgive me."

"Nothing to forgive. Duchess is a hereditary title. It really doesn't mean that much anymore. About the only thing it really means is that I don't have to stand in line in government buildings, but that will probably change very soon. When my father was born, it was very important, but most of that kind of pomp is just a memory now. My father made sure I had a degree, so I wouldn't starve, but now, I only take cases that interest me."

"You are very lucky," Mom said.

Jocelyn smiled. "And my vineyard produces wine which sells very well in the city."

"Good heavens!"

"I'll also make sure Katherine doesn't travel alone. Someone will always be with her, so she won't lose her passport again." Jocelyn smiled broadly and winked at me. "In fact, I've never been to Oslo, either, so I might go with her."

"I was going to volunteer for that," Lenci said softly.

"I always love to have you around," I said.

"We'll see what we can do," Jocelyn assured her.

"See, Mom? I won't be by myself." *I'll have more company than I know what to do with.*

"Then I shouldn't worry." Mom sighed.

"I'll call or email regularly."

"And I'll make sure she comes home every other year or so."

"And I'm going to visit them next year," Amy added.

I smiled at Mom and nodded. Then I changed the subject. "Will Pam be home tonight? I have some clothes that will fit her if she wants them." I did want to say good-bye to my sister. I'd called her last week and explained things I hadn't told my parents.

"Yes, I think so, but I never know until she's here. Hold on, I'll call her at work and make sure she does come home so she can say good-bye to you." She got up to go inside.

"She's taking it better than I thought she would," Amy said.

"It's only because she likes Jocelyn and Lenci." I nodded. "Now I have to get past Dad."

❖

Dinner was over, and all my boxes were put into storage or given to Pam. Amy and Lenci had already driven away. We'd meet them at the ferry.

"Good luck, Kath," Pam said as she hugged and kissed me. "And I really like Jocelyn. You did good this time." She whispered in my ear. "Is this a three-way?"

"Sort of," I answered, smiling.

"Aha...my boring big sister is finally getting kinky."

"More than you know." I chuckled as I hugged her. "There are three other women who live there, too."

Pam grinned at me, her eyes wide.

"Take care of yourself," I told her. "And be careful. If you decide to get married, give me two weeks to get home."

Pam laughed in my face. "That won't happen if I have any say in it." We gave each other more hugs and kisses.

Then I turned to Dad. He took me into his arms. "Be careful," he said in his father voice. "And if you need anything, let us know."

"I will, Dad," I whispered as I hugged him tightly and kissed him on the cheek "But I don't think I will. I have my own money, and I'll be working some."

"Well, if you need anything at all, please call."

"Please don't worry about me, Daddy. We're going to be fine. This is a big move, but I know in my heart it's right."

"If you're sure, then go off with my blessing. I like Jocelyn. I have good feelings about her."

"You and Mom will have to come visit. That would be a nice vacation for you. You'll only have to pay for airfare. Food, lodging, and a car will be taken care of."

"It is a thought…if I can get your mother back on an airplane."

"Well, she can't drive from here. I'll work on her from my end, too."

He held me to him for a long time, then kissed me on the forehead like he used to do when I was small.

I turned to kiss and hug Mom. "Make sure you email," she reminded me. "Your father will worry." I knew she would, too.

"Of course, and I'll call, too," I said. "I don't want either of you to worry. I'll be fine. *We'll* be fine. This makes me very, very happy, Mom."

"Then I'm very pleased for you, darling." My mom was trying so very hard to be a modern, accepting mother that she went out of her way not to voice her concerns. If she had them, she'd voice them eventually, but not when we were parting. "I like both of them. Jocelyn seems to have a handle on everything."

"She sure does, Mom." I answered. "I don't think there'll ever be anyone I want more than her. I really love her, and I know she loves me. Who knows? Maybe next year, we'll come back and get married."

Mom nodded happily, kissed me, and patted my cheek.

"I love you," I called back as I got into my car. Jocelyn and I waved as I pulled onto the street.

"Your father had tears in his eyes," she whispered as we turned onto Route 101.

"Mom did, too."

"And now you're ready for your new life."

I reached over and took her hand. "I've been ready for months."

"Are you still worried about the other girls?"

I took a deep breath. "It will be different this time. I won't feel as vulnerable, and they'll have to accept that I'm there for the long run."

"You get to set your own terms now. If you want any of them... or all of them...you have the right to do it, but you and I will save at least two nights a week to be alone together."

"One night in your room and one in mine?" I couldn't stop smiling.

"Or in the dungeon. We can't leave that out."

I smiled. "No, we can't, Mistress."

I could feel her studying me. "Will you still kneel to me if I request it?"

"Of course. That was one of the things I looked forward to. I knew it meant that you were getting ready for something...and I always enjoyed what you were getting ready for."

"Let's not change that," she whispered. "I so enjoy hurting you."

I tried not to smile. "And I enjoy being hurt by you. It's the foundation of our relationship." Yes. We were going to have a relationship, a strong one, even with the others around us. We were going to be Mistress to Mistress. *Watch out, girls.*

About the Author

Nanisi Barrett D'Arnuk had a successful music career as a pianist and conductor and performed and traveled around the world several times. She was the first open lesbian to conduct on the stage of DAR Constitution Hall is Washington, DC. She has lived in the Northeast, the Pacific Northwest, and the central South.

When M.S. curtailed traveling and performing, she turned to her writing. She has written mysteries, romances, and erotica. She now lives on thirty acres of wooded land in south central Oklahoma with her partner, their family, five dogs, and a flock of chickens and ducks.

Books Available From Bold Strokes Books

All the Paths to You by Morgan Lee Miller. High school sweethearts Quinn Hughes and Kennedy Reed reconnect five years after they break up and realize that their chemistry is all but over. (978-1-63555-662-9)

Arrested Pleasures by Nanisi Barrett D'Arnuck. When charged with a crime she didn't commit, Katherine Lowe faces the question: Which is harder, going to prison or falling in love? (978-1-63555-684-1)

Bonded Love by Renee Roman. Carpenter Blaze Carter suffers an injury that shatters her dreams, and ER nurse Trinity Greene hopes to show her that sometimes hope is worth fighting for. (978-1-63555-530-1)

Convergence by Jane C. Esther. With life as they know it on the line, can Aerin McLeary and Olivia Ando's love survive an otherworldly threat to humankind? (978-1-63555-488-5)

Coyote Blues by Karen F. Williams. Riley Dawson, psychotherapist and shape-shifter, has her world turned upside down when Fiona Bell, her one true love, returns. (978-1-63555-558-5)

Drawn by Carsen Taite. Will the clues lead Detective Claire Hanlon to the killer terrorizing Dallas, or will she merely lose her heart to person of interest urban artist Riley Flynn? (978-1-63555-644-5)

Lucky by Kris Bryant. Was Serena Evans's luck really about winning the lottery, or is she about to get even luckier in love? (978-1-63555-510-3)

The Last Days of Autumn by Donna K. Ford. Autumn and Caroline question the fairness of life, the cruelty of loss, and what it means to love as they navigate the complicated minefield of relationships, grief, and life-altering illness. (978-1-63555-672-8)

Three Alarm Response by Erin Dutton. In the midst of tragedy, can these first responders find love and healing? Three stories of courage, bravery, and passion. (978-1-63555-592-9)

Veterinary Partner by Nancy Wheelton. Callie and Lauren are determined to keep their hearts safe but find that taking a chance on love is the safest option of all. (978-1-63555-666-7)

Forging a Desire Line by Mary P. Burns. When Charley's ex-wife, Tricia, is diagnosed with inoperable cancer, the private duty nurse Tricia hires turns out to be the handsome and aloof Joanna, who ignites something inside Charley she isn't ready to face. (978-1-63555-665-0)

Journey to Cash by Ashley Bartlett. Cash Braddock thought everything was great, but it looks like her history is about to become her right now. Which is a real bummer. (978-1-63555-464-9)

Love on the Night Shift by Radclyffe. Between ruling the night shift in the ER at the Rivers and raising her teenage daughter, Blaise Richilieu has all the drama she needs in her life, until a dashing young attending appears on the scene and relentlessly pursues her. (978-1-63555-668-1)

Olivia's Awakening by Ronica Black. When the daring and dangerously gorgeous Eve Monroe is hired to get Olivia Savage into shape, a fierce passion ignites, causing both to question everything they've ever known about love. (978-1-63555-613-1)

The Duchess and the Dreamer by Jenny Frame. Clementine Fitzroy has lost her faith and love of life. Can dreamer Evan Fox make her believe in life and dream again? (978-1-63555-601-8)

The Road Home by Erin Zak. Hollywood actress Gwendolyn Carter is about to discover that losing someone you love sometimes means gaining someone to fall for. (978-1-63555-633-9)

Waiting for You by Elle Spencer. When passionate past-life lovers meet again in the present day, one remembers it vividly and the other isn't so sure. (978-1-63555-635-3)

While My Heart Beats by Erin McKenzie. Can a love born amidst the horrors of the Great War survive? (978-1-63555-589-9)

Face the Music by Ali Vali. Sweet music is the last thing that happens when Nashville music producer Mason Liner and daughter of country royalty Victoria Roddy are thrown together in an effort to save country star Sophie Roddy's career. (978-1-63555-532-5)

Flavor of the Month by Georgia Beers. What happens when baker Charlie and chef Emma realize their differing paths have led them right back to each other? (978-1-63555-616-2)

Mending Fences by Angie Williams. Rancher Bobbie Del Rey and veterinarian Grace Hammond are about to discover if heartbreaks of the past can ever truly be mended. (978-1-63555-708-4)

Silk and Leather: Lesbian Erotica with an Edge, edited by Victoria Villaseñor. This collection of stories by award-winning authors offers fantasies as soft as silk and tough as leather. The only question is: How far will you go to make your deepest desires come true? (978-1-63555-587-5)

The Last Place You Look by Aurora Rey. Dumped by her wife and looking for anything but love, Julia Pierce retreats to her hometown only to rediscover high school friend Taylor Winslow, who's secretly crushed on her for years. (978-1-63555-574-5)

The Mortician's Daughter by Nan Higgins. A singer on the verge of stardom discovers she must give up her dreams to live a life in service to ghosts. (978-1-63555-594-3)

The Real Thing by Laney Webber. When passion flares between actress Virginia Green and masseuse Allison McDonald, can they be sure it's the real thing? (978-1-63555-478-6)

What the Heart Remembers Most by M. Ullrich. For college sweethearts Jax Levine and Gretchen Mills, could an accident be the second chance neither knew they wanted? (978-1-63555-401-4)

White Horse Point by Andrews & Austin. Mystery writer Taylor James finds herself falling for the mysterious woman on White Horse Point who lives alone, protecting a secret she can't share about a murderer who walks among them. (978-1-63555-695-7)